Lilies
IN
WINTER

The Intriguing Sequel to
Crushed to the Bone

ED J. THOMPSON

Lilies in Winter

Copyright 2024 by Ed J. Thompson

This is a work of fiction. Aside from reference to known public figures, places, or resources, all names, characters, places, and incidents have been constructed by the author, and any resemblance to actual persons, places, or events is coincidental.

Scripture quotations marked NKJV are taken from the New King James Version®. Copyright © 1982 by Thomas Nelson. Used by permission. All rights reserved.

ISBNs: 979-8-89298-892-6 (Print)

979-8-89298-893-3 (Ebook)

Printed in the USA.

To my siblings, Michelle, Karen and Hank.
Also to Ray and Gloria.

*But the mercy of the Lord is
from everlasting to everlasting
on those who fear Him, and
his righteousness to children's
children (Psalm 103:17 NKJV)*

Prologue

It was exactly 6:15 p.m. as the bus slowly pulled up to the crowded bus stop and the people waiting there began to file into one line. Michael picked up the two large bags containing the items that he just bought and patiently waited his turn to board. He was in no hurry. He hated shopping, and he was glad that he could finally leave the shopping mall and go home. Had there been a store in Schenectady where he could have bought a decent pair of jeans and shoes, he would have never come all this way to Albany. But he hadn't bought himself any new clothes in over a year and he was badly in need of the basics.

He blamed himself because he would have been home by now if he had started out first thing this morning as planned. The early weather forecast was clear and a seasonable 35°F, and yet he still struggled to get himself in motion. Now the sun was gone, and the temperature had dropped considerably. He hated the winter cold, and the month of February was one of the worst in upstate New York.

By the time that he got on the bus, the only window seats available were in the back. He found one and sat down just as the bus began to move. Almost immediately, a man approached. He was wearing a camouflage jacket with his pant legs tucked into his combat boots.

"Is this seat open?" he asked.

"Yeah," Michael reluctantly replied without making eye contact.

He moved over as close to the window as he could and placed his bags on the floor between his legs. He was bitter about having to move his stuff. There were other seats available.

"It's good to get out of the cold," the man said. "The heat feels good."

Michael did not respond.

"Are you from Albany?" the stranger asked as he briskly rubbed his hands together.

There was a large tattoo of a white flower on the back of one of his hands.

"No, I'm from Schenectady," Michael answered.

"About how long will it take to get there?"

"Um, 40 minutes."

"Oh really? That long?"

Michael shifted his body slightly to partially face the window.

Undeterred, the stranger intruded, "What do you do? If you don't mind me asking."

"Um, I just started a new job at a small law firm," Michael replied. "I'm kinda like the office manager, but not really."

"Oh, that's exciting," the man said.

Michael could tell that he wasn't going to be quiet.

"I'm not from here," he continued. "I'm just passing through. I'm a soldier."

"You in the army?" Michael asked.

"Yes, I am. My name is Michael," he offered. "What's yours?"

"My name is Michael too."

"How about that? Nice to meet you, Michael."

"Uh huh."

He couldn't get a good look at the guy because there wasn't much light on the bus, and he was careful not to stare. But considering his profile, he could tell that his travel companion was a big man. He was very muscular with large hands, and Michael felt the full weight of him a couple of times as the bumps and curves in the roadway caused them to rock together. It was like hitting a brick wall. He looked a little like he could have been Latino or something, but it was hard to tell.

"Did you know that the name Michael means, 'Who is like God'?" the G.I. asked.

"No, I didn't."

"Yup, it sure does," he continued. "Guys like us were created to stand with God against the enemy."

"Against *who*?" Michael responded, before he realized it. "I don't know what you're talking about."

"What don't you understand?"

"I mean, *I'm* not a soldier," Michael stated.

"You're wrong," the man insisted. "You have some of the same gifts as your father."

"You don't know my father! I'm nothing like my father!" Michael recoiled and looked away.

"Why do you say that?"

"It doesn't matter why."

He crossed his arms and sulked.

"You need to study your Bible more," the soldier maintained. "The gifts of God are passed from generation to generation. Your father can only run *his* race and fight *his* battles. *You* must fight *yours*."

Michael was beyond annoyed. All he wanted was to be left alone and to go home. He was in no mood to be lectured. No longer willing to be polite, he retreated entirely within himself.

He scolded himself now because he knew that he wouldn't have to deal with stuff like this if he had his own car. He really needed to address his fear of driving, but his anxiety had worsened over time, and it was now affecting other areas of his life. His mother was the only one who knew the depth of his phobia and she had mostly just helped him to hide behind it rather than deal with it. When she died four years ago, he was left to fend for himself.

"I'm sorry. I know that I am bothering you," said the interloper. "But this really is important."

"Alright!" Michael huffed loudly. "What is it?"

"Listen carefully," the man directed and leaned in. "It is important that you hear this. Do not fear any of the things that are to come. It is only a test. When your name is called, you must engage the enemy but do everything you can to resist him. Just do what you know to do. Again, don't be afraid for God is with you."

"Are you kidding?" Michael scoffed. "Who are you really?"

"Who I am is not important."

"Well, no offense but you are freaking me out a little," Michael asserted. "How about you just leave me alone?"

"Sorry, there is no need to be overly concerned. I am just trying to help you. Please remember what I said."

Michael wasn't quite sure what to say in response. So, he said nothing. He just looked away and fretted because there was a sense of conviction in the way that this pushy courier spoke.

Regardless, he was more than a little relieved when the man abruptly got up and, without looking back, took another seat closer to the front. Michael just turned his head and focused his attention back to the passing traffic lights outside the window until they arrived at the bus station in Schenectady.

By the time that he had made his way to the front of the bus, the man was nowhere to be found. He was relieved again because as a wimpish, insecure black guy, who had never been in a real fight in his life, he was basically defenseless. The last thing he wanted was a confrontation with a crazy stranger on the bus. With his luck, this dude was probably a trained guerrilla assassin with combat induced post-traumatic stress disorder who could pop off at any moment. He was just glad that this day was almost over.

Chapter 1

Goldberg & Epstein LLP was one of the oldest law firms in Schenectady, New York. Once very prestigious, it had long lost much of its prowess. The firm originally did a lot of commercial work in the capitol region, especially for General Electric Company (GE) at the turn of the 20th century when the company was flourishing. At one time, there were as many as ten attorneys working there. But now, just two lawyers and a paralegal, who specialized in bankruptcy and real estate law, made up the workforce.

The managing partner was Robert Epstein, a short, stocky guy in his mid-50s, who was the grandson of one of the original partners. He was a nice guy with a mean temper. If something set him off, he was a real bear. But typically, Rob was pleasant enough and easy to work for. On the bad days, everyone just took cover and waited for the storm to pass.

Michael got the job at Goldberg & Epstein through a temp agency. He was forced to get another job when the convenience mart, he worked at for several years, suddenly closed. He was supposed to just be filling in at the firm while their receptionist was out on maternity leave, but he was offered the job on a permanent basis when she decided not to return.

In addition to answering the phone, he opened the mail and did some filing and basic bookkeeping. Most of the real work at the firm was done by Jeffrey Sutter, the paralegal, who worked up every real estate closing in the office. Jeff did all the paperwork and Sarah Cohen-Smith, the lone associate attorney on staff, appeared at the closings and handled the bankruptcy matters. She was married to an attorney in town, and they had two young children. She basically worked part-time at the firm, as they scheduled four to six real estate closings every week.

Initially, Michael was intimidated by everyone at the firm, and he felt very much out of place. His associate degree was in liberal arts, not law. But the work was pretty much common sense to him, and they seemed to like him. It wasn't long before he was taking on additional duties, including filing papers at the courthouse. Because Michael was not used to having much responsibility, the new job helped build his self-confidence.

He had been at the firm about a month when he met Ira Goldberg for the first time. Mr. Goldberg was the retired partner who kept his office at the firm. He was 80 years old, but he managed to get along pretty well. Occasionally, he would drop in and spend a couple of hours sitting at his desk and talking on the phone. A little too strident to be called a "sweet old man" but was still very personable, and he loved to retell long stories about his younger days.

Michael didn't initially feel any special affinity toward the firm's elder statesman, who always insisted upon bringing goodies with him in the form of cookies, bagels, or pastries whenever he came into the office. It was an obvious ploy to get people to engage in conversation with him. Clearly, this widower was desperately seeking a friendly audience. He seemed more than just a little lonely.

"Mikey! Mikey!" Mr. Goldberg called out from his office one morning.

Michael got up from his desk and walked down the hall to the large corner office.

"Yeah," he asked while standing in the doorway.

"Have you seen my gold pen?"

He was a thin man of average height. His hair had thinned out pretty good on top and his ghostly complexion was highlighted by several age spots and blemishes. He also had wrinkled circles under his eyes, which were protected by thick framed glasses.

"I could have sworn that I left it here," he fussed.

"No… wait, is that it by your foot?" Michael pointed out.

"Oh, yes. There it is. Thanks."

"You're welcome."

"What's that on your wrist?" Mr. Goldberg asked.

"What? My bracelet?"

"Yes, what is it?"

"It's just a sideways cross," Michael responded. "My aunt gave it to me when my mom died."

"Oh, I'm sorry to hear. So, you know Yeshua?"

"Who?" Michael asked.

"'Yeshua' is the Hebrew name for Jesus."

"Oh, I never heard that before."

"Jesus was a Jew, you know."

"Yeah, I know."

"So, that means that he is the Jewish Messiah," Mr. Goldberg asserted.

"I thought that Jews rejected Jesus," Michael remarked.

"I'm Jewish. I believe in him. I am a member of a Messianic congregation."

"Does that mean that you are Christian too?"

"We prefer the term 'Messianic Jew' as ones who celebrate both the biblical and cultural heritage of the Jewish people."

"So, you don't like Christians?"

"That's not it at all," Mr. Goldberg corrected. "The true church is made up of both Jews and Gentiles. But we probably shouldn't have this conversation here, if you know what I mean. Maybe we can talk about it some other time."

"Oh… okay, thanks," Michael said and turned and quickly walked away.

He really didn't know what Mr. Goldberg meant. He didn't know any Jewish people. Although Rob and Sarah both were Jewish, they never talked about that part of themselves. The only thing he knew about the Jews was what he heard in church and what he had read in the Bible.

He also had studied the Holocaust in ninth grade world history class, but he still didn't really understand why people hated the Jews. To him, Jews are mostly white people, like the Italians and the French are mostly white people. Arguably, the black experience in America had framed that perspective.

Just because he was more than a little curious, Michael did a quick search on his laptop later that night and was surprised to learn that there were approximately 250,000 Messianic Jews in the United States and 350,000 worldwide. He felt stupid. He was always discovering things that others just knew but had somehow escaped him. The problem was it seemed to be happening a lot lately, and it was embarrassing. This added to his self-doubt, and he wondered what Mr. Goldberg thought about him.

For as long as he could remember, he felt misunderstood. As the youngest of the three Johnson brothers, Michael always believed that he didn't quite measure up. His father was a mechanic and an upright man who had worked very hard to take care of his family. However, because his siblings had serious deficiencies growing up, it always seemed to Michael that his dad had simply run out of both patience and love by the time he was born.

In response, Michael grew to lean heavily upon his mother. She was a homemaker and the most caring person that he had ever known. She died at the age of fifty-six after a nearly two-year battle with breast cancer. He was still dealing with the grief of losing her.

Michael lived alone in the family home. His father had taken an early buyout package offered by his employer, the City of Schenectady, and retired two years ago. He now spent most of the winter months in Arizona. At first, Michael wasn't sure that he could stay there by himself, but it turned out not to be that much of an adjustment. All he had to do was make sure that nothing happened to the house. His father still paid all the bills and returned home in the early spring to take care of the real maintenance that the house required. It worked out good for them both.

His only real friend was Leonard Rogers, a guy who he met in college. Leonard worked for his father at a business that sold headstones. He had an accounting degree, although he never took the state exams to be certified. He was a couple of years younger than Michael and had his own small apartment located close to downtown.

Unlike Michael, who still had a babyface and was handsome in a nerdy kind of way, Leonard's face bore the scars from a bad case of teenage acne. He also wore thick glasses that blurred his blue eyes, and he was frumpy in a way that firmly cemented his status as a social misfit.

However, Leonard was bright and witty and easy to be around. It was a shame that most people never took the time to get to know him because he had a good heart too. He was a sensitive soul who was very troubled by the pain he saw in the world. This was why he preferred to hide out rather than face people. He and Michael mostly played videogames and watched movies together. But their real connection was that neither man felt esteemed nor valued.

Indeed, the two nonconformists shared a worldview that celebrated their lack of goals and vision for their lives. Although Michael knew better, he couldn't make himself think or act differently. Perhaps he was more than a little depressed and needed some professional help, but he simply lacked both the strength and the motivation to change anything about himself.

As a result, he had grown accustomed to living his life only for today with very little concern about tomorrow. At thirty-six years of age, he was mostly invisible.

Chapter 2

Michael was the first one in the office every morning. The firm was located on the second floor of a small downtown office building. He was supposed to get there by 8:30 a.m. He turned up the heat, put on the coffee and checked the phone for messages. The regular office hours were 9:00 a.m. to 5:00 p.m., Monday through Friday. The firm was closed on all legal holidays, and all the Jewish holidays. They never scheduled the first real estate closing before11:00 a.m. and the two senior attorneys rarely arrived before 10:00 a.m.

Jeff always came in at 9:00 a.m. sharp. He was 38 years old, and he had been with the firm for nearly ten years. He had shoulder length brown hair and a stocky build. He was a no-nonsense kind of guy and a hard worker. He was rarely away from his desk in his small, cluttered office and he never wasted time. Although Jeff was a bit standoffish, he was a decent guy and Michael really liked him.

A married father of three, Jeff really knew his stuff. One thing for sure, his work was indispensable to the firm and Rob was lucky to have him.

"Good morning," Jeff said one frosty morning as he walked through the door.

Michael was sitting at his desk in the reception area. Jeff was bundled up in a big winter coat, hat, and scarf. He was carrying a backpack on one shoulder and a thermos in his hand.

"Good morning," Michael responded without looking up.

"You might want to ask the building manager to salt the front steps. They are very icy in certain spots. I almost slipped and fell."

"Okay."

"I'm not sure if the Tate closing is going to happen," Jeff muttered. "We still don't have a cleared title."

"Do you want me to call Sarah and tell her that it is off?"

"No, not yet" Jeff replied. "Let me make a couple of phone calls first."

"Okay."

"Oh, and you should probably turn on the heat in Mr. Goldberg's office. I think that he is coming in today," Jeff reported.

"Today? Really? I mean with the weather and all."

"I think he has a conference call or something today with the Mackey Foundation," Jeff informed. "He lives for that stuff. He's a tough old goat. He should be fine."

"Yeah, he seems hardcore. Hey, he was telling me the other day that he is a Messianic Jew."

"Really?" Jeff questioned and raised one eyebrow. "Rob gets mad when he tells people that."

"Why?"

"I don't know. I don't fully understand it. All I know is that they got into a big fight or something about it this one time."

"Really? I didn't know."

"I'm surprised that he said anything to you about it."

"No, it was nothing," Michael asserted. "I probably asked him about it."

"Well, you might not want to mention it to Rob," Jeff said dismissively before scurrying off to his office.

Michael considered the morning to be the best part of his workday. He didn't handle stress well and this time was often like the calm before the storm. They regularly faced many dead-lines, and he could feel that pressure seep down to his front office position. Unlike his predecessor, Michael didn't type or prepare documents. But he *did* make all the copies needed, put the documents together in backers, prepare mailing labels and envelopes, and made sure that everything was delivered or placed in the mail on time.

Fortunately, most days were quiet. If not for the soft music coming from the small radio that he kept on his desk, there would have been nothing but the occasional sound of the printer and the phone ringing to break up the silence. Overall, it was the perfect job for an introverted guy.

Mr. Goldberg walked through the door at 10:30 a.m. Michael never exactly knew when he was planning to come into the office. He wore a fur hat and a khaki-colored trench coat that probably wasn't heavy enough considering the extreme cold temperature. He was also carrying a small white box of pastries.

"Top of the morning to you, Mikey," Mr. Goldberg said enthusiastically.

"Good morning," Michael said.

"How are you?"

"I'm good. How are you?"

"I am good too," Mr. Goldberg expressed. "Good thing that I like the cold. Otherwise, I'm living in the wrong place. Wouldn't you say?"

"Yes, that's right."

"Hey Mikey, what do you think about joining me for lunch today? The place around the corner has good soup."

"Well, I don't know," Michael hesitated.

"What's wrong? They let you eat lunch here, don't they?"

"Yeah, but I brought my lunch."

"Save it for tomorrow. I think that it's time that we got to know each other better. You don't want to hurt my feelings, do you?"

"No, I don't want to do that," Michael admitted.

"Good, then, it's settled. How's 12:30?"

"Well…okay," Michael softly replied.

"Good!" Mr. Goldberg exclaimed. "It's a date."

Obviously, Michael had no desire to go to lunch with Mr. Goldberg. He was caught completely off guard by the invitation, and he just didn't know how to say no. The old man had never shown anything other than a passing interest in him before. He had even insisted upon calling Michael by a nickname that he hated.

Typically, Michael ate his lunch at his desk. Even on nice days, the most he ever did was walk to one of the downtown restaurants and pick up a sandwich. He liked his routine and was bothered when he was forced to change it. However, today his typical lunch break would be interrupted.

They ended up going to a restaurant that was just a few minutes walking distance from the office. Michael had never been there before. It wasn't quite his style. It was basically a small bar surrounded by several tables. The room was only about half full. A waitress seated them at a table in the far corner away from the kitchen as Mr. Goldberg requested.

"You ever been here before Mikey?"

"No."

"Do you like tomato soup? The soup here is terrific."

"No, not really," Michael disclosed.

"Well, there are other options."

Michael began looking over the menu. He was worried about the food taking too long and getting back to the office late. He only had an hour for lunch, and he had forwarded the phone to Jeff's desk. He really hated doing that because he felt that Jeff did enough already.

The two men read the menu in silence before dictating their selections to the waitress.

"So, tell me about yourself," Mr. Goldberg began.

"What do you want to know?"

"Where are you from?"

"I'm from here," Michael revealed.

"You were born in Schenectady?"

"Uh huh."

"Do you have family?"

"Yeah, my father is in Arizona for the winter. I have two older brothers too, but they are not here."

"How old are you, Mikey?"

"I'm thirty-six."

"Really, thirty-six? You look much younger. You must have good genes."

"I don't know," Michael said and shrugged.

"You're not married?"

Michael repelled by the question. "No," he said.

"Is there someone special in your life?"

"Nope."

"Why not?"

"No reason."

"I get the feeling that you don't like talking about yourself," Mr. Goldberg acknowledged.

"Not really."

"Why do you think that is?" the attorney probed.

"I don't know. I just don't. Why do you want to know?"

"Because I have been watching you. I'm just curious."

"Watching me?" Michael cringed.

"Nothing bad," Mr. Goldberg reassured. "It's just that I have a good feeling about you, that's all. My guess is that there is much more below the surface than meets the eye."

"Really? Cause I'm nobody special."

"Well, that remains to be seen," Mr. Goldberg spoke.

Michael felt uncomfortable and shifted his weight in his chair. He wasn't used to compliments, veiled or otherwise. His thoughts suddenly turned to wanting to return to the office.

"Mind if I ask you one more question?" Mr. Goldberg solicited.

"No, go ahead."

"How long have you been a Christian?"

"Uh, basically my whole life. My whole family is. We went to church a lot. My parents taught us to love God."

"Well, good for you," Mr. Goldberg remarked. "That's really great, Mikey."

They were interrupted by the waitress delivering their food.

"Okay then, since you don't want to talk about yourself, let's turn the table, shall we? Do you have any questions for me?"

"Yeah, how long have you been a Messianic Jew?"

"Let's see, almost thirty-six years."

"Wow! Why did you convert? If you don't mind me asking?"

"No, not at all... It's a long story."

"I mean…you don't have to."

"No, I like talking about it," Mr. Goldberg explained. "My parents were Ashkenazi Jews. I was born in Russia. I had two brothers too. We were all born there. My family came to the United States to escape persecution in Europe. We were in Northern Africa for a little while and then I was raised in New York City."

"Africa?"

"Not long though," Mr. Goldberg followed up. "The goal was always to immigrate to the United States. I don't remember any of that. I was too young."

"Oh," Michael said and took his first bite of his hamburger.

"Even though we were culturally Jewish, religiously we were atheist. Unlike you, I was taught that God was a myth. My father thought that people who believed in God were foolish. And I believed that way too for most of young adult years, even after I was married, and we had our kids."

"So, what happened?"

"My mother died," Mr. Goldberg said matter-of-factly. "I took it hard, very hard. She was in good health and hadn't been sick. My father was sickly for years before he died years before. But not her. About a week before she had a heart attack, she called me and said that there was something that she wanted to tell me. She said that it was important. I went to her house in the

Bronx the next day. She was different, anxious. I just remember being worried. That's when she told me about Yeshua, the Messiah. At first, I thought she was crazy. But she spoke with such assurance and joy that it caused me to shiver inside. I knew in my heart that I needed to listen. She was a good woman. Apparently, she had secretly become a believer several years before."

"Oh, wow!" Michael exclaimed. "You never suspected."

"No, never. Of course, my father knew, but he made her keep her faith a secret. I cried like a baby then and there. I wasn't sure why. I just couldn't help myself. She put her hand on my shoulder and prayed to God to reveal himself to me."

"You think that she knew that she was going to die soon?" Michael wondered aloud.

"You mean like a premonition or something?"

"Uh huh."

"I'm convinced of it," Mr. Goldberg declared. "I prayed to God for the first time by myself the night after she was buried. I immediately felt a peace unlike anything I had ever known before."

"That's an amazing story!"

"I know," Mr. Goldberg conceded. "After that I started studying the Torah for myself in a way that I had never done before and compared it to the new covenant. I was hungry for the truth. And I found the evidence for Yeshua to be overwhelming."

"Did you tell your family? Your brothers?"

"No, not immediately. I told my wife first. Let's just say that she was less than impressed. My brothers had pretty much the same reaction. My two children too. I think that they were all convinced that I had completely lost my mind and they just wrote me off after that."

"I'm sorry," Michael commiserated. "That must be hard."

"Honestly, I try not to dwell on it. They feel like I rejected both them and my heritage, even though I still celebrate the Jewish holidays, like Passover and Rosh Hashanah. I don't really celebrate Christmas or Easter. We were never kosher. Look, I know that my family loves me in their own way, but they don't understand me, and they definitely don't want to hear anything about Yeshua."

"So, what do you do?" Michael pressed.

"I pray for them the same way that, my mother, Ruth Goldberg prayed for me. I trust Yeshua."

"Is that enough for you?"

"Yes, it is more than enough." Mr. Goldberg said with a gleam in his eyes. "I know without a shadow of a doubt that Hashem has not forgotten about his sacred covenant with Israel. I get that not all Jews will accept Yeshua. But the Bible says that there is a remnant of Jews who will be saved. I am standing on the promises in his word that they may experience the end-times spiritual awakening."

"Mr. Goldberg, I think that is so awesome."

"The Lord is worthy to be praised!"

"So, do you see them much?"

"My daughter lives in Syracuse with her family. She checks on me every so often when she remembers. My son Ari is a plastic surgeon in New York City. I never see him. I have four grandchildren and four great grandchildren. I get to see them occasionally."

"So, you're basically by yourself now?"

"Sounds to me like you are too."

"Yeah, maybe," Michael reluctantly admitted and quickly averted his eyes.

"Then, how about we become friends, Mikey? I could use a good Christian friend."

"But I don't understand why you would want to be friends with me," Michael resisted.

"You mean because I am an old man?"

"No, because I'm only the guy who answers the phone at your office."

"Like I said, I have a good feeling about you," Mr. Goldberg stated emphatically.

Michael smiled this time despite himself and let his guard down a little.

"Thank you, Mr. Goldberg."

"My friends call me Ira."

"Okay. My friends call me Michael."

Chapter 3

Ira and Michael quickly came together. Michael remained a bit skeptical at first, but his hesitation eased more each day. Ira began coming into the office more frequently and they talked when time permitted. Michael was always careful about what he said to Ira when other people were around. They often went to lunch at that same place, Rocky's, which had grown on him.

It turned out that they had several things in common too. Both men were quick-witted and shared a similar sense of humor. As a result, they enjoyed picking on each other. Additionally, they were both very stubborn and adverse to change.

Indeed, when Michael insisted that Ira get a cell phone, the battle was on.

"I already have a phone at my house," Ira argued. "If I don't answer, call back later!"

Michael thought taking Ira to a cellular store was a nightmare until he discovered that teaching him how to use his new phone was twice as tortuous. It took a week just to teach him how to answer it and even then, he continued to have trouble. When it rang, he kept hitting the decline button and when it cut off, he complained incessantly that "this cheap mass-produced product is garbage!"

"I have no idea why I let you talk me into getting this piece of crap!" Ira lashed out one day. "I'm never listening to you again!"

"That's your problem, you're not listening now. You never listen to anybody!" Michael shot back.

He really wanted Ira to get a laptop next. Ira was such an intelligent man, and he still was very curious about things. Michael was convinced that his new friend would love having all the information at his fingertips. However, Ira's old-school version of getting information still worked for him. He read the newspaper every day and watched the nightly news intently. And frankly, Michael was too afraid to bring up the subject of a laptop. He decided that it made more sense to retreat and live to fight another day.

Naturally, the tone of voice that they used with each other had become less professional and more familiar. Michael was completely unaware of it until Rob asked him about it.

"What's with you and the old man?"

"What do you mean?" Michael responded.

"I see that you guys go to lunch together all the time and always have your heads together. Is something going on that I should know about?"

"No, I like him," Michael explained. "I like hearing him talk about his life."

"His life?" Rob questioned with a surprised look on his face.

"You know, the things he's seen and the places he has been. I have never been anywhere. Did you know that he used to live in Africa?"

"No, I hadn't heard that."

"He's different from me," Michael explained. "He's interesting. Why is something wrong?"

"No, nothing is wrong," Rob conceded. "I just wanted to make sure that he wasn't forcing himself on you."

"No, nothing like that," Michael said.

"Well, if you say so. I was just asking."

Rob walked away without saying anything else. Michael was confused. He repeated the conversation to Ira at lunch later in the week.

"I wasn't sure why he was asking me that stuff," Michael solicited.

"Because he doesn't want us getting too close."

"But why?"

"Well, for one thing, he doesn't really want me around," Ira disclosed. "My father and his grandfather started the firm together. They met in law school, and they were good friends and became partners. We both inherited our shares of the firm from our fathers. Of course, I was here long before he came along. Although we are cordial, we never really saw eye to eye on a lot of things and there have been several bumps in the road along the way in our business relationship. He wanted to buy me out when I retired from the practice of law ten years ago, but I didn't want to sell."

"Why not?"

"Because my father started the firm and he left it to me," Ira explained. "I want to keep it in the family."

"That makes sense."

"I think that he is concerned about what is going to happen when I die."

"But that has nothing to do with me," Michael said.

"Right," Ira agreed. "I can't say for sure what he was after. But he's also not fond of Messianic Jews. He might be concerned that I am trying to convert you."

"Convert me?"

"I'm joking, but most Messianic Jews are largely shunned by mainstream Jewish communities around the world. They are afraid that we are going to preach Yeshua to their children and that they will convert. It's become a big problem in Israel."

"Israel?"

"Yes. There have been protests there outside of Messianic places of worship and many of us have a hard time getting jobs and finding places to live. Some people have been prosecuted by the government for supposedly violating the law by proselytizing to minors without the consent of their parents."

"So, you are telling me that Rob hates you because you believe in Yeshua?" Michael wondered.

"I don't think that he *hates* me," Ira stressed. "But a while back, he became angry with me when he overheard me talking to someone from my synagogue on the phone. It truly was an innocent conversation, but he came barging in and started screaming and shouting that he didn't want any of that talk in *his* office."

"How did it end?"

"Not well. But even though I thought that he was out of line, I agreed not to talk about my faith in the office. I just wanted to resolve the issue. He really offended me, but I felt that I needed to turn the other cheek. Do you know what I'm saying?"

"Uh huh, I get it," Michael sympathized. "Um, I'm really sorry that happened to you."

"Thank you, Michael. I appreciate it, but persecution for the sake of the gospel is an honor and a privilege. It wasn't like he could put a muzzle on me. The entire world is our mission field!"

While Michael appreciated how forthcoming Ira was about everything, he found the conversation much more disturbing than he let on. Rob was really *his* boss, not Ira. Rob was the one who hired him. This job was important to him, and he didn't want to get on Rob's bad side or be viewed as somehow conspiring with the enemy. He figured that it made more sense to focus on his job while he was in the office and not let Rob see him interacting with Ira too much.

*　*　*

Ira called one afternoon from home and said that he had walking pneumonia.

"Are you okay?"

"Yes, I'll be fine."

"Is there anything you need?"

"No, it's not that bad," Ira contended. "My doctor considered putting me in the hospital, but I told him that he was crazy if he thought that I was going to lay up in that germ-infested factory and catch some deadly infection that really does kill me. These people are out of their minds!"

"Maybe you should listen to your doctor," Michael calmly suggested. "You don't have a medical degree, you know. Maybe he knows what's best."

"No, he doesn't," Ira insisted. "I know what's best for me."

"Alright, alright, I'm not going to argue with you," Michael retreated. "My number is in your cell phone. Remember what I showed you? You just have to click on my name. You don't have to dial the number. Call me if it gets worse or if you need something."

"Okay, I got it. But I can take care of myself."

"Ira?"

"I said I got it!"

"Just don't forget."

Fortunately, Ira was right this time. He made a fast recovery. Michael called him twice on his cell phone just to check up on him and surprisingly Ira answered both times. But that was really only because he thought that Michael was testing him, and he couldn't resist the opportunity to gloat. Regardless, at least he finally learned how to answer the darn thing. It only took a month!

Chapter 4

How come you don't have a car?" Ira asked.

"Because I don't," Michael replied.

"That's not an answer. That's just a restatement of the question," Ira goaded.

"Because I don't have a driver's license."

"Why not?'

"Because I don't."

"There you go again with that circular argument. Are you doing that on purpose?" Ira wondered aloud.

"I'm afraid to drive," Michael confessed. "There I said it. Are you happy now?"

"Amaxophobia," Ira said.

"What?"

"Amaxophobia," Ira repeated. "It's the irrational fear of driving. What happened? Were you in a bad accident as a child or something?"

"No."

"Then what?"

"Nothing happened," Michael protested. "I already told you."

"You know, they have meds for that, right?" Ira asked. "Did you ever see a doctor?"

"No, I never saw a doctor."

"Maybe you should," Ira teased. "Doctors go to medical school. They know everything. Isn't that what you said?"

Michael was annoyed. Ira had a way of getting under his skin that made him want to scream. It was like no disagreement was ever really over with him. He always took the first chance that he got to deliver a comeback.

"Look, can you just drop it?"

"So, what are you going to do?" Ira questioned. "Just spend your whole life riding the bus?"

"Maybe. It's my life."

"Do you like girls?" Ira baited.

"What?

"You heard me. Do-you-like-girls?"

"What does that have to do with anything?" Michael resisted.

"Schenectady isn't exactly New York City where you don't need a car. How are you ever going to go on a date if you don't have a car?"

"That's my problem," Michael replied defensively. "Don't worry about it!"

"See, now I am worried about it!" Ira shot back. "I'm very worried. My best friend in the whole world is a big baby who doesn't know how to drive and who is never going to have a girlfriend. People are going to talk, and it is going to reflect poorly on me. I won't have it."

"Just mind your own business!"

"You *are* my business," Ira stated emphatically.

"What do you want from me?"

"I could teach you," Ira offered.

"Teach me?" Michael asked and snickered.

"What's wrong with that?"

"Are you crazy? I'm not letting some 80-year-old guy, who probably can't even see the road, teach me how to drive. How ridiculous is that?"

"Not true," Ira objected. "I'll have you know that I have never had an accident, and my eyesight is excellent. And need I remind you that I have a car and a license, and I've had a woman. So that makes me better off than you any day of the week."

Michael was incensed, but he refused to let it show. He was never good at controlling his anger. That's one of the reasons he had avoided his brothers as much as he did when he was younger.

A little thing could turn into a big deal in no time because they loved to antagonize each other. He fretted.

"Can you please just drop it? You can't possibly understand," Michael implored.

He sighed heavily.

"No, I don't want to drop it," Ira maintained. "Why would I do that? You can't just let that blister fester and get bigger and bigger. At some point you need to pop that sucker. Are we men here, or what? I think that you should take me up on my very kind offer. If you go out on the road with me one time, then I will drop it. But not until then."

Michael was silent. He rolled his eyes.

"Don't ignore me" Ira dug in deeper. "Did you hear what I said?"

"Yeah, I heard you… One time?"

"One time. That's the deal."

"Okay."

"Good, I'll take care of everything. See, now was that so hard?" Ira needled.

Michael knew that he was in trouble. He had never actually been behind the wheel of a car before. He had refused to take the driver's education class in high school. He had no idea how or why his fear developed, but just the thought of driving in traffic made him feel sick to his stomach. It was just something that he never wanted to do.

Ira wanted to go out driving the following Saturday morning. He suggested that they meet at the office. Michael seriously considered not showing up, but he knew that that was probably the worst thing that he could do. That would just stir Ira up even more. He barely slept that Friday night.

As planned, Michael waited in front of the office. Ira pulled up a few minutes later in a black, late model Volvo sedan. It was a nice car. Michael had only been in the car once before when they went to get the cell phone. Ira rolled down the window.

"Get in," Ira said.

"Where are we going?"

"It's a surprise," Ira said.

He had a wry smile on his face.

"I don't like surprises," Michael said as he plopped down and shut the door. "Why do you have on a motorcycle helmet?"

"Because I don't want to die when you try to drive!"

"No see, I'm not doing this," Michael stated and grabbed the door handle to get out of the car.

Ira hit the gas hard and drove off.

"Let me out of this car!" Michael demanded.

"No, it will be okay. Just you sit back and relax."

He hit the gas harder and slammed on the brakes when they came to the first light.

Michael was starting to feel a little queasy.

"Ira, I mean it!" Michael yelled.

"Oh, stop your bellyaching. Where's your faith, brother?"

"I'm not playing around," Michael begged.

"You're fine," Ira said. "I have only had two accidents before--only one was bad."

"I thought you said you never had an accident."

"I may have stretched the truth a little. I don't know."

Michael just looked straight ahead as his heart raced. He held on tightly to the handle overhead with his right hand. He didn't trust Ira, who was driving in traffic at a normal speed. He made several turns and intersection stops before he finally pulled into a small shopping plaza and parked the car.

"We are here," he suddenly announced.

"Here? Where?" Michael asked while looking around.

"Get out!" Ira urged. "Come on!"

Michael was furious as he followed Ira toward an outdoor mall storefront. The printed sign on the window read in big block letters, "Stanley Driving School."

"What's this?" Michael asked.

"Just hurry up," Ira directed. "We have an appointment."

A buzzer went off as soon as they walked inside. It was a lobby with several empty chairs lined up against a back wall facing a counter. A man walked through a closed door that was behind the counter.

"Good morning, Ira," he said with a big smile.

The two shook hands.

"Good morning," Ira greeted. "How are you this fine morning?"

"Blessed! This must be the young man you were telling me about."

"Yes, this is Michael."

"Hello, Michael. I'm Andy. Ira tells me that you would like to learn how to drive."

"Um, yeah," Michael said without looking at Ira.

"Do you have any driving experience?"

"No."

"Good," Andy said. "Just the way I like it. That means that you don't have any bad habits to unlearn."

"If you don't mind, I have a form here that you need to complete and sign," Andy continued. "Once you finish with that, we can get started."

He handed Michael a piece of paper and a pen. Michael was apprehensive. He kept thinking that Ira should have just told him they were coming here. It would have been so much easier that way, but with Ira that was probably too much to ask.

Ira and Andy conversed while Michael completed the two-page form. Apparently, they attended the same synagogue. Michael wasn't really paying attention to their conversation. There were a couple of questions that he wasn't sure how to answer, such as whether he suffered from anxiety. He just skipped them and quickly signed the liability waiver at the bottom of the form and put the pen down.

"You finished?" Andy asked and began looking over the form. "Okay, everything seems to be in order. How about you follow me? Ira, you are welcome to wait here, or you can leave and come back. We will be about an hour."

"I brought something to read with me," Ira said. "Michael, I will be waiting out in the car when you are done. And just remember that the greater one lives in you and helps us to defeat our fears!"

Andy escorted Michael to a large room in the back where there were four driving machines. They looked a little like a gaming cockpit that one might find at an arcade.

"You like videogames," Andy asked.

"Yes, I do."

"These machines simulate driving on the road like a video game," Andy explained.

"Ever play one of those games?"

"No."

"No?" Andy questioned. "Okay, so why don't you get in? It'll be painless. I promise."

Andy was right. It wasn't that bad, and it didn't feel like driving, not that Michael knew what that felt like. After the first couple of minutes, he loosened up and he didn't think about what he was doing. By the end of the hour, he was able to drive on what appeared to be a two-lane roadway with limited oncoming traffic.

Michael was proud of himself. It was relatively painless. He scheduled his next nine private lessons. Andy said that Ira had paid for them in advance.

Ira was reading the newspaper when Michael opened the car door and sat down. He looked straight ahead.

"So, how did it go?" Ira asked.

"Good."

"That's it?" Ira questioned. "That's all that you can say?"

"Leave me alone," Michael protested. "How's that?"

"Looks like someone has his nose a little out of joint," Ira teased.

Michael continued to look straight ahead. Ira started the car and slowly pulled out of the parking lot. He was no longer wearing his helmet. The ensuing five minutes or so of silence were deafening.

"I don't understand why you are so angry," Ira pestered.

Michael did not respond.

"Are you ever going to talk to me again?"

Still nothing.

"Do you want me to take you back to the office or drive you home?"

More of the same.

"Michael?"

"Why did you do that?" Michael finally asked.

He shot a piercing glance in Ira's direction.

"Aww come on. I was just having a little fun at your expense."

"Wasn't funny," Michael brooded. "It was mean."

"Sometimes I go too far, I know."

"You need to listen when people tell you stuff."

"Yeah, you're right."

"Take the next right. I live close to here" Michael directed.

"Okay."

"Take this left. It's the grey house on the corner."

"Here?"

"Yeah."

Ira slowly pulled the car into the driveway.

"Thank you," Michael said, "…for everything."

"Are you breaking up with me?" Ira wondered.

"No."

"Thank you. I know I was wrong. I really am sorry."

Chapter 5

Adat Yeshua was a Messianic Synagogue located in the far east city limits of Albany.

For months Ira had been trying to get Michael to go to his synagogue with him. Because Ira was so insistent, it was getting harder to say no. Michael knew that he just needed to bite the bullet and go. He wasn't resistant for religious reasons, or anything as serious as that. It was just that he feared that he would feel out of place. They finally planned that he would accompany Ira to Saturday service after his driving lesson. Fortunately for Ira, Michael agreed to go before he knew the service would last three hours.

The synagogue was located on a small rural roadway situated amidst several old factory and industrial buildings. It appeared to be a converted warehouse or something. There was no parking lot, so Ira just parked his car haphazardly on the side of the road. The front entrance led to a narrow hallway, which after several twists and turns, fed into one big open room. There were about 150 or so folding chairs set up facing an elevated platform.

Overall, the room was very plain and basic, without any crosses or symbols prominently displayed anywhere. There was Jewish music being piped in through two large speakers on both sides of the platform. It was 2:45 p.m. and, although the service was supposed to begin at 3:00 p.m., there were only a handful of people present. Of course, Ira wanted to sit in the front row, dead center.

To Michael's surprise, the service began promptly at 3:00 p.m. The rabbi's name was Benjamin Jacob Cohen. He was short with a small frame, and he wore black framed glasses. He also had a grey moustache and beard that completely covered the lower half of his face, including his lips. He appeared to be in his sixties. He wore a black suit and, over his shoulders, a white prayer shawl with twined and knotted fringes on the corners. He also wore a black yarmulke on his head.

The first part was a liturgical service, which began with the rabbi reading from the Torah. It readily brought back childhood memories of when he had to fight hard to stay awake in church so as not to incur the wrath of his father. Similarly, it would have truly been a nightmare if Ira caught him dozing off. At one point, he began praying silently in hopes that the service would pick up soon or else he was going to be in real trouble.

Fortunately, the readings were followed by more contemporary worship. Michael recognized a couple of the songs, and he was beginning to feel more at ease. Several people in the congregation, which was slowing growing in numbers, raised their hands as they stood and sang.

However, he was still caught completely off guard when a middle-aged man sitting nearby stood up and began dancing and spinning in circles in the aisle. Michael wasn't put off by it exactly. People in the Baptist church his family attended danced on occasion. It's just that for some reason, he hadn't anticipated that anyone there would be so demonstrative in their worship.

Thereafter, Rabbi Cohen went directly into his teaching. He was very funny, and Michael was surprised by that too. He was soft spoken and told stories about his family and life experiences that Michael could relate to and found very interesting. He referred to both the Old Testament and the New Testament. His central theme was the power of love to change lives and to elevate our present existence. Overall, Michael thought that the teaching was very good, although he started getting a little tired near the end of it.

Interestingly, no one left after the benediction. The service transitioned into a social hour and people seemed to just automatically break up into small groups. Michael was immediately concerned because he figured that this was just the excuse that Ira needed to never leave. He was a man who simply loved the sound of his own voice far too much to let this golden opportunity pass.

Michael's fear came true, as Ira introduced him to everyone.

"This is my best friend Michael," he said repeatedly and smiled broadly.

"Welcome Michael," Rabbi Cohen replied and extended his hand. "I have heard a lot about you."

"Thank you," Michael said.

"Did you enjoy the service?"

"Yes, I did. It was very interesting."

"What church do you go to?"

"I go to Grace Union Baptist in Schenectady."

"I'm not familiar with it," Rabbi said as he stroked his beard and slowly shook his head back and forth. "Please be sure to give our best to your pastor and please feel free to visit with us anytime. Any friend of Ira's is always welcomed here."

"Thank you."

At one point, Michael excused himself and went to the bathroom. Then he took a seat in the back of the room and just waited there. It was clear that Ira was in it for the long haul.

"You ready to go?" Ira finally approached and asked with exuberance.

"Yeah, I'm ready."

"Got time for dinner?" he asked. "I know a good restaurant not far from here."

"Yes, I have time. I'm not doing anything."

Ira was in a good mood. Being an extrovert, Ira was revitalized by interacting with everyone. It was like a drug to him. He was humming to himself in the car. Good thing it was only a short drive to the restaurant… except it wasn't a true restaurant. It was a greasy- spoon diner.

Ira had weird eating habits and also a cast iron stomach. He could eat anything. Unlike Michael who was strictly a meat and potatoes guy. Ira preferred places with "character" to the run of the mill restaurant. The more colorful the better.

"So, what did you really think about the service?" Ira asked over dinner.

"Like I said, I thought it was interesting. It was different in the beginning with the Hebrew prayers."

"Do you have any questions?"

"So, it's kinda like a mixture of Judaism and Christianity, huh?"

"In a manner of speaking," Ira agreed.

"What are the differences?" Michael wondered.

"Theologically, you mean?"

"Yeah."

"Not a lot really," Ira admitted. "As you know, Paul and the other writers of the new covenant were all Jewish converts. The gospel was preached to the Jews first and then to the gentiles. The early church was predominantly Jewish."

"But you said that you don't consider yourself to be Christian, right?"

"Yes."

"Why not?"

"It's complicated," Ira stated. "Some Messianics are members of Christian churches. But that would be a hard pill to swallow for me. Over the years, Christians have persecuted the Jewish people like everyone else. It is difficult to see yourself as a part of a group that has sought to destroy you."

"I get that," Michael affirmed. "But you said that orthodox Jews don't like Messianics either."

"That is certainly true."

"Do they even consider you to be Jewish anymore?"

"No," Ira acknowledged.

"So, it just seems like everybody wants to be separate and be in their own special group, yet that is not what the Bible teaches."

"I said that it's complicated. The Jewish people have been tormented and ravished all throughout history like no other people on the face of the earth."

"So have black people," Michael asserted. "And we go to church all the time with people whose ancestors put us in slavery."

"Yes, I know," Ira acknowledged. "Please don't take this the wrong way, but I'm not sure that it's the same thing. It seems that the further we're removed from the Holocaust the more the world forgets about what really happened there. One-third of all Jews were annihilated!"

"Is it a competition?" Michael pressed.

"No, that is not what I meant. It is just that literally the whole world has hated us. It is hard to forget that if you are a Jew."

"The same people who hate Jews today hate black people too, especially in this country," Michael insisted. "Rabbi Cohen just said that people choose other things over love and forgiveness, such as pride and selfish ambition."

"Yes, he did say that," Ira conceded.

"If we agree that there is only one God, who is the God of Abraham, Isaac, and Jacob, then there should be only one true church too, regardless of what we call ourselves or how we treat each other," Michael asserted before he caught himself. "Um…I mean, in my opinion," he quickly added.

He immediately feared that he might have spoken too brazenly and scolded himself for taking a chance at offending Ira. The truth is that this was all new to him and he was very interested in it. But he also didn't really know what he was talking about, nor was he capable of discerning just how sensitive a subject this really was.

Ira paused to take a bite of his dinner. He ordered a big messy mound of chicken and biscuits. It looked like a heart attack on a plate.

"Can you dance like that one guy?" Michael blurted out, changing the subject.

"I've been waiting for you to say something," Ira said and shook his head. "I give you credit. You lasted much longer than I thought you would."

"I just want to see you bust a move like that," Michael teased.

"No, you want to see me bust my ass," Ira countered.

They both laughed heartily.

Then Ira was noticeably quiet and distant. He looked pensive and began rubbing both eyes with his fingers.

"You alright?" Michael asked.

"Michael, in all seriousness, I need you to understand where I am coming from in all of this," he began slowly. "It's important to me that you do. See, even as our numbers are growing worldwide, Messianic Jews are heavily persecuted today, especially in Israel. There have been bombings at our synagogues, harassment, and vandalism. Our very lives are in danger every day solely because we choose to believe in Yeshua. Think about it: it is okay to be an atheist there, but you face severe persecution and discrimination the second that you profess Yeshua. Some of us have had to go underground. At the same time, most Christians, especially evangelicals in this country, are blind to all of it and instead they are staunch supporters of a government that actively discriminates against us. It makes me crazy!"

"Oh," Michael said. "I didn't know. I think I understand."

"Thank you."

"Have you ever been there?"

"Where? Israel?"

"Yeah"

"No, I haven't," Ira responded while looking slightly dejected. "Of course, I always intended to go, but Esther, that's my wife, was always the one who decided where we went on vacation, and she never wanted to go there. She said that it was too much trouble. I probably should have found a way to go by myself. It's probably one of the things that I regret most in my life. But it's okay, I guess. 'Next year in Jerusalem'."

"Next year in Jerusalem? I've heard that before. What does it mean?"

"It's the very last words of the traditional seder like Passover and Yom Kippur. It's a prayer that serves as a reminder of the past sufferings and reflects the obligation of Jews to live in Jerusalem, a city whose name means peace."

"Well, it's not too late," Michael presented. "Maybe you can still go."

"No, I'm afraid that that ship has sailed as far as I am concerned. Tell you what though, maybe one day you can go for me. How about that?"

"Maybe I will," Michael replied.

"For it is written, 'Wherever you go, I will go; wherever you live, I will live. Wherever you die, I will die, and there I will be buried'," Ira recited from scripture. They both were quiet for the rest of their dinner. Ira *had* to have a piece of apple pie for desert while Michael finished his burger. He felt bad for Ira, who suddenly looked like he had the weight of the world on his shoulders. Perhaps for the first time, Michael was beginning to see the true complexity of the world's problems. Not everything was black and white. He had been too yielding before, living with his head in the sand. That was a big mistake; he could clearly see that now.

"Hey, what do you say you drive home?" Ira asked as they walked toward the car.

He offered his keys to Michael.

"Me?"

"Michael, you've made some real progress. You really have; but you're going to have to learn to drive at night at some point. Now is the perfect time. There won't be much traffic at this hour."

"Well, I don't know…" Michael wavered.

"Come on. I know you can do it."

"Okay," he whispered and sighed heavily. "Let's go Miss Daisy."

Chapter 6

It was one of those crazy days. The power in the building went out twice. Then something went wrong with both real estate closings scheduled for that day, and everything was delayed. Both Jeff and Sarah were stressed. Michael was sitting at his desk getting ready to leave for the day when the phone rang.

"Hi, this is Rebecca Bernstein. I am looking for my father, Ira Goldberg. I don't suppose that he's there by any chance?"

"No, he is not here. I haven't seen him today."

"I've been calling his house, but no one answers. I'm starting to get a little worried."

"I know that he had a doctor's appointment today," Michael replied. "Have you tried calling him on his cell phone?"

"I didn't know that he had a cell phone."

"Yeah, he does," Michael disclosed. "Let me give you the number… Let's see… It's 518-547-2899."

"Okay, thank you. I'll try it."

"Let it ring when you call," he advised. "He sometimes for-gets how to answer it and just starts pushing all the buttons. It might take him a minute to remember. I put your name and num-ber in it already. Hopefully, he'll see it and answer it."

"Are you the one who has been helping him?" she asked. "He said that there was someone."

"Yeah, we have been hanging out a little. He's a good guy."

"Okay, if you say so," she replied and laughed to herself, "So, as you probably know, he is a very stubborn man. I don't like the fact that he is living there in that big house by himself. He had that heart attack a while back. I have tried repeatedly to get him to make other living arrangements, but he won't hear of it."

"What kind of other arrangements?" Michael wondered.

"You know, like a retirement place with assisted living," she stated. "I looked into it for him and there are some really nice ones out there."

"He never said anything to me about that."

"I'm sure he didn't… I'm sorry, I didn't catch your name."

"Michael Johnson."

"Michael, maybe you could take my number and call me if there is ever a problem with my father. I would really appreciate it."

"Yes, I can do that," he quickly responded.

The conversation left him feeling uneasy. He had never really thought of Ira as being someone in need of assistance with his daily care. Michael had a grandmother who was living in an apartment building for seniors in Schenectady, but she had a lot of health issues. Ira was highly functional compared to her and he didn't display any outward signs of having a disability or mental impairment.

Michael wasn't worried that something had happened to Ira. It was way too soon to go down that road. With Ira, just about anything was possible. He waited until he got home before he called Ira himself.

"You, okay? Your daughter called the office looking for you."

"Yes, I'm fine," Ira snapped. "They had me sitting in the waiting room at the doctor's office for hours. They claimed they had an emergency, but I didn't see them take anybody out of there on a stretcher. They just like to overbook so they can make their company mandated quotas. Shameful! Nothing but sheer greed! These doctors are just playing the system. I don't know who they think they're kidding."

"I thought that your son is a doctor."

"That's how I know," Ira contended. "My son lives to chase the almighty dollar."

"Do you like anyone in your family?" Michael wondered aloud.

"I don't know what you mean."

"Did you talk to your daughter?"

"Yes, I did."

"She was very worried about you."

"Really?" Ira replied sarcastically. "I find that hard to believe. I think that she just goes through the motions just to feel good about herself. She likes to tell people about *all* she does for me."

"I'm pretty sure that's not true. You know how difficult you are."

"Nonsense," Ira resisted. "I don't know any such thing! She hasn't been here in months."

"Trust me, you have issues. How come you never told me that you had a heart attack?"

"Aww, Becky told you that?" he complained. "It was nothing. It was before I retired, when my wife was still alive. I didn't give it a second thought. Felt like gas. I have always taken good care of myself."

"Are you kidding me? Look how you eat. I don't think that I have ever seen you eat a green vegetable. Not even once."

"Look who's talking," Ira countered. "The only vegetable you eat is the lettuce you just happen to find on your hamburger. Do you know how much fat is in a burger and french fries?"

"Well, we are not talking about me. You need to eat better."

"Why?" Ira asked flippantly. "Because I'm old? Well, let me tell you something. At this point in my life, I don't think that it matters what I eat. I don't drink anymore or play golf or chase women. Food is all I got."

"Give me a break! You never chased any women."

"Never you mind!"

Michael laughed. "You know that if you need help with something, you can call me, right?" he asked.

"I'm not helpless," Ira snapped.

"I never said that you were. I just meant that you have been helping me with my driving and all and I just want to return the favor."

"I don't want anyone feeling sorry for me."

"I don't feel sorry for you," Michael maintained. "I feel sorry for me for wanting to help you with anything."

"Am I really that bad?"

"Yeah, you are," Michael said with a chuckle. "You need Yeshua."

"Amen brother!" Ira agreed.

Chapter 7

ichael still spent a lot of time at his friend, Leonard's place; it wasn't like his social calendar was full otherwise. Truthfully, there was no other place in the world that he wanted to be. The fact is that the two of them had grown more than a little co-dependent in that neither one ever really expected anything from of the other except maybe benign companionship. It was probably the thing that Michael liked most about Leonard—absolutely no pressure.

So, he was really surprised when Leonard challenged him one day about Ira.

"You talk about that old Jewish guy a lot," Leonard contended.

"I know," Michael acknowledged. "It's just that if it wasn't for him, I still wouldn't have my driver's license."

"You still don't have a car so what good is it?"

"I told you; I am just waiting for my dad to get back to help me find a good used car. I have the money."

"But I don't get why you would want to hang around with an 80-year-old dude anyway. It's just weird!"

"Weird how?" Michael wondered.

"Oh, come on! He's older than dirt. How many guys you know our age who hang out every day with an old geezer?"

"A lot of people talk to their grandparents. Besides, we don't hang out *every* day."

"Seems like it," Leonard said.

"How would you know and why do you care? Are you jealous or something?"

"No, I'm not jealous," Leonard refuted. "But you do know that Jews don't even like black people, don't you?"

"That's not true," Michael contested.

"It is true," Leonard said and rolled his eyes. "Did you forget that I am part Jewish? My grandmother always said that black people are lazy and no good."

"That doesn't prove anything just because your grandmother is prejudice."

"Yes, it does," Leonard disputed. "Jews prefer their own. Everybody knows that. This guy just likes having you around because it makes him feel like he is doing his civic duty. You're like the stray dog that he picked up somewhere. It's called charity. Look it up!"

"That's not fair," Michael protested loudly. "You don't even know him."

"I don't have to know him to be right,"

"Maybe, we should just change the subject," Michael wisely suggested and looked away.

He was offended. He and Leonard had never had anything close to an argument before. It just never occurred to him that anyone would care if he spent time with a lonely, old man. But first Rob, and now Leonard. Michael didn't want to make more out of it than he should, but Leonard was right about one thing. It was weird.

As soon as he got home, Michael opened his laptop and did an internet search. There were several articles about the historical relationship between blacks and Jews. Apparently, there is a long history of both cooperation and tension in black-Jewish relations in the United States. Most northern Jews opposed slavery, while most southern Jews supported it. Jews were instrumental in much of the progress made in the Civil Rights movement in the mid-1950s to the mid-1960s. Apparently, the decline in relations began in the mid-1960's with the rise of black nationalism. At the same time, Jews were climbing the economic ladder at a remarkable rate. From then on, interactions between the two communities can best be described as mixed. Sadly, Michael was uninformed about it, having lived his entire life isolated in upstate New York.

The following week, Ira asked Michael to help him sort through his mail. So, he picked up Michael on a Sunday morning. Despite having good intentions, Michael rarely went to church. It was too much trouble to get there without a car. He tried to read his Bible a couple of times a week and he even had a weekly Bible reading planner, although he was always behind in his readings.

This was the first time Michael had been to Ira's home. It was beautiful, located in an upscale development east of downtown Schenectady. It was a picture-perfect colonial with a white picket fence and big oak tree in front. Considering that it was only early April, and most people hadn't even begun their spring cleaning yet, the yard was in pretty good shape. Some of the white perennials were starting to bloom.

Ira parked his car in the driveway and led Michael through a side door. They followed a short hallway into a kitchen that was clean and neat. There were a couple of dishes piled up next to the sink and the hardwood floors were in excellent shape. It was a good size room with a nice wooden table and chairs in the middle. It probably needed some updating, especially the countertops. Notwithstanding, Michael had to admit it was the nicest house he had ever entered.

Ira immediately pointed to a large brown cardboard box on the floor in the corner.

"The mail is in there," he said.

The box was filled to the top. Michael picked it up and placed it on the table.

"When was the last time that you went through it?" he asked.

"I take out the bills and I just dump everything else in there. My old housekeeper used to keep track of the rest of it, but she quit around Thanksgiving. The gout got her."

"So, this is all of your mail since November?" Michael questioned and shook his head.

"It's mostly junk mail. But I didn't want to throw anything away without double checking."

"Is it okay if I open it?"

"Yes, go ahead" Ira indicated.

Michael sat down at the table and began the sorting process.

"Why is it so cold in here?" Michael complained.

"It's not cold. Zip up your jacket if you're cold. You want something to drink?"

"No, thank you."

"Alright, I will be in the other room if you need me," Ira said.

It took almost an hour for Michael to go through everything. He made three piles; one was for junk mail, one for miscellaneous items, and the smallest pile was for correspondence that he wasn't sure about. He called Ira in and explained what he needed to do.

"Got it," Ira said. "Thank you. See, I knew that you were good for something."

"Don't you get lonely living in this big house by yourself?" Michael asked.

"Maybe, a little. But this house is full of memories of my wife. A lot of my life happened here. We loved it here."

"Have you ever considered moving to a smaller place?" Michael wondered. "Something that is easier for you to manage."

"I can't see myself living anywhere else."

"But isn't it hard to take care of all by yourself."

"The new housekeeper shops and cleans the house," Ira revealed. "And this one guy takes care of the lawn and the driveway in the winter, the same as always. I manage pretty good, I'd say."

"I don't know how you can stand this cold," Michael complained again and rubbed his hands together.

Ira shrugged his shoulders.

"Do you cook for yourself?" Michael asked.

"Oh, for goodness' sake, no! I mostly get meals delivered."

"So, I guess that you have it all figured out," Michael concurred.

"People want to write you off when you get to be my age. I know that it's not intentional necessarily, but I know the look. Sometimes they look at me like I have no purpose, like I am already dead, or close enough to it that I should be put out to pasture somewhere. You have no idea how that makes me feel. I'm not dead. I'm very much alive! I feel alive! Believe me when I say that Hashem, the Lord our God, is not through with me yet."

"I know you're not dead," Michael affirmed.

"Yeah, well you might be the only one," Ira said stone-faced.

Michael didn't know how to respond.

"Hey, you want to go to lunch?" Ira interjected into the awkward silence. "I know a great place."

Michael rolled his eyes. "Yeah right," he muttered.

Walking out of the house together, Ira handed Michael the car keys. Now, whenever they went someplace together, Ira asked Michael to drive. He directed Michael to yet another out-of-the-way restaurant that he didn't even know existed.

"What's this place?"

"It's Polish. You like Polish food? They have great golabki here. You like golabki?"

"I don't even know what that is?"

Ira laughed to himself.

Michael couldn't find anything on the menu that he wanted. He just ordered the cabbage soup, which he ended up not eating.

"Ira, did you know that about half of the civil rights attorneys in the south during the 1960s were Jewish?"

"Yes, of course," Ira answered. "Several of my classmates from law school went down south during that period. I considered going myself, but my father absolutely forbade it. One guy I knew, David Zimmerman was his name, went down and never made it back."

"What happened to him?"

"I'm not sure that they ever found out. Apparently, he got caught up in something in Mississippi and they found him brutally beaten in some alley."

"Was he a good friend of yours?" Michael wondered.

"I believe that David was…maybe a year ahead of me at NYU. But we were a small closely knit group, so I saw him a lot. He was a very nice guy. He wasn't religious or anything. None of us were. I just remember that he was always deeply passionate about ending injustice in the world."

"Do you wish that you could have gone?"

"Uh, I don't know," Ira reflected. "His family was never the same after he was killed. He had a wife and a baby. And it wasn't just David. A lot of people died."

"That's really sad."

"This is the world that we live in Michael."

"It's really bad," Michael reflected. "I mean, what's the point?"

"Point? There isn't one," Ira replied. "Live a life that you can be proud of. One thing about Judaism is that it has always emphasized the importance of community. That means doing things for other people."

"Is that why you help me out?" Michael solicited. "Charity?"

He spoke before he knew it.

"What?" Ira asked and froze in place.

"Big lawyer like you helping someone like me. Trying to live a life you can be proud of? Good deal, right?"

"Where is this coming from?" Ira asked and stared at Michael. He looked startled.

"No, I mean it's okay if it is," Michael said and cast his eyes downward. "I understand."

"You understand what exactly?" Ira pressed.

"You found a black guy who you can work on," Michael lamented. "Obviously, I'm a mess. You're doing a good thing."

"Let's get one thing straight." Ira defended. "I have never looked at you like that."

"People think that it's weird that you and me are friends."

"People like who?"

"Doesn't matter," Michael insisted.

"Matters to me. Is that what you think?"

"I don't know what I think," Michael admitted while looking dejected.

"Well, I'm not sure that is good enough, Michael," Ira challenged. "Not for me. I thought that you and I had an understanding."

"There is this guy I know, who is part-Jewish, and he said that there is no way that you consider me a real friend because Jews don't like black people."

"And you believed that crap?" Ira fumed.

"I don't want to." He lowered his head.

"Michael, in the new covenant it says that there is neither Jew nor gentile in Yeshua," he replied softly. "We are one. No matter how the world views people, it shouldn't define the way we see each other- not you and me."

There was an awkward silence.

"Okay, you're right. I'm… sorry," Michael sheepishly replied.

"Are you sure?"

"Yeah, I'm sure," Michael whispered and slowly raised his head and looked Ira in the eyes.

"Friend, in many ways you're all I got," Ira chokingly expressed. "You should know that by now."

Michael felt terrible. He never meant to hurt Ira and he certainly never planned on telling him what Leonard had said. It just slipped out. On some level he needed to say something and get it off his chest. It was festering. But now expressing his frustrations had cast a shadow and was eating away at him like a rabid dog. He tossed and turned in bed that night, *all* night.

When his mother died, he just figured that he was destined for a mediocre existence for the rest of his life. And he was okay with that because he couldn't think of one single thing that he really wanted—other than to be left alone. But recently he was starting to notice that something was changing within him. There was a stirring inside that was never there before. He wasn't sure exactly what was happening or why. All he knew was that, like his friend Ira, he didn't want to be discounted and devalued. Nope, he wanted to matter too.

Ira never revisited the topic of their conversation that day. He acted like it never happened. But Michael couldn't forget— and he didn't want to. Perhaps this was just the shaking that he needed. He was awakening from his self-imposed exile into a world of possibility and opportunity. His extended hibernation had ended at last, and like a grizzly bear confronting the outside world anew, he now found himself wide-awake and famished.

Chapter 8

Michael loved his truck. His dad found a used two-year old Jeep in mint condition with only 15,000 miles. He also insisted on paying for it. He just told Michael to save his money. Initially, Michael was concerned that a Jeep might be too much vehicle for him, but when he drove it, he was surprised to discover that the bigger frame actually made him feel safer.

He knew that he needed to go back to school, but that was a mountain too high to climb. School was never his strong suit. Not that it was too hard for him, because it wasn't. Rather, he was just bored out of his mind most of the time and content to just go through the motions of everyday life. The only reason that he even had his associate degree was because his dad made him go to community college. Now, in his heart, he knew that it was time for him to complete his studies the right way.

Oddly, he suddenly hated his clothes. He never quite noticed that everything he owned was dark and lifeless. It wasn't just the way he looked in them, but the way they made him feel. He felt like a stranger wearing a dead man's clothes.

Honestly, he never much cared about what he wore before. He never wanted to wear anything that drew too much attention or could trigger someone to make fun of him. But he felt different now. He bought a bunch of new outfits that better reflected his new persona.

Unfortunately, Leonard became a casualty of his new attitude. Michael found himself making excuses as to why he couldn't hang out at Leonard's place. It wasn't that he was angry with Leonard, he just suddenly felt out of place around him. Almost overnight, he lost his appetite for childish things, and he didn't want to just sit around anymore. He knew that Leonard didn't understand and was hurt. He truly felt bad about that, but he had a new desire for something more.

"What's going on with you?" Ira asked over lunch one afternoon.

"What do you mean?"

"You seem different lately."

"Different how?" Michael questioned.

"You're eyes. Did something happen? You got a girl?"

"No."

"Well, it's something," Ira persisted. "You just don't want to tell me. It's probably a girl. Good for you."

"It's not a girl."

"Why? Don't you like girls?"

"I'm not gay if that what's you mean," Michael asserted.

"I kissed a man one time," Ira goofed.

"No, you didn't."

"Yes, I did," Ira laughed. "On the lips!"

"You're just messing with me."

"No, I'm not," Ira teased with a straight face.

"Alright then, who?" Michael challenged and crossed both arms across his chest and leaned back. "When did this supposedly happen?"

"I don't want to tell you now that I see how closedminded you are," Ira maintained. "Your generation knows absolutely nothing about true liberation."

Michael raised his eyebrows and sighed to himself. "See, I knew you were making it up."

"Nope. You're wrong, sonny. I don't always tell the truth, but I never lie. I never said it was a romantic kiss."

"Tell me then."

"Never mind," Ira rebuked. "You have your secrets and I'll have mine. How about that?"

"You say too much crazy stuff," Michael responded dismissively. "I want to ask you something serious anyway."

"What is it?"

"Remember when I told you that I only have an associate degree."

"Yes, I remember."

"Well, I am thinking about going back to school," Michael divulged.

"Oh, really?"

"Yeah, I checked, and I can have my bachelor's degree in a year and a half if I start this summer."

"Degree in what?"

"Liberal arts."

"What do you want to do with it?" Ira wondered.

"Um, that's the thing. I…um," Michael hesitated. "I was thinking that maybe…"

"What?"

"I'm not saying for sure…"

"Uh oh…," Ira remarked and appeared dumbfounded.

Michael sat up straight in his chair.

"What?" Ira exclaimed. "Good lord! Don't tell me that you want to go to law school!"

"Well, yes… I was thinking about it," Michael forced himself to say. "Why? Is that a problem?"

"No, it's not a problem," Ira replied and laughed freely. "I think that's great, Michael. I really do!"

He was grinning from ear to ear and shaking his head back and forth. "Really? I mean, you really think that I could be a good lawyer?"

"Of course, I do."

"Then why are you looking at me like that?"

"It's nothing, really. Michael, I just happen to believe that you can do whatever you set your mind to do. I fully expect that you, my friend, will change the world."

Chapter 9

Ira fell. He went out to get the mail and fell in the driveway. He hit his head and possibly lost consciousness for a second or two. Fortunately, Mona, the cleaning lady, heard him moaning and rushed out to help him up. She became frightened by the amount of blood covering the back of his neck and called 9-1-1 emergency. Not surprisingly, they had to force him to go to the hospital.

Michael arrived at the emergency room just in time to sit with Ira for several prolonged hours. Ultimately, they didn't find anything seriously wrong with him, except for the raised oozing gash near the crown of his head that required several stitches. They decided to admit him overnight for observation.

Ira didn't want Michael to call his daughter, but he called her anyway. He called the first chance he got, as promised. She didn't sound overly concerned and thanked him for letting her know.

Ira was scheduled to be released from the hospital the next morning at 10:00 a.m. When Michael arrived at his room at 9:30

a.m. to pick him up, there were two women standing next to the bed. One appeared to be in her fifties and the other one was about half that. They were both attractive, although Michael was careful not to stare.

"Hi Michael," Ira said.

He was fully dressed and sitting on the edge of the bed. All three turned their attention to Michael as he walked through the door.

"Hi," Michael replied.

"This is my daughter Becky and my granddaughter Leila."

"Hi," Michael repeated.

"Hello Michael," Becky said. "Nice to meet you."

"Hi," Leila whispered.

"Nice to meet you both," he stated.

"Thank you for letting me know about my father," Becky offered. "Otherwise, we never would have known."

"Thought I told you not to call her," Ira complained and looked hard at Michael.

"Well, I'm glad that you didn't listen to him, Michael. My father never lets anybody help him with anything."

"Because I don't need any help!" Ira insisted.

"Is that right?" Becky argued. "You could have died if the housekeeper hadn't heard you."

"Please don't overreact," Ira scolded. "It was a simple fall."

"Okay, Dad, I don't want to fight," Becky conceded. "We'll take you home now."

"Michael can take me home," he protested.

"I'm sure that Michael has things to do," Becky maintained. "Besides, I need to go to the house. There are some things that I left there that I have been meaning to get."

"It's okay, Ira," Michael said. "I'll call you later."

The tension in the room was palpable and Michael was glad to get out of there. He was a little concerned he had made a mistake calling Becky and that Ira might be angry with him, but he really didn't have a choice. Ira's family had a right to know that he was injured. His own family was dysfunctional enough that he didn't want to get in the middle of whatever Ira had going on with his.

* * *

Ira made a speedy recovery. He came into the office just two days after he was released from the hospital. He didn't mention his daughter or seem bothered in the least that Michael had called her. Michael was sitting at his desk when Ira called out to him.

"Yes Sir," he answered from the doorway.

"Can you close the door? I need to speak to you privately about something."

"Yeah."

Michael shut the door and walked up to the side of the desk.

"I need to ask you a big favor," Ira said.

"Sure, what is it?"

"Well, hear me out first before you say yes."

"Okay."

"I called my attorney this morning. I need to change some things that I had in place. I would like to make you my health care proxy and give you my power of attorney."

"I don't even know what that means," Michael said.

"Well, basically, it just means that if something should happen to me and I become incapacitated for some reason, you would be the person authorized to make decisions about medical treatment and some of my personal affairs."

"Me? Why me?" Michael resisted.

"Because I trust you."

"Does this have something to do with your daughter?" Michael wondered. "I know that…"

"Not really," Ira interrupted. "I love my kids and grandchildren. I really do. But they don't know me, not like you do."

"How can you say that?" Michael questioned. "Don't you think that they are going to be mad if they have to listen to me, a perfect stranger?"

"Probably," Ira hedged. "I have a will too and trust me they will be fine. But they don't accept or understand what Yeshua means to me and I'm just not confident that they will do things the way that I want."

"But I don't know what you want either," Michael objected.

"Yes, you do. I trust your judgment."

"But why can't you just talk to them?" Michael asserted. "I'm sure that you can work something out."

"It's not that easy. I'm sorry to put this all on you Michael, but I told you that you are all that I have."

Michael paused a moment to think. He pressed his lips tightly together and was starting to feel a little anxious. He knew that this could mean trouble for him down the line.

"Okay, if you are sure," he finally said.

"Thank you, Michael. I can't tell you how much this means to me. You know, this is only just in case something happens to me. So, don't worry about it. I'm not planning to go anywhere anytime soon."

But Michael was worried—very worried. While he appreciated that Ira had so much confidence in him, he was pretty sure that trust was misplaced. All his life, he had done everything that he could to avoid taking on too much responsibility and having to make any major decisions. Although he was no longer walking around with his head in the clouds, he was still naïve. There was much he still needed to learn about life.

This unsettled him for the rest of the day. He feared that Ira had put him in a precarious position unnecessarily. He had come to accept the fact that Ira was unpredictable. But Ira's tough exterior served as an appropriate covering for an equally unbending spirit. He oftentimes made things a lot more difficult than was otherwise necessary.

Indeed, although Ira's heart was mostly in the right place, he could only be pushed so far before he struck back with reckless abandon, even with family. In this regard, Ira was a lot like Dale

Johnson, Michael's father, who was bullish in both word and deed. Michael doubted that either one of them had ever backed away from a fight, even when wisdom dictated that they do just that.

Chapter 10

This time around, school was different. He was paying attention. Everything just seemed easier than he remembered. Michael had no recollection of ever asking a single question in any class before, that included all his high school years as well. But now his curiosity was peaked, and he found himself fully emersed in his studies and engaging with others in class. It felt both strange and exciting to him.

Ira was the only person to whom he mentioned his newly discovered desire to become a lawyer. Michael didn't even tell his father, who was excited enough when he told him about his decision to go back to school to get his bachelor's degree. Michael was concerned that people would laugh at him, and his confidence was still a little too fragile.

The fact is, there was nothing in his past that would prove he had the fortitude needed to accomplish such a lofty goal. He simply needed a little more time to be able to stand up to public scrutiny. Until then, he was keeping his cards close to his chest.

Another vulnerable area in his life that he needed to address was his interactions with the opposite sex. He never had a girlfriend, only a couple of secret crushes. The few times that it appeared that someone might be interested in him in that way, he immediately panicked. He was okay with platonic relationships, and there had been a couple of them. But he never could handle anything more.

He had always pretended that he didn't care what people thought about him, but that was only a defense mechanism. The truth was that he never really liked himself and he just assumed that no one else liked him either, which included every girl he knew. Thus, he had done everything that he could to make himself invisible to just about everyone.

However, he actually cared a lot about what other people thought. But he believed he was born with low self-esteem. The Bible says that a man is as he sees himself and he always saw himself as one who will never measure up.

Accordingly, as a kid, he never cleaned his room or picked up after himself because he didn't see the point of investing that much effort in anything. Nor did he fully appreciate it when other people, like his mother, did those things for him. To him, chores and personal responsibility didn't really have any value at all. More than lazy, he was deceived by the spirit of apathy.

* * *

Michael had his first real date just as his first semester was ending. A classmate from his English literature class asked him if he wanted to go to a movie. He said yes without even thinking it through, which probably was a good thing. She was just a girl who sat next to him in class. He had only spoken to her casually a few times and he hadn't really thought about her that way. She texted him her number and they agreed to meet the following evening. He was apprehensive most of that day.

Her name was Yolanda Williams. She was an attractive twenty-two-year-old black woman. Yolanda was five foot nine, with a medium build and short hair that she wore in a bob. They met at the theatre downtown and afterward they walked together to a coffee shop around the corner.

"I can't believe that you are thirty-six years old," Yolanda said. "I would have sworn that you were in your early twenties."

"I get that a lot," he replied.

"So, you decided to go back to school or something?"

"Yeah, I already have my associate degree. I decided that I needed to finish up."

"Do you have a job?"

"Yeah, I'm the office manager at a law firm."

"Oh, that's why you are so smart," she replied.

"Smart?"

"I saw some of the grades you got on your papers," she acknowledged. "You seem to like the stuff that we read."

"Um, I don't know if I *like* it, but I understand it a little."

"Well, that puts you way ahead of me."

"What's your major?" Michael asked.

"Business management. I'm not really sure what I want to be when I graduate."

"Well trust me, you have plenty of time to decide. Look at me."

"Are you divorced or something?" she wondered.

"No."

"You don't have a girlfriend?"

"No."

"Why not?"

"No reason," he said. "I just don't."

"You seem really shy," she commented. "Are you?"

"I don't know what I am honestly," he admitted. "I really just want to try new things, you know. I promised my mother before she died that I would take chances with my life. I'm just finally starting to do that."

"Oh, I'm sorry to hear about your mother," she said.

"Thank you… Where are you from?" he asked.

"Albany. I live there with my mother. I have a two-year-old daughter."

"Oh, really? What's her name?"

"Olivia."

"Nice name," he said.

"Thanks. Her father was my high school boyfriend. Obviously, he's not in the picture anymore. Turns out that he was kind of a jerk."

She looked disgusted and crinkled her nose up slightly. She was cute, although he thought he saw deep sadness in her eyes.

"Sorry," he whispered.

"No, it's good," she revealed. "Me and my daughter are better off. You can believe that!"

"What's it like being a mother?"

"Hard!" she exclaimed as her eyes got big. "Oh my God! I don't know what I would do if I didn't have my mom to help out. Getting pregnant really forced me to grow up, you know. I was so naive before. It was like I became a grownup overnight. Now I'm just trying to figure it out one day at a time."

"It might sound strange, but I am pretty much in the same place," he confessed. "I'm just trying to figure it out too."

"It doesn't sound strange at all," she affirmed and smiled warmly.

She was easy to talk to and Michael was somewhat relaxed for most of the evening. This was a big step for him, and he was determined to see it through. Standing next to her car in the parking lot at the end of the evening was probably the most stressful part of all. They chatted there for several minutes before she looked at her watch and said that she really had to go. She then leaned in and kissed him gently on the lips. He kissed her back. He didn't faint. She smiled and got into her car, and he watched her drive away.

He was *so* proud of himself! He turned up the music, sang aloud, and danced in his jeep all the way home. Although he liked Yolanda, she was not really the true source of his contentment. He was finally experiencing the confidence he was missing. He was beginning to feel like a real man.

Yolanda was a nice person, but she was a little too intense for Michael. She started calling and texting him all the time. He finally had to tell her that he just wanted to be friends at this point. She said that she understood. Unfortunately, things didn't work out with her.

* * *

With each passing day, Michael searched for small changes he could make to improve his life. After catching a glimpse of himself coming out of the shower one morning, he decided that he didn't like the way that he looked and that he needed to get in better physical shape. He always hated exercise, so he wasn't exactly excited about the prospect of going to a gym. All the men in his family loved sports except for him. He never understood what all the fuss was about and was mostly turned off by jocks and all their sports talk.

Nevertheless, once he put his mind to it, his physical transformation was easy. It turned out that he did have good genes after all. Although he hated running, he liked riding the bike at the gym. Also, to his surprise, he rather enjoyed the weight machines. He lost ten pounds in short order without dieting and still managed to gain both strength and muscle mass. His face thinned out too. Suddenly, he looked really good, and he felt even better. Everybody seemed to notice his makeover too, which embarrassed him immensely.

"Are you ready now to tell me what's going on with you?" Ira asked one day.

"I don't know what you mean."

"You're lying. You look completely different."

"No, I'm not," he insisted. "It's not a big deal. I just needed to make a few changes in the way that I was living."

"But why now?"

"It's hard to explain. I just feel like something is pushing me to get moving. I haven't been able to shake the feeling. I'm sorry, but there really isn't any other way to explain it. I have no idea what I'm talking about."

"Hmm…I must say that is really interesting," Ira replied.

"I know. But that is why I didn't say anything. Because I don't know what to say. People are gonna think that I'm crazy."

"You're not crazy," Ira exhorted. "A lot of people have changed their lives dramatically on a dime. That's really what happened to the apostle Paul, right? I give you all the credit for responding to that leading."

"Honestly, it hasn't been that hard and it's long overdue," Michael admitted. "So, I don't think that I deserve any special credit."

"You'd be surprised the number of people who are willing to drive in the same lane of traffic and in the same direction even though they know that they aren't really getting anywhere."

"That's a good way of putting it," Michael reflected.

"Change is never easy for anyone," Ira said. "I think that you need to give yourself a break. You're doing good, kid."

Chapter 11

Michael received a call from a parole officer advising him that his older brother Christopher was getting out of state prison. He was serving time for selling drugs. Michael had no idea exactly how long Christopher had been there this time around, but it had to be about 10 years. He last saw Christopher at their mom's calling hours when the corrections officers brought him. But they didn't actually speak to each other.

Just before Christopher was released, Michael's grandmother passed away suddenly. She was eighty-three years old, just a year older than Ira. Even though she lived in Schenectady, Michael was never close to her and rarely saw her. He understood that she had a hard life as an alcoholic involved in the street life. But that is all that he really knew about her. She was his father's mother and the only grandparent that he had left.

"Sorry for your loss," Ira said from the front passenger seat of his car.

"Thank you. How did you know?"

"I saw the obituary in the newspaper."

"You read the obituaries?"

"Yes, I always look for my name first," Ira joked.

"You know, if you had a laptop, you could look up all the obituaries online," Michael not-so-innocently remarked. "Even the ones from out of town."

"How many times do I have to tell you that I don't want a computer?" Ira protested. "You're worse than an old Jewish woman with your nagging."

"I'm just trying to make life easier for you."

"Really? Well…no!" Ira spoke with blunt force.

"Alright. Got it," Michael relented. "But you seriously need to lighten up. Seriously."

"You seriously need to drop it!" Ira sniped.

"Why are you in such a bad mood? You seem crankier than usual and that's saying a lot for you."

"No, I'm fine," Ira said in a softer tone.

"Okay then…tell me this, do you believe in heaven?" Michael posed.

"Yes, that's random, but of course I do," Ira confessed. "Are you asking me what I think happens when you die?"

"Yeah, exactly."

"Honestly, I have struggled with the concept of heaven," Ira admitted. "Before I came to know Yeshua, I thought that this life was all that there was. This was heaven to me, and it was all about how we live with others in the here and now. As hard as it was to make the jump to becoming Messianic, it was even a bigger jump for me to believe in a place in the sky where the streets are paved with gold, and we all fly around with angels who look like fat babies."

"That's funny," Michael quipped, "But we must live on somehow, right?"

"My mother didn't just lead me to Yeshua, but she also changed my perspective on eternity when he saved my immortal soul. I am looking forward to the day when I will see my Savior face to face, and I will be wherever he is. I believe that with all my heart."

"Me too," Michael shared. "But I'm also confident that I will see my mom again. I just know it. So, I'm okay."

"That's true," Ira agreed. "There really is just a thin veil that separates us from them now. We know that our loved ones aren't just in our past, they are in our future too. That is why I don't really have any fear of death."

"Really?" Michael replied. "Because I definitely do."

"Yeah. I get that," Ira said and nodded his head. "You are a young man, Michael. You have your whole life ahead of you. But it's different for me. I have already experienced all the highs and lows that come with living in this world. I'm not afraid to die because it is impossible for death to cheat me out of anything at this point."

His voice sounded strong and impassioned. Michael was sorting through his thoughts and didn't say anything. There was a minute or two of prolonged silence.

"But you know what I do fear?" Ira continued.

"No. What?"

"I don't want my children to die and be forever lost. I think that my mother felt that way about me too and that is why she desperately wanted me to hear what she knew to be true about Yeshua. My wife died an unbeliever. I can't tell you how much that haunts me. I just can't let the same thing happen to my children and grandchildren."

"I don't think that I know what you mean," Michael articulated. "You can't make someone believe if they don't want to. They already know about your faith. It's their choice."

"All true. But I just know that Hashem has a plan and that his plan is much bigger than me. You know how you say you will see your mom again, and you know it beyond a shadow of a doubt?"

"Uh huh."

"Well, I have the same assurance about my family," Ira reflected. "So, I just have to do my part, which means that I have to end well. If I do that, then he will finish what he started in my dear mother, and what she passed on to me. That means that I will one day see my children's children in the place where Yeshua dwells."

Michael's heart was racing as Ira spoke. He was completely undone by every word. They resonated within him and gave him more hope. Simultaneously, his own love for God and for his friend provoked him to look beyond himself.

He slowly pulled Ira's car into the medical center parking lot. He drove up to the front of the building and stopped. They were right on time for Ira's doctor appointment. He watched patiently as the old man opened the door and got out of the car.

"I'll find a parking spot and be right in," he said.

* * *

Michael decided that he needed to take a more active role in Ira's health care. Not just because he now had a document in his possession giving him Ira's proxy, but also because he was tired of listening to Ira complain about going to his appointments. Turns out that Ira's primary care physician was open on Saturday mornings, which meant that Michael could accompany him. Moreover, the appointments had quick turnovers since the office closed at 1 p.m. on Saturdays. There wasn't as much waiting around.

Aside from the typical aches and pains affecting the elderly, Ira was in excellent health. He had an issue with his thyroid and high cholesterol. He did not take heart medication, although he saw a cardiologist once a year. He also didn't show any loss of mental acuity. His biggest disability was his overall ornery disposition, which unfortunately was a chronic condition. This had obviously gotten worse over time and for which there was no known treatment.

Surprisingly, Ira didn't seem to mind having Michael involved in his affairs. He was pretty open about everything.

Michael never expected or took any money from Ira. Other than paying for their meals together and for the driving lessons, Ira never attempted to make their relationship financial. Theirs was a friendship based upon mutual admiration and respect.

However, Michael was becoming increasingly annoyed about one thing. Ira was riding him all the time about not having a girlfriend. Even his dad didn't do that. The truth is that he was working full-time, taking classes almost every weeknight and helping Ira as much as he could. So, he didn't really have time for much else. But Ira thought that he was missing out and he wasn't shy in the least about bringing up the subject every chance he got.

In response, Michael would make every effort to divert the conversation and sometimes it worked. Otherwise, he just had to grin and bear it. Apparently, Ira's wife was the love of his life. They met on a blind date when he was a young lawyer just out of law school. She was a schoolteacher and came from a conservative Jewish family. He said that she was the most beautiful girl that he had ever seen and that he was smitten immediately. They were married just six months after they met.

Evidently, they were good together and had a good marriage. He said that she was always very supportive and understanding, except for when it came to his religious enlightenment. Concerning that matter, they had agreed that he would keep that part of himself separate from their marriage. She died unexpectedly after fifty-two years together and a brief battle with pancreatic cancer. His loss cut deep.

"I have been married and I have been single, and without a doubt, having someone to share your life with is the better way to go," Ira opined.

Notwithstanding, Michael didn't have to be talked into marriage. His parents had set the perfect example of just how great marriage can be. They were hopelessly devoted to one another, and their lifelong commitment will always be before him as a testament to the sanctity of holy matrimony.

But obviously, it wasn't going to be that easy for him. He still needed time to figure out who he was and what kind of man he wanted to be before he joined himself with someone else. He knew that he was doing the right thing by taking his time, but there simply was no talking to Ira about it. On top of everything else, Ira's wife must have been one of the most patient women who ever lived!

Michael noticed that every so often when Ira was tired or forgot that he wasn't alone, a sadness came over him that seemed to overtake him like a torrential rainstorm. He looked like a lost little boy. Michael always pretended like he didn't see it. He had no idea how often that happened or what exactly triggered it. But the lesson for him was clear: everybody has pain. Those were the only times when he ever felt sorry for Ira.

Many of the changes taking place in Michael were spiritual, but he was unaware. His mother's passing was rock bottom for him. He was so used to being overlooked and suffering in private and her illness thrusted his pain out into the open where everyone could see it. He had also gotten used to taking everything for granted. He took his mother for granted his whole life. And he had taken God for granted too.

Somewhere deep inside, he always knew that God was real. But he never desired to know more about him. What people didn't seem to get about Michael, and about Ira, was that they were cut from the same cloth and blessed with many of the same gifts. Hidden among them, was the dying wish of both of their loving mothers: that their sons would come to know Jesus on a personal level.

* * *

By the end of his second semester back in school, Michael had earned an "A" in all four of his classes. However, his grade point average from his transferred associate degree was not very good. Getting his G.P.A. high enough to get into law school was going to be no small feat. As a result, there was added pressure on him.

Ira kept telling him not to worry about his grades and to just do his best. But he was wasting his breath. Michael felt like he had no room for error this time and the anxiety from it kept him up at night. He was literally torturing himself.

Beyond his college grades, he started to reflect on his youth and the regret began to build. What was bothering him the most was the realization that he had squandered so many opportunities. No first prom. No first-time partying with his friends in the park after dark or breaking curfew. No first kiss or teen love. He just missed out on so many rites of passage solely because he was afraid to live. He had wasted his youth feeling sorry for himself and he was paying the price now for having done so. Although he understood somewhere inside that there was nothing to be gained from crying over spilled milk, he couldn't help brooding over what might have been.

Just by chance, he ran into an old classmate at the supermarket.

"Michael? Michael Johnson?" a voice called out from behind him.

He turned around to see a familiar face. She was a tall, thin, white woman. The first thing he noticed was that she was wearing way too many earrings in both ears. Her dyed blond hair was completely supported by brown roots. She also had an odd black spider tattoo just above her cleavage.

"Is that you Michael?"

"Yes, it's me," he cautiously replied.

He smiled at her even though he wasn't exactly sure who she was at first.

"I can't believe it!" she exclaimed. "I hardly recognize you. Remember me? Beth Moyer."

"Oh yeah, from high school. Of course," he said.

"Oh my God!" she squealed in delight and laughed and giggled to herself. "Imagine running into you like this. How have you been? You look great."

"You look good too," he kindly reciprocated. "I'm doing great."

"You still live here in Schenectady?" she wondered.

"Yes, I do. I work downtown. What about you?"

"I live in Troy now," she answered. "I'm married with three kids. Can you believe that? My oldest is in high school! She's sixteen. Seems like my whole life is a whirlwind of taking somebody here or there. Most of the time I don't know if I am coming or going. My mom still lives here."

"Sounds like you need a vacation," he joked.

"You have no idea. But I can't get over seeing you like this. You probably don't remember, but you were my lab partner in ninth grade biology."

"Sure, I remember," he replied and laughed. "We almost burned the school down."

"That was your fault," she alleged.

"That's not how I remember it."

"We were both so crazy," she reflected. "I have mentioned you several times to some people over the years."

"Me?"

"Yeah. One day I asked you, 'How come you never smile?' Do you remember what you said?"

"No," he admitted.

"You said, 'Because it hurts when I do that'," she recalled. "I have never forgotten that. It made me cry. It was one of the saddest things that I had ever heard anybody say."

"Wow, I really said that?" he bemoaned while shaking his head.

She paused a moment.

"So, what happened?" she pressed.

"What do you mean?"

"What changed for you?" she pushed. "I bet it was a girl… It was, wasn't it? Tell me, did you meet some amazing woman who stole your heart and changed your life?"

"No, I'm sorry," he whispered. "It wasn't anything quite so dramatic."

"Then what? I'd really like to know," she implored.

In her eyes, he saw sincere desperation. It seems that just about everyone wants the fairytale.

"I just woke up one morning and decided that pain is just pain. It's not everything and it doesn't have to define you," he explained.

A look of surprise covered her face.

"Oh! That's a really good way of looking at it," she muttered. "You know, I always liked you, Michael. I always thought that you had *something*."

Chapter 12

Christopher showed up at the house unexpectedly. But it wasn't a complete surprise. He had been out of prison for about a week.

"Hey bro!" Christopher exclaimed while standing at the front door with a big grin on his face.

"Christopher!"

Christopher reached out and warmly embraced his brother. Surprisingly, he looked good.

"Look at you," he said. "Oh my God! You look like a straight-up playa!"

"So do you," Michael replied.

There was no mistaking that they were brothers. Although Christopher was taller and considerably more muscular, they both looked like their father. Oddly, Michael never noticed until now.

"You look like you've been working out," Christopher complimented.

"Look who's talking. Come on in."

"The house looks good," Christopher said. "Where's Dad?"

"He's in Flagstaff, Arizona. There is a retirement community out there that he likes. He goes every winter."

"I'm surprised that he didn't sell the house after mom died."

"Have a seat," Michael said and pointed toward the sofa. "I think that it was hard for him to even think about selling the house. It was tough going for him for a while. By the time that he retired from the city, he needed a change of scenery in the worst way. He's better now. I think that he might even have a girlfriend. She's a preacher or something. He hasn't really said much about her, but I hear them talking on the phone."

"A girlfriend," Christopher repeated and tried to let it sink in.

"Yeah, I know," Michael remarked and raised both of his eyebrows.

"Well, good for him," Christopher commented. "I was really worried about him."

"He's still a tough dude," Michael replied. "What's going on with you?"

"Nothing much," Christopher said. "I live in a halfway house. I have a job working in a warehouse and I start tomorrow. I'm just taking it day by day you know. What about you? I want to hear about you."

"Me?" Michael responded. "Well, I work at a law firm as the office manager. I really like it and they treat me well. I'm back in school and I will probably graduate next year."

"You live here by yourself?"

"Yes."

"Do you ever see TJ?"

"No," Michael replied. "He didn't even come to the funeral. Dad sees him sometimes, but he never talks about him."

"I would like to maybe try to find him and see if there is some way that I can help him."

"*Really*?" Michael asked with more than a little skepticism in his voice.

"He's our brother," Christopher replied. "Just because he's sick doesn't change anything."

"I know," Michael uttered. "I'm just surprised that you would…"

"I've changed," Christopher interrupted.

"Okay," Michael responded.

"I have," Christopher insisted. "You have too."

"I know," Michael admitted.

Christopher sat up straight and kind of braced himself against the arms of the chair. He looked cornered.

"Michael, I know that you don't trust me. I messed up a lot and I was a real jerk to you when we were growing up, even before the drugs. So, I am not making any excuses. I'm really sorry. I can't tell you how bad I feel. When I look at you now,

I see how much better I could have been if only I was smart like you."

"Like me?" Michael said and instantly jerked his head back in shock. "You've got to be kidding!"

"Yeah, like you," Christopher stressed. "Believe me, I have been around enough knuckleheads to last me the rest of my life. The problem with most of us is that we think that we have it all figured out and that we are smarter than everybody else. But we really aren't smarter than anybody. You never acted like that. You never did. You just laid low until you were ready. Now look at you."

"Some people would say that I was just a lazy slob for most of my life," Michael acknowledged almost apologetically.

"Don't listen to them. They don't know what the hell they are talking about! Dad always said that it takes time to become a champion."

Michael couldn't believe what he was hearing. He was hard pressed to recall even one kind word that Christopher had ever said to him before. He was five years older than Michael and they were never on the same page. In fact, Michael did every-thing he could to avoid both of his brothers most of the time, especially Christopher who could be physically abusive. But his words had a special meaning and impact for Michael because he knew how hard it was for his brother to say these things.

"You know how I look at it," Christopher continued. "Mom held you close until it was time for you."

Michael's heart dropped. An uneasiness was rising in his belly.

"Um… I don't know what to say."

"You don't have to say anything. It's true. I just want you to know how sorry I am about everything. I'm proud of you, man."

They spent about an hour catching up until Michael had to leave for class.

"Uh, this is hard, but I really need to ask you something," Christopher solicited.

"What is it?"

Christopher licked his lips and hesitated. His lips began to quiver, and it was obvious that he was fighting hard against his emotions. Michael could feel his heartache.

"Um… I don't know how… but you are the only one that I can ask. I just really need to know the truth. I was wondering if…you knew if mom was mad at me when she died?"

He looked desperate and his eyes were reddened and pooling. He was panting slightly.

"I don't understand. Why would she be mad at you?"

"You know…because I always let her down. I keep thinking that maybe if I…"

"Christopher, mom wasn't mad at you," Michael spoke earnestly. "She loved you."

"I know, but …"

Christopher began sobbing. It was one of those heaving cries that came from the gut. Michael easily recalled the times as a young boy when Christopher would agonize over the loss of every youth football game. There were instances when he was inconsolable.

"No, listen," Michael interrupted. "You have to stop this!"

He put one hand on his brother's leg and stared deeply into his eyes. He had forgotten how emotional Christopher could be. Of the three Johnson boys, he was by far the most tenderhearted about some things.

"Please, listen to me!" Michael demanded. "A few days before she died, she told me that she considered us to be the best thing that ever happened to her, the three of us. She told me to tell you and TJ that all she wants from us is to pursue God until we get to the place where we are truly happy. She made me promise. I'm sorry. I would have told you. I just never had the chance to."

"It's okay… I miss her like crazy man!" Christopher said. "I'm not sure I can live knowing that I caused her pain." His whole face was a puddled mess.

"Then promise me!" Michael's voice had suddenly changed. There was a tone and an edge to it that even surprised him.

"Huh?" Christopher remarked.

"Promise!" Michael demanded.

"What?" Christopher mouthed with a puzzled look on his face. Perspiration was starting to drip from his brow and chin. His eyes were big.

"You know… I know you do! Promise me!" Michael repeated in the same tone.

Christopher took several deep breaths. He was choked up again and he was trembling.

Michael moved in ever so slightly and glared at his older brother. Face to face, his eyes shot out darts of fire as they bore into Christopher like bullets from an assassin's rifle. He was angry. But more importantly, at that moment, he was completely devoid of sympathy for Christopher.

"I'm gonna make it this time. I promise," Christopher spoke softly.

"Say it again!"

Christopher swallowed hard. "I promise. I'm gonna make it." He nodded his head up and down and stared back at Michael.

The tension in the room had reached a breaking point. Both were barely holding it together. Michael was the one who looked away first.

* * *

They didn't speak at all as he gave his brother a ride downtown. Christopher wanted to be dropped off on some street corner. They shook hands and Christopher turned and started to get out.

"Hey, do you want to come live at home?" Michael asked. "I could talk to Dad."

"Um …no," Christopher said. "I appreciate it, but please don't. It's time for me to man up. I can't do it that way."

"Okay, I understand," Michael softly replied.

* * *

It was two weeks before Michael saw Christopher again. He wasn't worried. He knew that his brother was okay for now. Obviously, he had a lot to contend with.

Christopher just showed up at the front door again.

"Hey, come on in," Michael said.

"What's up?"

"Nothing much," Michael replied. "I was just getting ready to have some lunch. You want a sandwich?"

"Yeah, I could eat."

"Come on in the kitchen. Where have you been?"

"Just working," Christopher reported. "It looks the same in here. You guys haven't changed a thing."

"What is there to change?"

"I don't know. Just some upgrades. I bet you that refrigerator came with the house."

Michael looked in the direction of the refrigerator and shrugged.

"Maybe. Who died and made you Suzy Homemaker anyway?" he prodded.

"I know, right?" Christopher replied with a chuckle. "I'm just saying, bro."

"Yeah, well you try telling Dad that it's time to upgrade."

They both chuckled.

"When is he coming home?" Christopher asked.

"Middle of April," Michael responded. "He's afraid that something might happen to his lawn if he's not here to watch it grow. He definitely doesn't trust me."

"We should dig the whole damn thing up just to mess with him."

"That's not funny," Michael rebuked. "We both know that would be the last thing that we ever did in this lifetime."

"Yeah, I know."

Michael placed everything on the table.

"Help yourself," he said. "What do you want to drink?"

"Anything. Doesn't matter."

"Soda okay?"

"Yeah, that's good."

Michael sat down at the table across from Christopher. He started making his sandwich.

"So, what's the plan?" he asked.

"I don't know what you mean?"

"What is your game plan for the future?" Michael directed.

"You sound like an old man," Christopher responded. "I don't have a plan."

"Then how do you know what to do next?"

"I need time."

"Okay, take your time," Michael said. "But just not too much time. You're already behind."

"The main thing is for me not to start using again," Christopher asserted.

"Yeah, I get it," Michael agreed.

"There is always gonna be that temptation, you know," he presented. "And we both know that I have never been good at fighting it."

"Maybe you just never had a good enough reason to fight it before," Michael suggested. "Everybody needs a reason for living."

Christopher suddenly seemed uncomfortable.

"Maybe," he replied. "But it's not like I have all these different choices, because I don't."

"But what do you see yourself doing? What job would make you most happy? You must have given it some thought."

"I think that I might really like working with kids."

"What do you mean working with kids?"

"You know, maybe coaching football," Christopher reflected. "Helping them to make better choices. Better choices than I've made…"

"Oh, I can see that," Michael exhorted.

"But who are we kidding? Nobody is going to let me work with kids. I'm a convicted felon."

"We don't know that," Michael argued. "Not if you work hard and prove yourself. You already look like you play for the New York Jets. Besides, what do you have to lose?"

"Nothing, probably," Christopher conceded.

He took a big bite of his sandwich.

Michael continued, "The way I see it, you need to know where you want to go before you start driving the car. Otherwise, you are just wasting time… and your gas."

"You know who you sound like?" Christopher asked. "You sound just like…"

Michael abruptly interrupted, "Don't say it! I mean it!"

Christopher erupted in laughter. Michael jumped to his feet.

"I have something for you," he announced.

He walked out and returned moments later with a medium-sized white plastic bag.

"Consider it a welcome home gift."

"What is it?" Christopher asked as he carefully opened the bag. "Is this a cell phone?"

"Yes, I already set it up for you."

"Wow, thank you," Christopher said. "You know, I have never had one before."

"You're welcome. Now I have a way to reach you."

"Okay. I really appreciate it. Just don't tell my parole officer before I see him next week. I need permission to have a cell phone."

"Oh, sorry I didn't know," Michael apologized.

"No, it's okay. I see him on Wednesday."

Michael drove Christopher home. It was just a big old multifamily house located at the end of a city side street. There was a big metal barrier across the road perpendicular to the house with a large yellow triangle-shaped sign on a post that read, "Dead End."

The irony was not lost on Michael.

Chapter 13

The two brothers managed to get together a couple of times a week. Michael still did not have a whole lot of free time, but he recognized the importance of staying connected. He reluctantly agreed to let Christopher train with him at the YMCA. Obviously, Christopher knew his way around a weight room. He made Michael vomit twice and thought it was funny.

Christopher was very sentimental and liked to reminisce about the good old days when they were young and growing up together. Michael didn't even recall most of the events that Christopher fixated on, but it was clearly cathartic for him to just be able to talk about them. For Michael, those simply weren't the best of times. However, being a high school football superstar and their father's pride and joy was apparently the highlights of Christopher's life.

Michael was hesitant to ask Christopher any questions about prison or his drug use. He wasn't just a user; he was also a small-time dealer. He had several arrests for selling drugs in various quantities and had been given numerous chances to get his life right. Michael was unable to make the connection in his own mind about how anyone can go from being a football star one day to selling crack and cocaine on the streets the next. Sadly, almost everyone had written Christopher off, including their dad.

"I met this honey," Christopher announced during one of their training sessions at the YMCA.

"Where?"

"At work. She works in a different section than me."

"You think you are ready for a girlfriend?" Michael asked. "Whoa, who said anything about a girlfriend? She's not my girlfriend. I just like her, that's all."

"Did you sleep with her?" Michael asked directly.

"Yes, but..."

"Does she know that you are on parole?"

"I don't know. Probably not," Christopher muttered.

"Don't you think that is something that she might want to know?"

"I think you're making this bigger than what it is," Christopher maintained. "Women out here know the score."

"Really?" Michael asked with a big scowl on his face. "That's what you think?"

He stared at his brother in disbelief. Christopher was purposely avoiding his gaze.

"Lighten up, Lucy!" Christopher exclaimed. "We are just kick'n it. You know, having a few laughs. That's all it is."

"Just remember that you still have a lot of things to figure out," Michael lectured. "You want to go 'kick it' with some girl, fine go ahead. But just be honest with her about who you are and what it is that you are doing. If you want to stay clean, then you have to come clean with everyone too."

Christopher rolled his eyes. "Some things never change, Michael. You're still no fun at all."

"You don't say?"

"I dropped you on your head this one time when you were a baby and never told anyone. That probably was a mistake, huh?"

Christopher laid down on the weight bench and waited for Michael to get in place to spot him.

"Fun is what got you into trouble in the first place," Michael argued. "Playgrounds are for kids. Men don't have fun. They work so that their kids can have fun."

Christopher did a set of twelve reps. It was truly amazing how much the guy could bench press.

"Wait a minute, don't even try telling me that you don't ever just take the edge off with one of those college honeys," Christopher asserted.

"You took the edge off when you were in high school and got somebody pregnant," Michael pointed out. "You need to listen to what I'm saying."

"No, I don't," Christopher disputed. "You're not my parole officer."

"I'm not, but I'm trying to help you same as he is."

* * *

Michael continued to make the grades in his classes. But that didn't stop him from obsessing about them all the time. He was supposed to take the Law School Admission Test (LSAT) in the upcoming summer, and he was already having nightmares about it. His prep course for the exam was in two weeks. Ira said that he didn't even remember taking that exam.

"Stop it already!" Ira shouted into the phone. "You're going to drive yourself crazy. Just do the best you can. It'll all work out. Trust me."

"You keep saying that, but it's not really that helpful," Michael pointed out.

"Would you feel better if I told you that that test was the hardest exam that I ever took in my entire life and that you are in big trouble?"

"Well, no," Michael reasoned. "I don't want that either."

"Then let it go. Worrying about it never helped anybody."

"Maybe I can't help it."

"Anyway, do you realize that when you go to law school that you are going to have to move away and that we won't be able to see each other? You don't sound too worried about that and frankly I am a little hurt by your lack of consideration."

"Not if I go to Albany Law School."

"Is that where you want to go?"

"Yeah, I think so," Michael disclosed. "You're not getting rid of me that easily. I'm not through with you yet."

"How did I ever get so lucky?" Ira responded in jest.

"Besides, this is not a good time for me to leave home with my brother and all," Michael explained.

"How's he doing?"

"Okay, I guess," Michael hedged. "I feel like he is just holding on. He really needs a break before he does something stupid."

"What kind of break?"

"I don't know …something. He wants to coach kids. Maybe if he could find something like that, it might go a long way with him."

"What about the Boys and Girls Club?" Ira suggested. "There must be something that he could do there. I used to serve on their board. I could make a call?"

"You think that they would give him a chance?" "I don't see why not," Ira remarked. "You want me to reach out?"

"Uh, yes. If you don't mind. I hate to ask."

"Nonsense, I'll do it as soon as I hang up with you."

"Thank you."

"Oh, it's nothing," Ira remarked.

"Not to me," Michael admitted.

"Oh Michael, I've been meaning to tell you something."

"What?"

"I met a girl!" Ira exclaimed.

"You met a girl?"

"I did. At synagogue," he announced.

"Ira, you-met-a-girl?" Michael slowly enunciated.

"Not for me, for goodness' sake. For you! A nice Jewish girl. I think you'll really like her."

"Here we go again," Michael muttered in disbelief.

"What? You don't like Jewish people now? I've been thinking, if you marry a Jewish girl, then your children will be Jewish. Wouldn't that be something? I think that would be fantastic!"

"Half Jewish," Michael contended. "Our children would be half-Jewish."

"No," Ira refuted. "According to traditional Jewish law, if the mother is Jewish, then the children are Jewish. So, there you go. What do you think? I could introduce you?"

Michael was not amused in the least. Ira was really getting on his nerves with this obsession of his. "Why don't we just hold off on that for now," he replied calmly. "You know how busy I am. Let me think about it and get back to you."

"I know what you are doing Michael Johnson," Ira snapped. "You need to meet me halfway on some of these things. That's what friends do for each other. You are a very stubborn person, you know. Would it kill you to throw me a bone every once in a while?"

* * *

Ira really came through. He got the Boys and Girl Club to take on Christopher as a volunteer youth counselor. They agreed to work around his schedule at the warehouse and his parole officer signed off. Christopher was so nervous before his interview.

He and Michael practiced together the night before. Michael asked him questions about himself and Christopher aimlessly fumbled his way through. It was truly painful. But according to Ira, it didn't really matter how he did in the interview, the decision had already been made.

Initially, Christopher getting that position was like a successful bypass surgery: it released blockages in the arteries of the heart. The pain went away immediately. He gushed with enthusiasm for the club's programming. Every conversation with him inevitably led to a discussion about something that he has observed there or some idea that he had to make things better. He quickly learned the names of every kid there and earned their respect.

It probably didn't hurt that he was six foot four and 195 pounds of solid muscle. Michael just listened to him politely. Most of the time he didn't have a clue what his brother was talking about, but it was good to see him so engaged. Ira told Michael that he heard that everybody there loved Christopher.

Notwithstanding, Christopher's Achille's heel continued to be the family curse—the lack of self-confidence. His insecurities had worked against him from a very young age to the point where he was always questioning his intellect, abilities, and decisions. He ultimately resorted to masking his private pain with drugs and sex. Even if he had been fortunate enough to pursue a football career after high school, inevitably he would have done something stupid to prove himself that would have gotten him kicked off the team.

This meant that Christopher was existing in a vulnerable state. Even a minor setback could revive his inner demons. As a result, Michael was always a little on edge when it came to his brother. Ira suggested that he go see Christopher's parole officer. He said it might not be a bad idea to discuss these issues before they grew into monsters.

As he sat in the waiting room at the parole office, Michael felt a little like he was going behind Christopher's back. There were several other people waiting there too, including a young black woman with three kids under the age of five who were completely out of control. He watched in disbelief as they ran around in circles and raised hell.

Fortunately, he only sat there for about five minutes before the door opened and a tall white man called his name. He introduced himself as Richard King. He was a nerdy looking guy. His glasses covered too much of his face and he wore jeans with an orange mickey mouse sweatshirt and cheap sneakers. He appeared to be in his late thirties or early forties. He gestured for Michael to follow him and led the way down a narrow hall and into a small conference room where there was only one small round table with two chairs.

"Please have a seat," Mr. King said. "What can I do for you?"

"Thank you for agreeing to meet with me. I'm here about my brother, Christopher Johnson."

"Is there a problem?"

"No, no problem," Michael indicated. "I'm just a little worried about him because I have been trying to help him adjust."

"What do you mean? He is adjusting fine, as far as I know. Is there something in particular that I should be aware?"

"No, that's not it. I guess my question is whether there is anything in particular that I should be doing to help him stay out of trouble. He's very emotional. When things are good, then he's fine. But when something bad happens, he can't always be trusted to make the right decision."

"That's very insightful," Mr. King complimented. "I figured as much. It sounds like you are concerned that he will start using again."

"Yeah, a little," Michael admitted.

"Well, I can tell you that he gets drug tested regularly and he hasn't had a problem so far. The guys who do best on parole are the ones who have determined that they would rather do anything than go back to prison. You can't always go by what they say, it is more about what they do. And you're right, the key for your brother is going to be how he handles the hard times, you know, like the fights with the girlfriend or getting fired or something. Until then, you just don't really know."

"Right," Michael agreed. "He's really hard to read."

"Keep in mind that he was incarcerated for a long time," Mr. King emphasized. "A lot of things have changed since he went away. There are many things that you and I just take for granted that are new for him. It's hard. I'm not gonna lie."

"Do you think he needs a counselor or somebody to prepare him for what's coming?" Michael inquired. "Maybe to help him through it?"

"I think that what he needs most is a really good support system," Mr. King opined. "Basically, he needs to know that somebody who he cares about believes that he can make it. Right now, he is full of self-doubt that he either doesn't recognize as being there or he doesn't want to admit to himself."

"That makes sense to me," Michael acknowledged.

"Whatever you do, don't coddle him," Mr. King warned. "Keep your expectations high and let him know when he disappoints you. Push him hard. His pushing back at you is a good thing."

"Okay," Michael said. "Thank you. This helps."

"I have to say that I have been a parole officer for going on twelve years now and you are the first person who has come to see me on behalf of a parolee to ask what they could do before there was a problem. I suspect that the biggest thing that your brother has going for him is probably you. I know that you were behind him getting in at the Boy and Girl's Club and you deserve a lot of credit."

"I don't want any credit," Michael said. "I just want my brother to have a life worth living."

Michael was glad that he went to see Mr. King. If nothing else, it gave him confidence that he wasn't completely missing the mark with Christopher.

Still, he was concerned that if he rode his brother too hard, that it would have the opposite effect and push him further away, resulting in Christopher running out and doing the exact opposite of what he was supposed to do. That is pretty much what happened with their father. Michael's knew he had to keep Christopher talking and listen for signs of trouble brewing.

A few days later, the brothers hit the gym together again. However, going with Christopher was frustrating as he garnered attention from everyone there. He initiated interaction with everybody. As a result, guys were always coming over and asking him for workout advice, and the women kept smiling and flirting with him. Michael just wanted to get in and get out, whereas Christopher wanted to make an event out of being there.

"You're always so distracted when we work out," Michael complained.

"Distracted how?"

"When you're not talking to somebody, you're looking at yourself in the mirror."

"I don't look at myself in the mirror," Christopher argued.

"I have no idea how you got so vain."

"It's not my fault if chicks dig me," Christopher said with a smirk on his face.

"More like, you dig you," Michael criticized.

"You're just jealous."

"You're crazy. Do you still have that girlfriend?"

Christopher suddenly looked annoyed.

"I told you man that she wasn't my girlfriend," he protested.

"Well, are you still being friendly with her in that special kind of way?"

"As a matter of fact, no," Christopher replied defensively. "I told her that it was too soon for me and that I wasn't ready for a relationship."

"Really? You told her that?" Michael challenged.

"Yup. I also told her that my pain in the ass kid brother was all up in my business and that you didn't approve of her. She was very upset. I gave her your name and address. I think she's looking for you."

"Well, I think you did the right thing. I guess that she is going to have to just find herself another pretty boy," Michael joked. "Maybe a younger one, too."

He spontaneously spun around to face the mirror and flexed his upper body.

"You think that she might like this?" Michael provoked.

"Seriously, I'm not even trying to live without a woman," Christopher said. "Might as well just have stayed locked up then."

"I never said that you had to," Michael argued. "I just said that you need to be honest with the women you're mess'n with."

"It's the same thing," Christopher reasoned.

"No, it's not!" Michael resisted. "You start running game again, you're gonna get jammed up again. It never worked for you before. Why do you think that it will work this time? Is it too hard for you to find and open your heart to someone you really care about?"

"Yeah, it is," Christopher argued.

"Okay, do it your way then and let's see what happens!" Michael snapped.

"I will!"

"Good, then it's settled!"

He walked over to the other side of the room and stared at the big screen that ran upcoming announcements and inspirational quotes on a continuous loop. He wasn't angry as much as he was frustrated. Besides, getting upset with Christopher was a complete waste of time. In the end, you never won.

Michael was starting to wonder if he was the right guy to be helping Christopher after all. It's not as if he had all the answers. He was still struggling to find his own way out. Their dad had always preached that an undisciplined life will always produce many regrets in the end.

He wasn't worried about Christopher becoming a hindrance because frankly that wasn't even a possibility. Still, there was no way of knowing if his brother's bad habits would be a distraction to himself causing him to not follow through when it mattered. This uncertainty made Michael uncomfortable.

They were both quiet in the truck on the way home from the gym. Michael always just pulled into the driveway when he dropped Christopher off. He never went inside. Christopher didn't want him to. After shifting into park, Michael waited for his brother to get out.

"Michael, I need to ask you one more thing about mom and I promise that I won't ask anything else," Christopher finally said.

"What is it?"

"I know that she was in a lot of pain when she died, but how bad was it really? Dad said something about it before, but they gave her drugs, right? She probably couldn't feel anything?"

"Why do you want to know?" Michael asked and shifted awkwardly in the seat. "I don't see how any of this is going to help you."

"Yeah, but I just really need to know," he demanded. "I keep having these nightmares and she's calling me to help her, you know. She's moaning and whatever and calling my name."

"That never happened. She was often in severe pain, but not every minute," Michael asserted.

"Was she alone when she died?"

"No, she was never alone. Both Dad and Auntie were there with her pretty much all the time… I'm not gonna lie, it was bad. The pain meds did help a little, I guess… There was a smell. I will never forget that smell. That must be what death smells like… When I was around, she always pretended to be better than she was. She would have pretended with you and TJ too. She really didn't look that bad. She never lost her hair or anything. It just got grey all over. She was thin and frail and one morning she just died."

Michael could tell that Christopher was crying even though he didn't look directly at him. He didn't react himself, although his own grief had resurrected inside, and the dark cloud of despair was hovering over him once again like a heavy shadow. It hurt to swallow. This was the reason that he never talked his mother's passing and refused to think about it. There was a place in the corner of his heart where he had buried most of his pain and he resented being forced to go back there.

"Okay. I got it," Christopher said and kind of rocked back and forth slightly. "Thank you."

Chapter 14

ichael's score on the LSAT was in the top 35th percentile, which was actually better than he was getting on the practice exams he took. But he was convinced that it wasn't going to be good enough to get him into Albany Law School. He went to a community college for his first two years. He was competing against people who had gone to much more distinguished colleges and universities.

"So, I don't understand why you aren't happy about this. You did damn good in my opinion," Ira said before coughing into the phone.

"I don't know what I was hoping for," Michael admitted. "I always knew that it was a longshot."

"Most things worth having typically are," Ira asserted. "Somebody didn't do right by you, Michael. You are such a defeatist. You need to figure out a way to get out of the prison in your mind. That is why we are taught in the New Covenant to renew our minds daily."

"I'm just being honest."

"No, you're not," Ira dismissed. "The human mind is the battlefield of demons."

"You are probably right," Michael admitted.

"I'm always right," Ira joked. "You should know that by now."

"No, you're not," Michael replied curtly. "Hey, why are you breathing like that?"

"How am I breathing?"

"It's like you're struggling a little to catch your breath or something. You don't feel that?"

"No, I don't feel anything," Ira claimed. "It's probably just this cell phone getting bad reception. I told you that this thing is junk."

"Alright, but you need to pay attention to how you are feeling. Remember what Dr. Evans said to you about that."

"I'm not listening to him," Ira objected. "He doesn't know what he's talking about half the time. Do you want to go to lunch tomorrow to celebrate the future Michael Johnson, Esquire?"

"Are you coming in?"

"Yes, I was hoping to," Ira replied.

"Okay. Remember, no more donuts!" Michael admonished. "Nobody eats them."

"Okay, I'll see you tomorrow."

Ira hadn't been coming into the office as much as he once did. Michael attributed that mostly to the nice weather and how much Ira liked to pester the guy who took care of his lawn.

He also didn't like the sun. He seemed to get around better in the cold.

Most of their recent interactions were on the phone. As much as he complained about his cell phone, Ira now had Michael on speed dial, meaning he pushed that button every chance he got. Michael kept telling him to just leave a message and that he would call him back as soon as he got out of class or whatever he was doing. But it didn't make a difference. All of Ira's phone messages began the same way, "Michael, this is your best friend Ira…" The first message was always followed up by several other calls in rapid succession.

"Who is that blowing up your phone like that?" Christopher once asked. "You must have really put the whammy on some girl. Huh, Michael?"

Michael was sitting at his desk the following morning when Ira walked in and handed him a white box of baked goods and grinned.

"Hey, what's up with your face?" Michael wondered.

"My what?"

You're all blue."

"I am? Let me see."

Ira turned and started walking down the hall toward the bathroom. Michael followed closely behind.

"Oh, it's not that bad," Ira said as he examined himself in the mirror.

"Yes, it is!" Michael declared. "Come on, let's go! We have to go to the emergency room."

"I'm not going to any emergency room!" Ira protested.

"Yes, you are! You could be having a heart attack or something."

"I'm not having a heart attack!"

"Oh my God! Listen to your breathing!" Michael said in a panic. "I can't believe you!

Let's go!"

"No!"

"I'm not playing with you!" Michael shouted. "Come on now before I drag you!"

Michael ran into Jeff's office and told him what was going on.

"Go!" Jeff directed. "I'll tell Rob when he comes in. Call us and let us know what is going on as soon as you can."

They took Ira's car because he was parked closer. Suddenly, Ira looked bad. Michael helped him get into the front passenger seat. He was beginning to wonder if maybe he should call 9-1-1. But he decided to just follow through with his original thought.

Michael's heart was racing. He told himself that he needed to calm down. He kept glancing over at Ira, who was slouched over in his seat taking deep, shallow breaths. He looked like he was half dead.

Ten minutes later, Michael pulled up to the ER entrance and slammed on his breaks. He jumped out of the car and ran into the hospital.

"Help!" he shouted. "Somebody, please help me!"

"What's wrong?" the woman sitting at the desk behind the window asked.

"My friend needs help. I think he's having a heart attack."

"Where?"

"Outside, in the car up front."

The woman turned and shouted to someone, and two guys came running out. They ran up to the car and started attending to Ira. It was hard to tell if he was still conscious. Michael was nervous and anxiously watched from the sidewalk as they worked on his friend. Two more guys came out and they eventually put Ira on a gurney and rushed him inside. A nurse approached as soon as he walked back inside and started asking him a lot of questions, most of which he didn't know how to answer.

"Look, I'm sorry. I don't know how long he has been in pain or the last time that he had anything to eat. I told you; he lives alone. You are asking me a lot of stuff and I don't have any idea!"

"I understand," the nurse said. "Please just sit tight. I will try to find out what is going on. Okay? Just stay here."

"Okay."

So many different thoughts were running through his mind. The overriding one was that Ira was going to die and he was already starting to feel some grief pangs. He knew the feeling well.

"I'm sorry, sir, but you need to move your car," a security guard interrupted his dip into the pool of gloom.

Startled, he jumped to his feet. After finding a parking spot, he called Ira's daughter. She didn't answer. He left a message.

He tried to sound calm. He reminded himself of the need to remain positive.

As soon as he walked back inside, his phone rang. It was Rob. Michael told him everything that he knew, which wasn't much. Just as he hung up with Rob, Becky called.

"Michael, what is going on with my father?"

Her question sounded like an accusation of some kind.

"I don't know," he replied. "They are working on him now."

"Is it his heart?"

"I don't know for sure, but I think so," he acknowledged. "He showed up at the office and his face and lips were blue. He wasn't in pain, but he was out of breath and very weak."

"He really came to the firm in that condition?"

"I had to force him to come here to the ER."

"I see," she said. "Okay, I will be there as soon as I can. Thank you."

The waiting room was starting to fill up. Michael was a bit of a germophobe, and he didn't want to sit there with all the sick people. One guy came in with blood all over the front of him and sat down a few seats away. Michael eventually got up and moved to the other side of the room. He was starting to feel a little queasy.

"Hi Michael," the nurse interrupted.

"Hi."

"Your friend is stable now. He did not have a heart attack, but there is definitely a problem. His oxygen levels were dangerously low when he came in and that is why he was so weak. We are giving him oxygen and that should make him feel better for the moment. We need to run some more tests. We are going to admit him and once we get him settled in his room you can see him. Do you have any questions?"

"Do you want me to wait here?"

"Yes, please. We have a room for him, but I don't know how long it will take for us to get him there. He is going to be in the cardiac unit."

"Okay."

Michael was relieved. At least Ira was stable. But he could tell that this time was different and there was probably something very serious going on with him. Michael's anxiety level was starting to rise again, as he wrestled with his fears.

He was still sitting in the ER waiting room two hours later when Becky and her daughter arrived. He watched as they approached the receptionist. He could not hear what was being said, but it seemed like Becky was giving the receptionist a hard time. He was just about to get up and walk over when Becky turned abruptly and headed in his direction.

"These people! I tell you. Have you heard anything?" Becky asked.

"Yes, they said that he is stable and that they were going to admit him and run some more tests," Michael replied.

"Did they say what kind of tests?"

"No, just that they were going to test his heart," Michael offered.

"But it wasn't a heart attack?" Becky solicited.

"No, they don't think so. His oxygen was low and that is why he was so tired."

"Have you seen him?" she asked.

"No, not since we got here."

"Okay I'm going to go see if I can find out anything more."

She turned and walked intently back toward the receptionist window while Becky's daughter had a seat next to Michael.

"Hi, I'm Leila, we met before."

She sat down. She wore a white t-shirt and jean shorts and sandals. She had shoulder length curly brown hair. He thought that she had nice eyes.

"Michael," he said. "It's nice to meet you again."

"Do you know if my grandfather has been having problems breathing for long?"

"Not that I am aware of," he replied. "I spoke to him on the phone yesterday and he seemed okay. His breathing sounded a little raspy. He said that it was nothing, so I didn't think much about it."

"Well, it's a good thing that you are keeping track of him," she stated. "He hates when people hover over him."

"Oh really? I hadn't noticed," Michael joked.

They both laughed through a slightly awkward moment.

"What do you do exactly? I mean, I know that you work at the firm, but what is it that you do there?" Leila asked.

"I'm the office manager."

"Oh, and that's why you help my grandfather out. It's part of your job?"

"No, I met him there, of course. But we just started talking one day and became friends."

"Really?" she asked. She looked genuinely surprised.

"Yeah, we found that we have some things in common."

"Like what?" she pressed. "If you don't mind me asking."

"Well, we like to provoke each other, for one. He likes that I give it right back to him."

"That's odd," she commented. "As far as I can tell, he usually hates it when anyone challenges him about anything."

"It's an act," Michael said definitively. "You gotta look past it."

"Well, he's pretty good at it," she responded.

"I know… And there is also our faith. We talk a lot about that stuff."

"Oh, I see," Leila replied. She was clearly thinking about something.

"Look, your grandfather is a really good guy," Michael expressed. "I think that he feels misunderstood by people. I just happen to know what that feels like."

Becky walked back to where Michael and Leila were sitting.

"They said that we can go up to the waiting room near the cardiac unit," she said. "I need to call Ari. He's impossible to get ahold of."

The three of them walked toward the elevator and took it to the third floor. The signs were confusing, and they needed to be directed to the waiting room. It was a plain room with a few chairs and a television on the wall. There was a bathroom in one corner. No one else was waiting there.

"I'm going to try to call Ari again and see if I can find some coffee somewhere. Either of you want anything?"

"No." Leila said and shook her head.

"No, thank you," Michael followed.

He looked at his watch. It was almost 3:00 p.m. He couldn't believe it. Seated there, they watched an old sitcom on television. Michael was not familiar with it. He didn't find it to be particularly funny.

"So, what do you do?" he asked at one point.

"I teach first grade," she replied.

"Oh, wasn't Ira's wife a teacher."

"Yes, but she taught high school."

"Do you like it?"

"Yes, very much," she answered. "I like the little ones. Watching them learn new things is a rush for me. They are so funny. I have never met a six-year-old who wasn't excited to learn."

"That's pretty cool," he said.

"Do you like your job?" she asked.

"I do," he said. "I'm in my last year in college. I get my bachelor's degree in the spring."

"Oh, that's great," she said. "Then what? Are you going to stay at the firm after you graduate?"

"I really don't know. Maybe."

They just stared at the television while they talked.

"Are you close to your grandfather?" Michael asked cautiously. "The reason that I ask is he never talks much about his family."

"Honestly, I was always a little afraid of him when I was a young girl," she explained. "He wasn't exactly warm and fuzzy. He was always fighting with my mother and so I just stayed away from him. My grandmother was the nice one."

"Oh, I see."

"He used to make funny faces at me, when no one was looking," she said with a hint of a smile. "I would make them back and it was kind of our secret game. He could always make me laugh."

"I'm telling you, he has a good heart," Michael emphasized. "Right now, he's just a little lonely and a little sad."

"See, that makes me sad," she whispered.

"Me too," Michael confessed.

Becky strolled back into the room. She was carrying a boxed container with three coffee cups in her perfectly manicured hands, which she plopped down on the table.

"I know that you guys said that you didn't want any coffee, but I got you some anyway. God only knows how long we will be sitting here."

"Thank you," Michael said.

"I finally got Ari," Becky announced. "He is going to make a phone call and see what he can find out."

"Oh," Leila said.

"Ari is my brother," Becky said turning to Michael. "He's a surgeon in New York City."

Michael just nodded his head.

"I left a message for your father too," Becky continued at Leila. "I told him that he needed to pick up dinner. Maybe you should call Roger. It doesn't look like we are going to be back in time for your date."

"Yeah, I was planning to call him in a little while," Leila answered.

"I'm sorry about all of this, honey. I don't understand why they have to be so slow."

"It's okay," Leila replied. "We just got here."

A doctor wearing blue scrubs walked in.

"Hi, I'm Dr. Chin. Are you here for Ira?"

"Yes, I'm his daughter," Becky said.

"Nice to meet you all," he said. "Ira is doing better. We have ruled out a heart attack based upon his blood work. He was having a lot of trouble breathing and we gave him oxygen, which seems to be doing the trick. But we also performed an echocardiogram, which is an ultrasound picture of the beating heart, which unfortunately did show some malfunction. I'd like to do a catheterization tomorrow on the right side so I can see exactly what is going on there.

"What's that?" Michael inquired.

"That is where we go in through the neck and thread a catheter to the right side of the heart. It's pretty painless. We don't have to sedate him to do this. Hopefully, we'll know exactly what we're dealing with. Do you have any more questions?"

"Have you spoken with my brother, Dr. Ari Goldberg?" Becky asked. "He said that he was going to call you."

"No, I haven't. He may have called, but I haven't had any time to return any of my calls today yet. I'm sorry about that. Do you have any other questions?"

"Is this serious," Michael pressed.

"He's eighty-two years old and his heart is not functioning properly. So, yes. It's serious," the doctor admitted.

Michael could feel himself tighten up.

"But let's just see what the catheterization shows, shall we?" the doctor suggested. "No sense in getting ahead of ourselves."

"When can we see him?" Michael inquired.

"Now. He's resting. Just ask them at the desk what room he's in."

"Okay, thanks," Michael said.

Ira was asleep. He had a clear tube in his nose. There was also a heart monitor attached to him and you could see how his heart was beating on the screen. There was a beeping sound and the monitor screamed out at one point. It startled Michael and he was embarrassed. They were quietly standing there for several minutes before Ira opened his eyes.

"Hi, Dad," Becky said. "How are you?"

"I'm good," he whispered with a slight groan.

"You really gave us quite a scare there, you know."

"It's Michael's fault," Ira asserted. "I told him not to bring me here."

"Now don't you go blaming Michael," Becky replied. "He was just trying to help you."

"I want to go home!" Ira blurted out.

"Dad, you can't go home. They still need to do some tests to figure out what is wrong with you."

"There is nothing wrong with me!"

"You have to trust the doctors," Becky said.

"No, I don't!" Ira barked. "Now I'm telling you that…"

"Ira, enough!" Michael said and stepped forward. "Cut it out right now! I mean it! I know that you don't feel well, but don't you even think about taking it out on other people."

"I don't want to die in this hospital!"

"You're too mean to die!" Michael said before he knew it. "Now settle down!"

"Alright, don't get your panties in a bundle," Ira shot back.

"Now listen very carefully," Michael slowly articulated. "We want to know how you really feel. Does anything hurt?"

"No, I'm just tired."

"Then close your eyes. Go back to sleep. We will be right here."

"Okay."

Ira closed his eyes. He appeared to fall asleep almost immediately. The three of them sat down in the chairs at the end of the bed.

"Michael, that was amazing," Leila said. "You are so good with him."

Just then a nurse walked in and started fidgeting with the monitor. She also examined the needles in Ira's arm and adjusted the blankets covering him.

"Can I get anybody anything?" she asked.

"No, thank you," Becky replied.

"Mr. Johnson, when you get a chance there are some authorizations that we need for you to sign out at the desk."

"Wait, what do you mean?" Becky challenged. "I'm his daughter."

"Yeah, I know. But Michael Johnson is the health care proxy listed in his chart. That's you, right?" she asked while looking directly at Michael.

"Yes," Michael answered softly.

"Then can you please come out and sign the authorizations before you leave today?"

"Yes, I will," he stammered.

"Thank you," the nurse said.

Becky had a bewildered look on her face, and she looked to her daughter for support. Leila quickly put her head down. They were each tense. It felt to Michael like the temperature in the room had gone up suddenly by twenty degrees. He wanted out of there in the worst way.

From that moment, Becky had no use for Michael. She was not necessarily outright rude, rather she went out of her way not to acknowledge him and to exclude him in any of the discussions. She insisted that the nurses address her directly and she refused to make eye contact with him.

"Uh, Michael, do you happen to know the security code to my father's house?" she sarcastically asked at one point. "I don't want to get all the way over there and find out that it was changed too, without my knowledge."

In response, Michael decided that he needed to take the high road and ignore her as much as he could. But that was easier said than done. She was clearly angry and determined to take it out on almost everyone, but especially on him. She was relentless. She made him uncomfortable, and he hated being around her.

Chapter 15

Ira was diagnosed with Pulmonary Arterial Hypertension (PAH). Specifically, he had high blood pressure in his arteries that go from his heart to his lungs. This is different from the run of the mill high blood pressure condition. In his case, the arteries in his lungs had become narrowed or blocked. Although it could be treated, there was no cure for this disorder. Because of his advanced age, his life expectancy was one year.

Ira had almost no reaction to the diagnosis or to the prognosis. His demeanor did not change in the least. It was as if he didn't hear a single word the doctor had said. His only question was when he could go home.

In contrast, Michael was visibly shaken, and he was doing everything he could to play it off. But he wasn't sure what to think about all of this. He wasn't in shock exactly—he was just anxious and wounded.

Obviously, this was going to be an incredible challenge. There was a part of him that just wanted to go somewhere and hide, like he did when his mom was sick. However, his maturity helped him recognize that this was no longer a real option for him. Everything was different this time. He needed to be there for Ira until the end. That's all that really mattered.

The treatment plan was minimal. Other than oxygen, the doctor only prescribed anticoagulant medication to help reduce the risk of blood clots and a diuretic to remove excess fluid from the body caused by heart failure. At Ira's insistence, he was going to be released in a couple of days.

Rob seemed genuinely upset when Michael told him what the doctor had said. Michael asked that he not share the news with the others just yet. Rob graciously offered that he could take whatever time off that he needed to help with Ira.

Fortunately, Michael was only taking one class that summer. Once Ira was home, he was going to talk to him about getting someone to take care of him at least part-time. The doctor recommended that they hire someone full-time, but Michael knew that Ira was going to be resistant to the idea. He needed to tread lightly.

* * *

As soon as he got off the hospital elevator, he could hear Ira yelling all the way down the hall. Michael hurried toward his room. He got there just ahead of a nurse who was also rushing to get there.

"Hell no!" Ira shouted. "There is no way! You must be out of your mind!"

"But Dad, just…"

"You heard what I said…"

"Hey! Hey! What's going on?" Michael asked as he entered the room.

The nurse stood in the doorway.

"Did you know about this Michael?" Ira asked.

He was already out of breath and panting.

"Calm down," Michael directed. "Did I know about what?"

"She wants to put me in some nursing home!"

"It's not a nursing home," Becky argued. "It's assisted living where you can have twenty-four-hour care!"

"I don't care what you call it. I'm not going!"

"Can we all just calm down, please?" Michael asked in a normal tone. "Ira if you get yourself all worked up, then you are not going anywhere. They are not going to discharge you tomorrow or any time soon. Right?" Michael said and looked at the nurse who was still standing there.

"Yes, that is correct," the nurse responded.

"Is that what you want?" Michael prodded. "We can figure all this out later, but I need you to settle down. Now sit back. Is this pillow good? Do you need another one for your arm?"

"No, that's good," Ira said with a sigh and slid back in the bed.

"How about some water? Do you want a little water?"

Ira shook his head no.

The nurse turned and walked away.

"Becky, can I talk to you please?" Michael asked and gestured toward the door.

She followed him to the family waiting room.

"What do you think you're doing?" Michael demanded.

He was angry and he was doing all that he could to suppress it.

"I'll tell you what I am doing," she shouted. "I have spent the last couple of days calling everybody that I know and using every connection I have trying to get my father in a place that will take proper care of him."

"Well, who asked you to do that?" he questioned.

"Nobody had to ask me! He's my father, not yours! I suggest that you remember that!"

"I know that he is *your* father, but you don't get to decide these things by yourself!"

She took a step closer to him and was now threatening him with her body language. Leaning in, she screeched, "We don't need your permission before we …"

"Actually, I think that you do need my permission," he abruptly interrupted. "I have the health care proxy. Not you!"

"I don't care what piece of paper you have, and I don't appreciate how you are talking to me!"

"And I don't appreciate you trying to go behind my back," he countered. "Look, it doesn't have to be like this. I am more than willing to work with you. I know that you are trying to help, but it is not good to get him upset. That is the opposite of what we should be trying to do here."

"I didn't mean to get him upset, but I'm worried to death about him dying in that house by himself. I can't move back here. What are you going to do, Michael? Quit your job and move in with him?"

"I think that we can find some reliable people who provide home care," Michael urged. "I'm telling you that he is going to die as soon as we take him out of his house. Is that what you want?"

Her eyes shot open wide.

"How dare you!" she exclaimed. "No, that is not what I want! I can't believe that you would ask me that! This is outrageous!"

"Then let me talk to him," Michael proposed. "We both know that he is never going to listen to you."

"Maybe not, but please don't think for one second that I trust you," she declared. "I see how you have worked your way into everything."

"Actually, you are just angry because Ira gave me his health care proxy instead of you," he argued. "Maybe you need to ask him why he did that. And maybe you should try to make some peace with him before it's too late. You only have one father. But that's your choice. I really don't care what you do, or if you trust me."

"I hardly need a lecture from the likes of you!" she shrieked.

"Apparently, you do. So, let me tell you something lady. If you ever pull another trick like you did today or do anything else to get Ira this upset again, I'll do everything in my power to limit your access to him. That's a promise!"

Michael turned and stormed out of the room. His heart was beating so fast. He couldn't remember the last time that he was this angry about anything and he didn't regret anything that he had said to her. She needed to be brought down a peg or two.

He had done a little research on the effect of the power of attorney in New York and found that as Ira's "agent", he had broad legal authority to make all the decisions for him. It was like Ira had handed him a blank check. Becky couldn't do anything without Michael, and it was time that she realized it.

When he walked back into Ira's hospital room, Ira was lying there asleep in bed. As Michael approached, he slowly opened his eyes.

"Where's the ice princess?" he whispered.

"She's in the waiting room."

"Did you give it to her good?" he asked with his eyes suddenly all aglow.

"I know what you're doing," Michael replied critically. "And I don't appreciate being used like that."

"Hashem calls the young man because he is strong," Ira preached. "But he also calls the old man because he is wise."

"Yeah, well you're not as wise as you think you are," Michael lectured.

"Doesn't matter as long as you are as strong as I think you are," Ira said with a smirk on his face.

"Should I be worried?" Michael asked.

"How many times do I gotta tell you that you worry too much?"

* * *

Becky found a woman who had a home healthcare business with a good reputation. The woman indicated that they could start almost immediately. Becky insisted on staying with Ira the first two nights after he was released from the hospital, before the start of the contract period. After that, there was an aide scheduled to be with Ira all the time.

Just as Michael had predicted, Ira wasn't too thrilled about having people in his house. But he didn't much like the alternative put to him by Michael either, the same option first presented by his well-meaning daughter. Specifically, the threat was that he would not be able to stay in his house if he wasn't nice to the people who were there to help him.

Although Becky was cordial, there was a lot of tension between her and Michael. Fortunately, she was not there every day, and their interactions were limited. The bigger problem, in Michael's opinion, was that Ira had no patience with her at all. It wasn't necessarily all her fault; it was just that she had a knack for always saying or doing something that got Ira going. It didn't make sense how little she knew about her father. As a result, Ira refused to meet her halfway. It was painful to watch.

Chapter 16

Michael remained very dedicated to his job. He hated not being in the office and was determined not to let Ira's illness interfere with his work responsibilities. It was hard that first week that Ira came home. Michael felt like he needed to be at Ira's house for some part of each day to keep him calm. But he quickly became more confident that everyone was settling into a routine and Ira was less on edge. His fall classes were on Tuesday and Thursday nights and on those two days he couldn't see Ira at all.

"Hey Michael," Rob called out early one morning from his office. "Can you come in here please?"

Michael was surprised because he didn't know that Rob had arrived. He was surprised again to find a man sitting across from Rob when he walked in.

"Michael, this is Ira's son, Dr. Ari Goldberg."

He was a middled aged man with a full head of dark curly hair and dark framed glasses. He wore a blue suit with a white-collared shirt and no tie. Michael didn't think that he looked anything like Ira, or Becky for that matter. His legs were crossed, and he made no attempt to stand up or to greet Michael.

"Hi," Michael said cautiously.

"Michael, Ari has something that he wants to talk to you about," Rob said. "So, I'm going to leave you gentlemen alone."

Rob stood to his feet and walked out of his office. Michael turned and faced Ari directly.

"What can I do for you?" he asked.

"Well, for one thing, you can stay the hell out of my family's business," Ari said.

He slowly stood to his feet. He was about Michael's height, but he was very thin.

"Excuse me?" Michael questioned.

"You heard me," Ari barked. "I want you to crawl back into whatever hole it is that you crawled out of and stay out of our affairs! My sister told me what an arrogant little prick you are, and I came here to tell you that I will have none of it!"

"I'm sorry, but what did you call me?" Michael asked.

"You heard me. I don't give a damn what papers *you* got my father to sign. If you continue to stick your nose where it doesn't belong, I will bury you. I know a lot of people and I can make you wish that you were never born. I don't think you know exactly who you are dealing with."

"Why don't you tell me?" Michael baited.

"Leila told me that you are in that same religious cult that my father got himself involved in and I hate everything that you stand for. I am asking you nicely to just walk away. It's as simple as that homeboy!"

"Are you finished?" Michael asked.

"Actually, that is all that I really came here to say. I am warning you. I want you to stay away from my sister and stay away from my father or I will come down on you like a ton of bricks. Are we clear?"

"Yes, we are clear," Michael replied

"Good," Ari remarked. "Then we understand each other."

"Well, not exactly," Michael contradicted.

"What don't you understand?"

"We are alone in this office right," Michael asked sarcastically while pretending to look around. "That means that there is absolutely nobody here to stop me from knocking you clean out. I mean, I could literally beat that smug look off your face by punching you repeatedly in your right eye and you would be completely at my mercy."

"You wouldn't dare!" Ari sneered. He sounded whiny.

"Wouldn't I?" Michael goaded. "You don't know me like that. I think that you have made the mistake of thinking that just because I am in a 'Christian cult' that I am somehow weak. Believe me when I tell you, that is far from the truth and the kind of mistake that could get you seriously hurt."

"I'm not afraid of you!" Ari shouted.

"Good, that makes us even," Michael postured.

"Look, I just want you to leave my father to me and my sister," Ari explained. "You have no vested interest here, so it should be easy for you to just move along."

"Who are you kidding?" Michael asked mockingly. "We both know that you don't care anything about Ira. You probably can't even remember the last time that you even saw him."

"Again, that's my business, not yours!" Ari interjected.

"But the part that you are overlooking is that Ira chose me, not you or your sister, to handle his affairs now. And we all know why he did that, don't we? Bottom line: I'm not going anywhere! If you want to fight about it, then bring it on, little man!"

"You are going to regret this!" Ari bellowed. "I can promise you that!"

"I seriously doubt it," Michael gloated. "But feel free to give it your best shot."

"You're nothing but a thief and an opportunist!" Ari spewed.

Ari's face was completely flushed, and he was perspiring heavily above his lips. His eyes bulged and twitched.

"That's all you got?" Michael mocked. "Ira was right, you really are a putz."

Michael turned and walked out. He was surprised to find Rob was standing in the hall just outside the doorway. Rob seemed embarrassed that he was caught. Presumably, he overheard everything and had facilitated this ambush. Rob walked passed him and quietly closed the door. Michael was infuriated.

Ari remained in Rob's office with the door closed for several minutes, which annoyed Michael even more. He kept imagining the two of them sitting in there and plotting against him. He was still fuming inside when they finally came out together. They were making small talk and laughing. Michael didn't look up from his desk when Ari passed by him.

He was earnest when he told Ari that he wasn't afraid of him. However, unless he was badly mistaken, Ari was caught off guard by Michael's brazen response. That is, there was a moment when Ari blinked, and he appeared to be very much intimidated by Michael. It was written all over his face.

Regardless, in hindsight, it probably wasn't the wisest move to have threaten Ira's son the way that he did. But Ari had it coming. He was the one throwing his weight around and he drew first blood. Michael's dad had always insisted, over their mother's strong objection, that his boys not run away from a fight. His decree was "if someone hits you, then you better hit him back harder." Although Michael never got in any physical fights himself, that way of thinking was ingrained in his psyche and imbedded in his DNA. He could feel it. A part of him liked going at Ari and Becky.

Rob didn't say anything to Michael about what happened until the following morning. He approached Michael and asked to speak with him.

"How are you?" Rob asked as he sat down at his desk.

"I'm good."

"I wanted to talk to you about what happened yesterday with Ari. I must say that I was really bothered by the whole thing."

"Me too," Michael said.

"And frankly, I was very surprised and disappointed at your behavior," Rob continued.

"My behavior?" Michael repeated and feigned surprise.

"Yes, you basically challenged Ira's son to a fist fight right here in my office."

"I didn't *challenge* him."

"I heard you," Rob insisted. "You can't deny it. It should go without saying that I cannot tolerate that kind of thing happening here. This is a place of business." He seemed nervous. "Michael, everybody here really likes you and you are a good worker. I like you and appreciate everything that you have done, but…"

"Wait a minute," Michael interrupted. "Can I ask you a question?"

"What is it?"

"I always thought that you and Ira were 50-50 partners here, but he told me that that is not the case."

"Excuse me?" Rob resisted.

"Ira said that his percentage is 52%. Is that true?"

"I don't understand how that is any of your concern," Rob objected.

"Well, because I am trying to figure something out. See, I'm thinking that if this is true and if I have Ira's power of attorney, then that means I now control his 52%. Is that right, or am I missing something?"

Rob froze in place. "He gave you his power of attorney too?"

Michael looked Rob directly in the eyes without saying anything.

"But why would he do that?" Rob questioned.

"I thought you knew. You mean Ari didn't tell you?"

"No, I thought you only had the health care proxy."

"Hmm…that's so interesting," Michael toyed. "Must have slipped his mind. But anyway, what do you think? Am I missing something? Because I need to understand."

Rob sat straight up in his chair.

"Michael, what exactly are you trying to do here? Are you threatening me?"

"I'm not trying to do anything, you wanted to talk to *me*, remember? Something about how surprised and disappointed you were at my behavior. But you're right, I interrupted you. I don't mean to be rude. What did you want to say to me?"

Rob leaned over and put his head in his hands and rubbed both eyes with his palms.

"Nothing…let's just drop it please," Rob said with a grumble and deep sigh. "You can go."

"Are you sure?" Michael pressed. "Because I really want to hear what you have to say."

"Yes, you can go," Rob directed. "Thank you."

"Okay," Michael replied. "Just let me know if you change your mind and want to talk about what happened yesterday."

Michael was laughing to himself by the time that he had reached his desk. He had anticipated that Ari wanted to get him fired. Although he really didn't want to lose his job, the truth is that his days at the firm were probably numbered anyway. After he graduated, and Ira was gone, his life was inevitably going to change in many ways.

After work, Michael went directly to Ira's house. It was Wednesday and he didn't have any classes. He hadn't seen Ira since Monday and he was anxious to check in on him. He assumed that Ari had gone to see his father too while he was in town, and Michael was concerned about how Ira had tolerated that reunion.

He was sitting in the living room when Michael arrived. He had the clear oxygen tube in his nose, and he was watching the evening news. The aide was sitting there too. She was a Ukrainian immigrant with blond-streaked hair and appeared to be in her forties or fifties. Ira seemed to really like her. She said hello and excused herself.

"How are you today?" Michael asked.

"I'm good."

"Did you get some fresh air today?"

"No, it was too hot," Ira complained. "How are things with you?"

Ira looked pretty good for the most part. He was dressed in his typical buttoned–down blue dress shirt and khaki slacks. Only the oxygen tube and tank gave away the fact that he was not well.

"Good. I met Ari yesterday," Michael disclosed.

"Yes, I heard that the good doctor paid you a visit too."

"He came to the office."

"And how did you two fellas get along?" Ira asked mockingly.

"Fine."

"You're lying," Ira rebuked.

"The better question is, how did it go with you and him?" Michael insisted.

"Aww, he's mad about you," Ira admitted. "He doesn't like you very much, you know. I've noticed that you don't really play well with others. Why do you think that is, Michael?"

"Did you fight with him?"

"No, he never confronts me head-on," Ira revealed. "He's smarter than Becky that way. He knows not to try to push me."

"I don't understand what happened with your children."

"What do you mean?"

"It's not normal."

"I don't know if I really know either," Ira reflected. "Esther and I were socially conscious when we were young. I told you how I even wanted to go down south to help with the civil rights movement. She loved her disadvantaged students and was always fighting for them. Somehow our kids turned out completely opposite of us in that way—both of them. Becky's idea of helping the poor is buying girl scout cookies. Ari is in medicine just for the money. He hates the sight of blood, and he doesn't even like people. We probably gave them too much. It's hard to say."

"But you can't just throw the baby out with the bathwater, right?"

"They're not babies," Ira asserted.

"You know what I mean."

"Esther, to her credit, decided a long time ago that she would just accept our kids the way that they were, warts and all, which is essentially what she did. Bless her heart! But it was harder for me because I wanted so badly for them to do better."

"And so that's it? You're okay with leaving things this way?"

"I'm doing no such thing," Ira replied.

"Then what?"

"I can't say," Ira insisted.

"You can't or you won't?" Michael challenged.

"Same thing."

"No, it's not."

"Listen," Ira said. "I have always prayed for my children, and I will continue to do so until the day I die. We have gone around and around with this thing for years and they have made it clear that they have little use for me. It's in the Lord's hands now."

"Okay," Michael replied and threw his hands in the air.

"What happened with Rob?" Ira changed the subject.

"I can't say," Michael followed suit.

Ira laughed.

Chapter 17

Christopher got in trouble with his parole officer. He refused to take a random drug test. Mr. King called Michael. He said that Christopher had exactly one hour to come down to his office and take the drug test or he was going to submit a request to his senior parole officer to issue a parole revocation warrant against him.

Michael had to call his brother's cell phone several times before he answered.

"Christopher, what is going on?"

"I don't know what you are talking about," Christopher alleged.

"Your parole officer just called me and said that they are going to violate your parole for refusing to take a drug test."

"Well, why did he call you?" Christopher asked. "I'm a grown man. He needs to deal with me man to man."

"Are you crazy?" Michael challenged. "Do you want to go back to prison? Is that it?"

"No, I don't want to go back to prison. I told him that I took some cold medicine with codeine by mistake and that I probably wouldn't pass the test. He was making me take it anyway. So, I just walked out."

"But that doesn't make any sense," Michael argued. "He said that your parole could be violated for just refusing to take the test even if your urine isn't dirty."

"I don't care," Christopher whined. "They can't just treat people like this."

"Listen, you are literally one hour away from the police looking for you," Michael noted. "I suggest that you get yourself back there as fast as you can and take the freaking test! If it comes back positive, then we will deal with it. But right now, you are in a no-win position if you continue to refuse."

"But this isn't fair," Christopher bellyached. "I tried to be honest with this dude and he is still trying to hold it against me. He's just out to get me."

"Do you remember the promise you made to me?" Michael interrogated.

Christopher did not answer.

"*Do you*?" Michael yelled into the phone.

"Yeah, I remember, but this isn't my fault!"

"So, you are breaking your promise?" Michael continued. "Is that what you're telling me? What about mom? She believed in you to her dying day. But you are going to go back to prison because you feel sorry for yourself. The hell with this!"

"I didn't say that…"

"Yes, *you* did," Michael spoke calmly and hung up the phone.

He was tired. Everywhere he looked these days, there was a living and breathing disaster coming at him. Simply because he was better equipped to deal with some things, didn't mean that he wanted to fight with somebody every other day.

And then on top of everything else, there was the little fact that his best friend was going to die. They hadn't talked about it specifically. They just continued where they left off before Ira got sick. Michael was not sure what Ira was thinking exactly. But he definitely wasn't depressed or withdrawn. Perhaps he was in denial. It almost seemed like Ira simply didn't care.

But Michael cared a lot. His mother's passing was the worst thing that he had ever been through. Now he was going to get shot in the heart again. He was trying not to think about it. But it was always in the back of his mind, even during school.

Christopher called him just as he was walking out of class. A big part of him didn't really want to answer his phone.

"Hey."

"Michael, what's up?"

"Nothing. Where are you?"

"At the crib. I passed the drug test."

"So, you took it?"

"Yeah, I took it," Christopher answered. "I'm sorry man. You were right."

"Christopher, you can't keep doing this."

"I know, I'm sorry," he apologized.

"I just wasn't thinking. Okay?"

"No, it's not okay," Michael contended. "You almost violated parole over something stupid."

"What do you want me to say?" Christopher pled.

"I don't want you to say anything," Michael replied. "I want you to do better."

"I'm trying bro," Christopher grumbled. "I really am."

"Not hard enough from what I can see."

"Man, why can't you just give me a break?" Christopher complained.

"Because you don't deserve one," Michael fired back. "You can't make anyone respect you. You have to earn it. You want your parole officer to respect you? Then earn it. And you can't do that by pulling the crap that you pulled today."

Christopher didn't say anything. He just kind of groaned.

"Look you are my brother and I believe that you are stronger than you know," Michael encouraged. "But it's your life. I can't live it for you."

"Okay, okay," Christopher agreed. "I hear you."

It was impossible to know if he was getting anywhere with Christopher. The truth is, it didn't feel like it. Christopher still liked working with the kids at the Boy's and Girl's Club, but his attitude sometimes created a tense situation. He told every-one what to do all the time and he became increasingly disgrun-tled when the staff didn't listen to him. His environment had improved but not his respect for authority.

These days Michael was barely holding himself together. But his driving force was he simply refused to let Ira down. Ira's life needed to end well, so he pledged do everything he could to make sure that happened. His conscience kept him taut in that direction.

* * *

Fortunately, all the drama around him suddenly took a respite. Becky called her father several times a week, but she stopped coming to Schenectady. Ari had crawled back into whatever hole he had crawled out of. And Rob was quiet. But Michael was smart enough to know that this was just the calm before the storm. Without a doubt, there were many more battles to be fought on this front before the war was over.

His stomach dropped a little when he pulled into the drive-way and saw Becky's car parked there. He hadn't seen her in several weeks. But he was determined not to let her get to him. If anything, she should have been the one avoiding him.

Leila was sitting alone at the kitchen table when he walked in. She smiled warmly when she saw him.

"Hi Michael."

"Hi," he said. "Where's Ira?"

"He's upstairs. They are helping him change his pants… he had an accident."

"Oh, okay," Michael said.

"So, how are you?" she asked.

"Good," he replied and looked away quickly.

"Is something wrong?" she wondered.

"No, nothing."

"You sure? You seem upset about something."

"No, I'm fine," he lied.

"Did I do something?"

"No," he snapped.

"I know that not everyone in my family has been nice to you," she acknowledged. "But that has nothing to do with me. I hope that you know that I am grateful for everything that you are doing for my grandfather."

"That's not what I heard."

"Well, what did you hear?" she asked.

"I heard that you think that me and Ira are in a cult together and I am using that to take advantage of him."

"I never said any such thing!" Leila exclaimed. "Who told you that?"

"Ari told me. I admit that I was really disappointed to hear that that is how you feel about me. But at least I know now," he contended.

"I swear, I never said anything like that to anyone!" she insisted. "I can't even remember the last time that I spoke to my uncle, and I have never had a conversation with him that involved you. He gets all his information from my mom, and I never told her that either. All she knows is that I think that you are good for my grandfather."

"Well, I'm sorry if I got it wrong," he meekly responded. "It's hard knowing just who and what to believe around here. But I want you to know that I would never do anything to hurt Ira. He has been nothing but good to me. I'm only here because he wants me here."

"I know that. I hope you believe me," she said.

"I do believe you," he uttered. "And I apologize for the misunderstanding."

"No need," she offered. "I think that I know what happened. But I really don't appreciate my uncle saying that."

"Maybe don't make a thing out of it," he urged. "They're your family."

"I don't care about that. I trust you."

"How can you trust me?" he wondered aloud. "I could be everything they say I am, or worse."

"But you're not."

"How can you be so sure?"

"Because I have a good feeling about you."

Michael fought the urge to smile with all his might and lost bitterly. She smiled back at him. He felt the heat.

Unfortunately, their tender moment was broken up by Becky's rushed entrance.

"Hello Michael," she forced herself to say.

"Um, hi," he replied.

"Did you know that both of my father's feet are badly swollen?" she asked in her typical accusatory tone.

"Yes, I did," Michael replied. "The doctor is keeping an eye on it."

"Why can't they get rid of the water?"

"I don't know. They aren't swollen all of the time. It seems to go up and down."

"Well, I was shocked when I just saw them." Becky said. "They look awful!"

"I will ask at his next appointment if there is anything else that they can do."

"I really would feel better if Ari could take a look at it," Becky stated.

"Me too," Michael said with a straight face and glanced at Leila.

She scolded him with her eyes.

"Okay, I guess we are going to have to get on the road," Becky decided. "Leila honey, are you ready?"

"Yes, let me go up and say goodbye."

Leila jumped to her feet and hurried out of the room.

"Michael, I am also very concerned that these aides aren't doing everything that they should be doing for my father. I mean, how do we know that they aren't sleeping on the job? You're not here at night. How would you ever know?"

"Ira seems to like them. He would have complained if he didn't. I think that you made a good selection with this company." "Thanks," she replied. "I think so too. Just let me know if there is a problem with them. I will be sure to address it immediately."

"I definitely will."

"Okay, tell Leila that I went to the car. I don't want to be late for dinner."

He was relieved to see her walk out of the door. He was determined not to take the bait from her. Almost everything she said had an edge to it. He could only imagine what plan she was devising as the end game.

"Where did my mom go?" Leila wondered upon her return.

Michael was seated at the table, staring at the stack of mail in front of him.

"She's waiting for you in the car."

"Okay," Leila replied. "I looked at my grandfather's legs and they don't look *that* bad."

"I know," he acknowledged.

"I'm sorry," she said.

"It's okay."

"Here, this is for you," she whispered. "It's my phone number. If you ever want to talk."

Michael was immediately flustered as he took the piece of paper from her.

"Um… Thank you," he muttered.

"See you later," she said as she turned and headed for the door.

He questioned whether her gesture was just friendly or if it implied a deeper interest. Regardless, he hoped he might have a chance. Obviously, he had noticed how attractive she was. A natural beauty, she was like a breath of fresh air. He hadn't allowed himself the luxury of really thinking about her as even a possibility—until that moment. He could not believe that this was really happening; he was over the moon.

"Michael, Ira wants you," Anna, the Ukrainian aide, who Ira apparently liked the best, interrupted.

Ira was sitting in the chair next to the bed. He had aged a lot the last few months. He looked thin and frail. His skin completely lacked color.

"Hi, Michael."

"Hi, what's going on?"

"What were you doing?" Ira wondered.

"The mail."

"The mail can wait," Ira stated. "Have you heard anything from Albany Law School yet?"

"No, and I hope you haven't told anybody about that."

"I haven't said a thing. But I have been praying."

"I told you it's a long shot," Michael argued.

"I like betting on long shots."

"How are you feeling?" Michael asked.

"I'm fine and I wish that everybody would stop asking me that. I can't stand all this fussing about."

"I know."

"And I don't want Becky trying to dress me. Keep her away from me."

"How am I supposed to do that? She's your daughter."

"I don't want her to," Ira said and sulked like a small child.

"Okay, I'll talk to the aides. It's not like she is here that often anyway."

"I know," Ira said. "But please tell them."

"Anything else boss?" Michael provoked.

"Don't call me that!"

Michael laughed.

"You got a girl yet?" Ira asked.

Michael tightened up.

"I told you to stop asking me that," he demanded.

"I just want you to be happy," Ira said defiantly. "Is that a crime?"

"I am happy," Michael insisted.

"No, you're not."

"You can't tell me if I am happy or not," Michael argued.

"Sure, I can. You are just now discovering what you're capable of. You need to settle down with someone. You won't be happy until you figure out who you really are, and you can't do that by yourself."

"And you know who I really am?" Michael questioned.

"Yes, I do because I know our destinies are tied together."

"You know you make me crazy when you say stuff like that."

"I don't know what else to tell ya," the old man quipped.

When Michael made his way back to the kitchen, Anna asked to speak to him. She was clearly upset.

"Michael, I'm sorry to have to bring this up, but I think that it's important," she said with an accent.

"No, what is it?"

"We like Ira. He's a little feisty, but he is funny too. But his daughter is hard to take. Every time she comes here, she wants to change the way we do things. That's bad enough, but she gets Ira so upset. Today, she wouldn't leave when I was trying to get him dressed. He wanted his privacy, you know, and he didn't want her to be in the room. She only left after he yelled at her. We were hoping that you could maybe talk to her."

"I'm sorry about that," he said. "I will speak to her."

"Thank you," she replied. "I don't want to start any trouble, you know. But I had to say something. I just want what is best for the client."

"I'm glad that you did," he answered. "He just told me too. I'll take care of it."

Michael was angry. He thought that he had made himself clear. He dreaded having to talk to her, but he really didn't have a choice. He waited until he got home before he called her.

"Hello, Becky. This is Michael."

"Is something wrong with my father?"

"Well, he wanted me to talk to you. He said that you refused to leave the room today so that he could get dressed. Is that true?"

"I didn't think that it was a big deal," she maintained. "I'm his daughter."

"It's a big deal for him," Michael replied. "He's entitled to his privacy just like everybody else."

"I was just trying to help."

"I know, but Ira is a very proud man. Would you want him in the room with you when you were getting dressed? I think that it makes sense to leave his personal care to the people that we hired to do that. He trusts them."

"I'm sorry," she said. "But this is all very hard on the family. Although the situation is less than ideal, we are trying to make the best of it."

"Well, it is hard on Ira too," he contended. "And he is the most important person now. Don't you agree?"

"Okay, I will leave the room when they are dressing him," she grumbled. "Anything else?"

"Yes, there is," he continued. "I have told the staff to let me know as soon as Ira gets upset about anything. They are going to call me immediately. I wanted you to know that because I didn't want you to think that they are going behind your back. I can't be there all the time. But I want to know everything."

"So, now you have people spying on me?" she asked. "Is that what you're saying?"

"Not just you," he resisted. "This applies to anybody who comes to the house. It's not personal."

"It feels quite personal to me," she declared.

"Well, I'm sorry that you feel that way," he articulated. "But thank you so much for understanding. Sorry for disturbing you. Please enjoy the rest of your evening."

Chapter 18

Michael was confounded. He couldn't decide if Leila wanted him to call her socially, or if she meant for him to call only if he wanted to talk about Ira. He debated the issue back and forth in his head for hours before he finally got up enough nerve to call her. He felt like a moron. But he somehow managed to stumble his way through asking her to dinner. She sounded excited and suggested that they meet halfway in Utica. She said that she knew a nice Italian restaurant just off the NYS thruway. It was a date!

He was nervous all day. Christopher was disappointed when Michael cancelled their workout, but he was a little more understanding when he learned that Michael had a date.

"You want to tell me about her?" Christopher asked.

"Nope."

"Why not? I'm your big brother. You're supposed to come to me with this stuff. You don't know everything. What does she look like?"

"Can we please not do this?" Michael begged.

"At least tell me this," Christopher needled. "Is she like a cheerleader? Does she wear those really short skirts? You know the ones where you see her underwear?"

He started panting and grunting loudly.

"You're a pig. Goodbye."

* * *

Leila was right. The restaurant was easy to find. He got there first and waited at the bar for her to arrive. He still wasn't sure that this was a good idea until he saw her walk in. She looked stunning. She wore a white off-the-shoulder top and a short skirt. She also wore black heels that made her look much taller than she was. His head was spinning.

"You look great!" he managed to say after the waitress had seated them and taken their drink orders.

"Thank you," she replied. "I hope that you don't think that it was too forward of me to give you my phone number the way I did. I have never done that before."

"No, I'm glad you did. I have been really looking forward to tonight."

"Really?" she asked.

"More than I should probably say."

"That's nice to hear," she said. "Michael, can I ask you a question?"

"Sure?"

"How old are you?"

"I'm thirty-eight."

"Really? I thought you were much younger. You look so young."

"I know, everybody says that. It probably doesn't help that I am still in college. How old are you?" he asked.

"I'm 28."

"Do you still live at home with your parents?" he wondered. "No way!" she expressed. "I would kill myself. You know how my mom is. My dad is not quite as intense as her, but it works out better for me if I have my own apartment."

"Don't you have a sister too?"

"Yeah, my sister Heather is two years older than me. She lives in Minneapolis with her husband and two kids."

"Are the two of you close?" he inquired.

"We were growing up," she explained. "But now it's kinda hard with her being so far away and with the boys. What about your family?"

"I live with my dad," he said. "My mom died not too long ago, and we are still trying to find our way out. I have two older brothers."

"I'm sorry to hear about your mother."

"Thank you," he said. "That was tough for me."

They dined together for over two hours. She was bright and caring and he really enjoyed talking with her. She was carefree and had a lot of stories about wild times on spring break with her friends in Miami and breaking her leg when she jumped from the backseat of a moving car. She made him laugh and forget all about the stress from college, his brother's parole, and Ira's declining health. Even though those things were on the backburner, he appreciated that she never brought up Ira or his problems with her family.

"How come you don't have a girlfriend?" she probed. "Even my mom thinks you are good looking."

"Let's just say that I was a late bloomer," he admitted. "Now, I'm just too busy."

"Oh, I see."

"What about you? Why haven't you settled down?"

"I guess I've had what you would call two serious relationships. One in high school and one in college. I got dumped both times."

"I can't imagine anyone dumping you."

"Well, it happened," she said and crinkled her nose. "How's Roger?" he boldly asked.

"You heard that?" she replied and giggled.

"Yeah, I heard."

"Roger is a nice Jewish guy. He is a CPA in my dad's firm and my mother loves him. But he's more her type than mine."

"What is your type?" he wondered.

"I don't know. But I am really starting to like guys who are into the geriatric crowd."

He laughed yet again.

They stared deeply into each other's eyes. He knew he was in trouble. The date ended with him walking her to her car.

"Thank you for dinner," she said. "I had fun."

"I had a nice time too," he replied. "Maybe we can do it again sometime?"

"I would like that," she confessed.

"Even with everything that is going on?" he finally questioned.

"Yes, I think that you are kinda great."

"Leila, I really like you too. But how would your family feel about me dating you? I think your mother would have a small stroke."

"More like a major heart attack for sure," she opined. "But I don't think that who I date is any of her business, do you?"

"No, but I'm pretty sure that she wouldn't agree with us, and this is already a tough time with your grandfather."

"I won't tell if you don't," Leila urged.

"But how is that going to work if…"

She suddenly jumped into his arms and pressed her lips against his. He was caught totally off guard and it took him a couple of seconds before he relaxed enough to completely lose himself in his first long, passionate, wet kiss. He felt like he was soaring. He was also aroused in every sense of the word and desperately hoped that she couldn't tell.

"That was nice," she whispered. "I'm sorry, what were you saying before?"

"I… don't remember," he bashfully admitted.

She giggled.

"Call me," she said and opened her car door.

"Okay. Goodnight."

He watched her drive away. He was calm on the outside, but inside he was shaking intensely. It was as if he had just hopped off a roller coaster at an amusement park and needed time to regain his bearings and settle down. Everything was happening so fast. He was completely out of his comfort zone.

He called her the next day and pretty much every day after that. They were opposites in almost every way. She saw the world as a place that needed to be experienced and conquered. Many of her questions began with, "Have you ever?" His answers were almost always in the negative. She was adventurous and wild, and he had no idea why she liked him.

Inevitably, the subject of religion came up.

"Is your brother-in-law Jewish?" he asked.

"Yes, Jake is very Jewish. His family is orthodox. They met in college. He's an environmental lawyer."

"Do you like him?"

"He's okay," she said. "He's a lot more religious than us."

"Ira is religious," Michael contended. "I know it's Christianity."

"I know. We don't really talk a lot about it."

"But you know that my faith is important to me," he presented. "My mom made me promise her before she died that I wouldn't turn my back on God."

"I'm not sure that it's fair for people to do that," she asserted.

"What do you mean?" he asked.

"To force people, I mean."

"She wasn't trying to force me," he clarified. "She just didn't want me to blame God for her getting cancer."

"Oh."

"It was kinda like that for Ira too. Not exactly. But his mother called him just before she died and told him about her secret faith in Jesus."

"Wait a minute!" she exclaimed. "You're telling me that my great grandmother was Christian?"

"Yeah, you mean you didn't know?"

"No."

"Ira is a very spiritual guy. He studied the Scriptures for himself searching for truth. How many people do you know who have done that? His faith is not blind. He's convinced in his heart that God is real."

"I always heard that he was just doing it to piss everyone off."

"Nope, that's not it at all. It cost him a lot. He loved your grandmother very much. She was literally the love of his life. But she wasn't open to his conversion from Judaism."

"I don't think you understand how hard that would have been for her," she argued.

"Yes, I do," he resisted. "We talked about it a lot. He never tried to convert her or blame her for rejecting him. He fully understood her position. He just wishes that it could have been different."

"This is all news to me," she said.

"I'm sorry," he apologized. "Maybe we shouldn't be talking about this."

"No, I'm not upset," she remarked. "It's just that my impression of him has always been so different."

"What if he's right about the existence of a God who has revealed himself to the whole world through a Jewish Messiah?" he inquired. "Does that change your impression of him? Look, I have only known Ira for like three years, so obviously I don't know everything about him. But I really respect him. He's honest about who he is and what he believes. Have you ever really talked to him? All he wants is for the world to be a better place. Yes, he's also difficult and… well crazy, but he's real and authentic. That's something, right?"

"At this point, it's kinda hard to know just what to think," she admitted.

Chapter 19

L eonard's father called Michael at home. He said that Leonard had overdosed last week and died. There was no service. He wasn't emotional at all. He just sounded tired. He wanted Michael to know.

Michael was in shock. Obviously, he knew that Leonard did some drugs, but he never ever saw him do anything other than smoke a little weed. But Leonard knew that Michael hated drugs because of his brother's addiction so he always kept that part of his life to himself.

As soon as he hung up the phone, Michael fast forwarded through his memory bank of all the times that they had spent together. All the laughs they shared came flooding back. His heart was heavy. He remembered the feeling and instinctively fought against it.

But oddly, he was also thankful to God. There was a time when both he and Leonard believed that life was meaningless.

Without a doubt, it was that mindset that had led, in no small part, to Leonard's demise.

"Oh, I'm sorry to hear about your friend," Leila said during their late-night telephone call.

"Like I said, I haven't seen him in over a year," Michael related. "But I probably did know him better than anyone else."

"Do you feel like you may have been able to save him if you were there?"

"No, I don't feel that way at all," he reflected. "I feel more like I probably would have been the one who found him if we were still hanging out. It may sound cold–hearted, but I'm glad that I didn't have to see that."

"No, I get it. I know a lot of people get trapped in their own world."

"It was a friendship that wasn't healthy for either one of us," he explained. "Leonard is a person who I couldn't bring with me into my future. If we were still friends, then I wouldn't be here talking to you now."

"Well, then I'm sorry to say, but I'm glad that you eased away from him," she articulated. "You did the right thing, for you and for me."

"Yeah, but it's still sad, you know."

"Yes, it's very sad," she agreed.

He was thinking.

"Hey, I told my sister about us."

"What?" he asked in a slight panic. "Why would you do that? What if she tells your mother?"

"She would never do that," Leila assured. "We used to cover for each other all of the time."

"What did she say?"

She hesitated. "She thinks we are doomed," Leila finally disclosed.

"Really, she said that?"

"She thinks that there are just too many obstacles in the way, that we are too different."

"So, we should what? Just forget about each other?"

"No, trust me, Heather has had her fair share of bad boys and early morning walks of shame. She understands the game. She's just worried about me."

"I'm not a 'bad boy'."

"My mom and dad think that you are."

"Well, what do you think?"

"I think that they don't know you."

"No, do you think that we are doomed?" he pressed.

"Heather says we are like Romeo and Juliet, except she calls you 'Homeo'," Leila said with a slight chuckle. "All I know is how I feel about you. I don't want to think about the rest of it. All these issues are other people's problems. We aren't doing anything wrong."

"I feel the same way," he commented.

"Oh my, I really have to go to bed," she finally said. "I'm looking forward to seeing you tomorrow. We should get there around four o'clock."

"Doesn't your mother wonder why I'm always there now when you guys are in town?"

"She just thinks that you have her car bugged," Leila kidded.

"If only there was a way," he replied jokingly.

"Goodnight, Romeo."

"Goodnight, Juliet."

* * *

Michael was excited all day. He couldn't wait to see Leila. Most of their contact had been by phone since their first date a month ago. Since then, he had seen her three times at Ira's house, and they had slipped away to the basement every time and made out like teenagers for about five minutes.

He decided that he would leave work a couple of minutes early, which meant that Jeff would have to close the office. He hated doing that, but it couldn't be helped. He didn't want to get delayed by the traffic and there was no way of knowing how long Becky would stay after he got there. He wanted more than a passing glimpse of his girlfriend.

He told Jeff that he had to do something at Ira's house. In the past, he would have cleared his leave time with Rob, but he was still angry about what happened with Ari. Now, he refused to ask Rob anything. He knew that he was being a bit childish, but the more that he thought about it, the more unrelenting he became.

There were three cars in Ira's driveway when he got there. He forgot that this was the day that Mona came to clean the house and prepared meals for the week. That meant it was unlikely that he would get to talk to Leila alone. He was already disappointed.

Mona was in the kitchen cutting up vegetables when he walked in. He knew she was wasting her time because there was no way that Ira was going to eat any of it. He shook his head.

"Oh, hi Michael. They are all in the other room."

"Hi, thanks."

"I left the mail in the box. It looks like mostly junk mail to me."

"Great, I'll check it later."

Michael took a deep breath and walked into the living room. Ira was sitting on the sofa with one of the aides. Becky and Leila were seated together on a loveseat.

"Hello everyone," he said.

He did not look directly at Leila.

"Hello," was the joint response.

"Ira, are you behaving yourself?" Michael asked.

"No," Ira replied.

"That's not true," Sandra said. "We had a good day."

"Good," Michael said. "Okay, I will be out here going through the mail if anyone needs me. Ira, I will check in on you in a bit."

Michael took the box of mail with him to the finished basement. Ira had a small office on the first floor that he could have used, but he wasn't comfortable going in there. He had been in the basement about thirty minutes when Leila walked on her tip toes down the stairs.

She rushed into his arms as he stood to his feet, and they kissed long and hard.

"No, you gotta go," he pulled away from her and whispered. "We're gonna get caught."

"I know," she replied. "That woman in the kitchen saw me come down here."

"I miss seeing you," he said.

"I miss you too."

They began kissing again.

"I have an idea," she whispered. "Your birthday is this week, right?"

"Yeah," he replied. "How did you know that?"

"Why don't you come to my apartment, and I'll make us dinner?" she begged.

"You want me to come to Syracuse where your mom could stop by at any moment?"

"She never comes over without calling first," she explained. "I want to celebrate your birthday together. No school, no Ira, just us."

"Okay," he whispered.

"Really?"

"Yes really! Sounds awesome. But you need to get out of here now."

"Okay, okay. I'm going."

They kissed again, and she hurried up the stairs.

He was overjoyed. His head was telling him to slow down and protect his heart. But he didn't want to. She was amazing! He didn't care about these other people. He was falling in love for the first time.

"Michael, it's Leila. We're leaving," she shouted down to him moments later.

"Okay. Thanks," he yelled back.

He debated whether he should run up and see them out. But he quickly decided to stay put. It made no sense to be reckless. His birthday was in a few days. He needed to be patient. So, he went up several minutes after he heard the door close, and the car pull away from the driveway.

"Did you eat your dinner?" Michael asked and sat down on the sofa next to Ira.

"A little. I'm not hungry," Ira replied.

"You need to eat to keep up your strength."

"So, how are you, Michael?"

"I'm good."

"I know why you hide out in the basement."

"You do?"

A small shock wave went through Michael's system.

"Because you don't like my daughter."

"I'm not even sure that *you* like your daughter," Michael regrouped.

"I told you, she's harmless. She's a lot like my wife's sisters. They just like to hear themselves talk. It makes them feel like they are doing something."

"Well, I'm just trying to keep the peace," Michael justified. "Can you blame me?"

"No, I guess not. How are you and Rob?"

"I don't know what you mean," Michael deflected. "Everything is the same."

"He said that you are angry with him."

"So, big deal. Why does it matter?"

"It is a big deal," Ira contended. "You never know what is going to happen and when you will need a friend."

"Rob is not my friend."

"You know what I mean," Ira pressed. "It's not like you to hold a grudge."

"I don't understand why you are defending him," Michael wondered. "He wanted to fire me."

"I'm not defending him," Ira disputed. "I'm on your side."

"Then what is it?"

"I want you to see that the key to a life well lived is not giving up on people just because they can't or won't do right," Ira explained. "Hashem never gave up on you or me. That's a big part of the Bible story. Unfortunately, too many people tend to overlook their harsh rebuke of others. Our God is the restorer of our souls even after we have failed him bitterly."

Michael took a deep breath and rubbed his forehead with his right hand. He knew that Ira was right, but he needed time to figure out the practical implications of what Ira was saying. This wasn't just about Rob. It was about Christopher too, and everybody else in his life who had let him down.

Ultimately, he wasn't sure that he could routinely overlook the shortcomings of others any more than he could disregard his own personal failures. People needed to be held accountable. Those who embraced their weaknesses ended up like Leonard. That's the part of his past that he had struggled most to overcome. No way was he going to let up and go down that road again.

Chapter 20

Michael was never a big birthday guy. Although his mom had always gone out of her way to make their birthdays special, he was never overly invested. In contrast, Christopher insisted on a "birthday week." Fortunately, their dad shared Michael's perspective and he always kept things from getting too out of hand.

The phone rang early in the morning while Michael was still asleep. He answered without first checking to see who was calling him.

"Happy birthday to you! Happy birthday to you!" his Aunt Wanda sang out.

Her voice sounded a lot like his mother's voice, although they did not really look alike.

"Thank you," he said.

"How are you doing baby?"

"I'm good."

"Do you have big plans for today?"

"Na, you know me," he lied.

"Well, I want you to be good to yourself today. You want to come over for dinner? I can make you something special."

"I can't but thank you very much. I am supposed to meet up with a friend later."

"Good for you. I never see you anymore. I'm gonna call you next week to set up a time for you to come for dinner."

"Okay, that sounds good," he said.

"Good," she replied. "When is the last time you talked to your father?"

"He called last night to wish me a happy birthday," he reported. "He's doing good. He was so determined to get to Arizona early this year to see his friends."

"Yes, he told me. Tell him to call me the next time you talk to him."

"Okay, I will," he promised.

"Alright. Happy birthday again, baby. I love you so much."

"I love you too."

He was wide awake now. He usually slept in on Saturday mornings until at least 9:00 a.m. and then spent the day doing homework. Today would be different. He didn't want to do schoolwork because it was going to be hard to concentrate. He didn't have to be at Leila's place until 7:00 p.m., which meant that he didn't have to leave home until 5 p.m. Until then, he was intending to just hang out.

Unfortunately, he couldn't relax. He tried everything that he could think of to settle himself. He did his laundry and surfed the internet, but it wasn't working. He received two more birthday calls from two of his cousins: one was his cousin Johanna, who was in medical school in Chicago. But neither conversation lasted that long. Attempts at napping proved equally futile. The day was dragging miserably. As the afternoon creeped in, he took his time getting ready for his special evening.

He left his house at exactly 5 p.m. He was anxious to get there, but he didn't want to arrive too early. He had never driven to Syracuse before, so he was concerned that he might get caught up in traffic or get lost trying to find Leila's apartment. Although he wasn't afraid to drive anymore, he was still a little apprehensive about driving in a lot of traffic.

Leila lived in an apartment building that looked like an old, converted school or something. It was located on the eastside of Syracuse. There was very little traffic and he arrived at 6:45 p.m. Rather than appear too anxious, he sat in his jeep in the parking lot for fifteen minutes before getting out. He had to buzz her apartment from the lobby entrance, and she unlocked the door for him. He was both nervous and excited.

"It's open," she shouted from inside.

He opened the door and walked into a nicely decorated living room. There was soft music playing and he could smell the food that she was cooking. She was standing in the kitchen.

"Have a seat. I'll be right there."

He walked over to a small table and looked at the photographs on display. He recognized Becky and assumed that the grey-haired man next to her was Leila's dad.

"Hey, is this Heather in this picture with you?" he asked.

"Yes, that's from last summer…no two summers ago."

"You guys look alike."

"Everybody says that, but I honestly don't see it," she replied. "She's so beautiful."

Leila was walking toward him. She was wearing a V-neck sweater and jeans. Her hair was loose and a little wild.

"You're beautiful," he said.

She walked into his arms, and they kissed.

"Happy birthday, Michael."

"Thank you."

"Here, come sit," she beckoned. "How has your day been so far?"

"Good. I'm not much for birthdays," he volunteered.

"So, why am I not surprised?" she asked sarcastically.

"No, it's just that I hate a whole lot of fuss."

"But it's your birthday."

"I know."

"I have a surprise for you."

"What is it?"

"Don't worry. It's not anything too crazy. I'll give it to you after dinner. Do you want some wine?"

"No, thank you," he said. "You never told me how you knew it was my birthday."

"My mom told me."

"Your mom?"

"She said that your birthday was the day before my dad's birthday, October 23rd."

"I wonder how she knew that."

"Maybe my grandfather told her."

"Yeah, that's probably it."

"Alright," she said and jumped to her feet. "Give me a couple of minutes to finish dinner and then I'm all yours. Don't go anywhere."

She hurried off to the kitchen. He already loved being there with her.

They had a wonderful evening together. She had prepared an amazing seafood dinner for them. They drank wine and laughed about everything. The outside world faded away as they embraced their connection of the heart.

"I have been meaning to tell you something," he said at one point.

"What?"

"Well, you know how I'm going to graduate in May?"

"Yes."

"Well, I have applied to law school," he revealed.

"Really? I didn't know that you wanted to be a lawyer."

"Just another new thing in my life," he said.

"How come you never said anything before?" she wondered.

"Because it's hard for me to even imagine it myself. I haven't told anyone, except Ira. Not even my family. And I only applied to one school in Albany because now is not really a good time for me to go away. I haven't heard anything back yet."

"I'm sure you'll get in," she affirmed. "You're so smart."

"Thank you, but right now I'm just playing it by ear. I have no idea what is going to happen."

After dinner she surprised him with a homemade birthday cake with candles. She also gave him a gift. It was wrapped in a small box with a big red bow on it. He was embarrassed as he opened it. Inside he found a sterling silver black braided bracelet with two small, engraved links. One read "Michael" and the other read "Leila."

"Oh, I love it!" he exclaimed. "Thank you."

"Don't worry. The names are really small so no one can read them," she remarked. "That way we can still be a secret."

"Good thinking," he said and kissed her again.

He stayed the night like he knew he would. He only struggled with it a little. Admittedly, not as much as he should have. Most men his age were already well settled with wives and kids. His dad had always preached abstinence. Right or wrong, he chose to not fight his desires any longer. Just before he fell asleep, he pulled her as close as he could.

"I love you," she whispered.

"I love you too," he replied.

* * *

When he opened his eyes, she was gone. Just for a second, he thought that he had dreamed all of it. Then he remembered the feel of her on his lips and smelled the coffee. He laid there for a couple of minutes reliving every inch of her and not wanting the moment to pass.

"Good morning sleepy head," she said. "I made you some breakfast."

She put the tray on the bed next to him.

"You didn't have to do that," he replied as he sat up and reached for the coffee cup.

She was wearing a white robe. She looked angelic. He could barely believe his eyes.

"Hi," he said and smiled big.

"How are you?" she asked and leaned over and kissed him.

"Best birthday ever!"

She laughed.

"Michael, you're amazing! Last night was amazing!"

"So, you like me like that?" he joked.

"Yes, but…"

"But what?" he asked.

"But how crazy is this?" she asked aloud. "We really are Romeo and Juliet."

He shrugged his shoulders and took a bite of his toast.

"You got any arsenic?" he teased. "Maybe we should just take our poison now and be done with it."

"That's not funny," she scolded.

"I'm sorry, but you said it yourself. We didn't do anything wrong."

"Didn't we?" she questioned. "It's not like we even tried to stop ourselves."

"But we're in love and love just happens," he argued. "Or did you not mean what you said?"

"Of course, I meant it. How could you ask me that?" she demanded and crossed her arms and pouted.

"Then we can't go back even if we wanted to," he rationalized.

"That's the problem, I don't see how I can ever let you go now," she reasoned. "So, I lose either way."

"What do you mean?"

"Heather is right. My family is never going to accept this. You and I are different in almost every way. And on top of everything else, you stole my grandfather!" She reached out and playfully punched him in the arm.

"I didn't steal him exactly, I just kinda borrowed him," Michael kidded.

She cut her eyes at him.

"Okay, okay. Let's just slow our roll a minute," he said. "Come here."

He patted the mattress, and she sat down next to him on the bed. He pulled her close and kissed her on the back of her neck.

"Baby, I know that this is really messed up," he began. "All I ask is that you do what is best for you always. Just so you know, I will never ask you to choose me over your family. I said I love you and I meant it. So, I will let you go if that is what you ever want, even if it kills me. That's my promise to you."

Chapter 21

Rabbi Cohen appeared at the law office unexpectedly. Michael recognized him immediately even though it had been nearly two years since he went to the synagogue with Ira. Of course, Ira talked about him enough that Michael felt like he knew him too. The rabbi smiled warmly when he saw Michael. He asked if they could talk.

Michael led his visitor into the conference room. He left the door slightly ajar so that he could hear the phone ring.

"Please have a seat rabbi. What can I do for you?"

"I'm sorry about coming here without calling first, but I decided to take my chances that you would be here."

He seemed more than a little anxious.

"Oh, that's not a problem," Michael reassured. "It is good to see you again."

"You as well…I just needed to talk to you about a few things," Rabbi said. "Ira doesn't know that I am here. I saw him a couple of days ago."

"Yes, I know."

"I was glad to see that his spirits are up."

"Yes, he's hanging in there," Michael stated.

"But he is going to die soon," the rabbi spoke without expression.

He was seated at the table with his hands crossed. He was leaning slightly forward.

"I know," Michael said sadly and looked away.

He was suddenly uncomfortable.

"How are you doing with all of this?" Rabbi Cohen asked.

"Oh, I'm good. People die, right? There's nothing that I can do about it."

"He is worried about you," the rabbi disclosed.

"About me?"

"Yes. He says that you had a hard time when your mother died and that you are hiding from your feelings."

"Well, I don't know where he got all of that from," Michael scoffed. "Yes, it's true that it was hard on me when my mom died, but you move on, right? This stuff happens to everybody. It's not like she just died yesterday. I think that I'm okay now."

"Well, those of us who have been blessed with good mothers know that the pain that comes with their passing is substantial," Rabbi reflected. "I have lost a child too and I honestly don't know which one was worse. Ira thinks that he has put you in the position where you will have to go through some of the same pain all over again. He regrets that greatly."

"But it's not like that for me, I swear," Michael implored. "There are good things happening in my life too that he doesn't know about. I'm not depressed or anything. I just don't know what to say to him."

"Why haven't you talked to him about his final wishes?" Rabbi asked.

"Because I didn't think that he wanted to talk about that stuff," Michael explained. "I wasn't avoiding anything. I was just trying to make it easier on him. I knew he would talk about it when he was ready. I thought that I was just following his lead."

"Trust me, he is not in denial, and he is not afraid," Rabbi advised. "Michael, I have watched many people die. It is one of the hardships of being in the ministry. Most people in the final stages of life want to talk if they are able. Nobody really wants to sit quietly waiting for death to come."

"This is all well and good and everything, but what exactly do you want me to do?" Michael asked boldly.

"It's okay to be angry, or sad, or frightened or whatever emotion rises up in us in times of despair," Rabbi encouraged. "We just can't go out of our way to avoid these feelings. We have them for a reason. They help us to cope and get through."

"I just want what is best for Ira," Michael asserted.

"Then forgive him for leaving you," Rabbi declared.

Michael tensed up immediately. Rabbi Cohen's words caught him completely off guard and began an emotional chain reaction inside of him much like a nuclear bomb explosion. His heart burst and his brain froze. Time stopped for him. He felt raw and exposed. The tears that had welled up in his eyes now poured out like rain and he was helpless to fight against them. Suddenly, he was staring face to face with the same anger and guilt that had been festering inside him since before his mother died.

"Are you alright, son?" Rabbi Cohen asked after a prolonged period of silence.

He handed Michael a tissue from his pocket. It smelled like menthol flavored cough drops.

"Yeah, yeah. I'm okay," Michael uttered and wiped vigorously at his tears.

He was shaking inside. Sitting there with the rabbi, he was embarrassed too.

"Would you like for me to leave you alone?" Rabbi asked. "We can talk more later."

"No, please," Michael forced himself to say. "I appreciate you coming all this way, and I want to hear you out."

"Unfortunately, events like weddings and funerals tend to bring out the worst in people," Rabbi expressed. "All of the family drama is shameful. It really is! Anyway, I believe that Ira wants to die in the Messianic tradition. But his family is likely to oppose that. I have seen these things get messy. You need to talk to him specifically about what he wants."

"What's the difference between the Messianic tradition and the Jewish tradition?" Michael inquired.

"In effect, probably not that much," Rabbi said. The Messianic funeral is a blend of both Christian and Jewish faith traditions, not unlike the service you attended with Ira. But this kind of service can be very hard even on Jewish family members who are accepting of Messianics, which of course is not the case for Ira's family."

"Okay, I'll talk to him," Michael pledged.

"If I were you, I wouldn't wait too long," Rabbi persisted. "Once Ira dies, then someone must carry out his wishes. Typically, that is the family. I don't know the law whether his family can legally disregard his wishes and do something different. But I have seen that happen."

"I understand."

"One more thing, in keeping with Jewish customs, we do not embalm the body. It is preferred that the body is buried within twenty-four hours of death, so there isn't much time. You should call me immediately."

He put a business card on the table and pushed it toward Michael, who picked it up and stared at it."

"Okay. Got it." Michael said and exhaled deeply.

"If you have any questions, you can call me at any time," Rabbi offered. "For some reason, I felt really pressed to come and talk to you today. I couldn't sleep last night because I was restless about it. I am sensing the presence of the Holy Spirit even as I sit here with you now. You see Michael, everything that we do on earth has an effect in the spiritual realm where God and the angels are. And the reverse is also true in that everything done in the heavenlies has impact upon the nations of the earth. The Lord has obviously brought you and Ira together for a reason. I believe that with all my heart."

"I don't know what to say," Michael confessed.

"You don't have to say anything," Rabbi spoke as he stood to his feet and gathered himself. "Ira trusts you. I do too. I have been praying for God to strengthen you. I'm here to help you as much as I can."

"Thank you."

Michael felt oppressed, like a dark cloud was hovering over him and he wasn't himself for the rest of the day. His stomach was off too, and he kept running to the bathroom. He tried to pass the feeling off as nothing more than him getting spooked by some of the things that Rabbi Cohen had said about happenings in the heavenlies that were somehow tied to him and Ira. He wasn't sure what any of that meant. But it was more than that. He was starting to think and feel some of the things that the old Michael Johnson thought and felt. Everything was working together to make him come unhinged.

* * *

"Michael, what's up?" Christopher spoke into the phone.

"Nothing," Michael answered.

"I was wondering if you could maybe give me a ride to the mall one day this week?"

"This week? Why do you want to go the mall?"

"I need to get a couple of things. It won't take long."

"Well, can you go tonight?" Michael wondered. "My class got canceled. My professor is sick or something. Otherwise, you are going to have to wait until the weekend."

"Yeah, I can go tonight. What time?"

"I'll pick you up at 5:30?"

"Okay, that'll work. Thanks."

Michael spent his lunch hour doing research at his desk. But he wasn't a lawyer, and he didn't really know what he was looking for. Sarah wasn't in or he might have asked her for advice. He was becoming more frustrated by the minute.

Finally, he rose abruptly from his chair and marched steadily down the hall. He knocked on the door once and opened it without waiting to be invited in. Rob was sitting at his desk and looked up just as Michael entered and walked up to the desk.

"Listen, I think that I might be in trouble with Ira," he announced. "I'm in way over my head. What I want to know from you is whether you are willing to help me or not. And I need to know now!"

 Rob looked startled. His mouth was opened slightly, and he seemed to hold his breath. He started to say something but then appeared to change his mind. He sat up straight and cleared his throat.

"Have a seat," he said. "Tell me how I can help you."

* * *

Christopher didn't stop talking from the moment that he got in the jeep. He really wasn't saying anything new or different. Michael just listened as he was more than happy to let his brother carry the conversation on his own.

"Hey, what's that on your neck?" Christopher asked.

"What? Where?" Michael reacted as he reached for his neck area.

"Right there," he gestured. "You wanna talk about it?"

"Nope."

"I didn't think so," Christopher said with a chuckle.

Michael was in no mood to walk around the mall. He was still reeling from his conversation with Ira's rabbi and only wanted some coffee and a quiet place to sit and think. They agreed to meet up in the food court in one hour.

As he sat there lost in thought, a small toddler walked up to him. She appeared to be about two or three years old. Her blond hair was sticking out of her pink fluffy hat and her cheeks were rosy red.

"Hi there," he said. "Aren't you the cutest thing ever!"

She just stood there looking at him and grinning brightly.

"Lily!" a woman's voice called out. "Lily get over here. Don't bother the nice man."

"No bother," he answered as the girl was led away by the hand.

His plan was to talk to Ira the next day and he wasn't looking forward to it. Thinking about the funeral service and such made him feel sick. Rabbi Cohen was right that he had gone out of his way to avoid the subject. Mostly, he was hoping that once Ira passed away that his role in the Goldberg family saga would be over. If Ira had a private lawyer and a will, then one would expect that everything that needed to be decided had, in fact, already been made known. But apparently, that wasn't the case.

He was so happy when he left Leila's apartment yesterday morning. This was the side of love that he had only heard about and never imagined could ever be true for him. His jeep pretty much drove itself home from Syracuse as he had no recollection of the drive. His head was completely in the clouds. If he closed his eyes, he could still feel her soft body pressed close to his own.

Unfortunately, it didn't take long for him to come back down to earth. His sense was that he was at a critical juncture in his journey to wholeness. He was convinced that there was still something important left for him to do. That is, there was still something he had to accomplish to completely bury his past and for his transformation to be complete. Whatever that was, he hadn't a clue.

Christopher wanted to eat dinner there at the mall. Michael was not hungry, but he bought a chicken sandwich and a drink just so that his brother didn't feel like he was eating alone.

"How was your birthday?"

"What?" Michael asked. "How did you know that it was my birthday?"

"What do you mean?"

"You never remember," Michael argued.

"Just because I didn't talk to you doesn't mean that I didn't remember," Christopher lied.

"You're so full of it," Michael balked. "Who told you? Auntie?"

"Yeah," he reluctantly disclosed with a sly grin.

"I knew it," Michael said. "I'm not that crazy."

"I remember the actual day that they brought you home from the hospital after you were born."

"No, you don't!" Michael challenged.

"Yeah, I do," Christopher insisted. "You had a big head, and you were all face."

"Is that right?" Michael mouthed without looking at Christopher.

"Yeah. And all you did was cry from the second you came home."

"Isn't that what babies do?" Michael asked sarcastically.

"Not like that. Somebody had to be holding you every second or you would let it rip."

"Sorry, but I don't believe anything you say."

"Don't pretend like you haven't heard this before."

"Even the truth coming from you sounds like a lie," Michael asserted.

"Geez, that's pretty harsh bro, don't you think?"

Michael suddenly heard what he said. "Yeah, sorry," he apologized. "I'm not having a good day." He dropped his shoulders and picked apart his sandwich in slight disgust.

"It's okay," Christopher replied. "So, is it serious?"

"Is what serious?"

"This love jones you got going on for whoever was sucking on your neck last night like a vampire."

"You talk like an old man," Michael mocked. "Nobody says 'love jones' anymore."

"Call it whatever you want, but you know what I'm talking about, don't you?"

Michael rubbed his forehead and looked away.

"Is she Spanish? I really like Spanish girls. She's Spanish, right?" Christopher pestered.

"No, she's not Spanish and you need professional help."

"Yes, she is," Christopher said with a wry smile. "She roughed you up last night too. That's what happened to your neck. Isn't it? Come on, you can tell me."

Michael rolled his eyes. His brother was seriously demented.

"What's her name?"

"Let it go, you pervert!" Michael demanded.

"Just tell me her name," Christopher insisted.

"I said no."

"Tell me or I'll tell auntie," Christopher threatened with a harassing lilt in his voice.

"Leila," Michael reluctantly divulged. "Her name is Leila. You happy now?"

"Is she the reason why you are being so ornery?"

"I'm just stressed."

"About what? School?"

"No, it's a lot of different things," Michael explained. "Let me ask you something. This may sound strange, but have you ever felt like you had a target on your back?"

Christopher stopped to think.

"Yeah, I have," he answered. "When you are the starting running back on the number one ranked team in the state you feel like that before every game."

"How did you handle it?"

"Coach used to tell me when I was nervous before a game to just close my eyes and dare myself to be great."

"Did it work?" Michael wondered.

"Sometimes."

They sat there for nearly an hour. Christopher loved to eat and went back up for a second helping of some fat saturated food and a sugary drink. He still didn't look like he ate all the junk food that he did. Sooner or later, it was going to catch up with him. And it wasn't going to be pretty when it did.

It began to rain just as they were walking to the jeep. There was a definite chill in the air and Michael turned up the heat as soon as he got inside. Christopher immediately began talking about what it was like to play football in the cold and started reliving one particular game he played in unbearable conditions. Once again, Michael wasn't listening to him closely. Rather, he was thinking about Leila and looking forward to calling her when he got home.

He followed the line of traffic out of the mall parking lot and passed by a covered bus stop. The wind had really picked up. There was a man standing there alone. He was a big guy in a military uniform and camouflage jacket.

Michael had to slow down just as he drove in front of the bus stop, and he almost came to a complete stop. He looked the man in the eye and the stranger peered back at him in return. Just then a faded memory resurfaced, and a rush came over him.

Chapter 22

It had been six months since Ira was diagnosed and he didn't really want to get out of bed that much anymore. When they brought him downstairs, he mostly just dosed off and on in his chair. He kept complaining that he was tired. But when he was awake, he was pretty much aware of everything that was going on. He always perked up a little when Michael was there.

"Have you heard anything yet?"

"No, but it's still early," Michael said as he stood next to Ira's bed. "Please don't worry about it."

"I'm not worried. You are,"

"You told me not to worry so I'm not," Michael fudged.

"Good."

"I understand that Rabbi Cohen came to see you."

"Yes, he was here."

"Did you have a nice visit? Did he pray with you?"

"Yes."

"He was asking me stuff that I don't know because we never talked about it," Michael reported.

"Like what?"

"Like what kind of services do you want."

"I don't want one," Ira disclosed.

"What do you mean? There has to be a service."

"No, there doesn't," Ira refuted.

"Yes, there does. Are you doing this to save me somehow? Cause I can do it."

"No, that's not it. Most of the people I know are not here anymore. It's much easier this way."

"I just think that you deserve to be properly honored," Michael expressed.

"I have been properly honored by *you*."

"Me?"

"You've been my lifeline. I prayed and *he* sent me *you!*"

Michael was completely taken aback and took a minute to respond. "Then what?" Michael inquired.

"Cremation."

"Cremation?" Michael repeated in disbelief. "You never said anything about that before."

"You never asked," Ira answered bluntly.

"Anything else?"

"Burial with other Messianics. Ask the rabbi. He should know."

"Okay, only if you are sure," Michael hedged.

"I am sure. The burial is probably the most important part."

"Right. Is that it?"

"Yes. And don't look back," Ira entreated. "I want you to be strong like you are."

Michael nodded.

"I'm not sad," Ira proclaimed. "You shouldn't be either. I'm going home."

"Okay."

"I'm counting on you Michael."

"Okay," he said again and took a deep breath.

That went much better than he thought it would. He was afraid that he would breakdown in front of Ira, and he knew that was something that he simply couldn't do. All day he kept thinking about different ways that he could delicately bring up the subject. He never doubted that Ira definitively knew what he wanted. It was just a matter of making it as easy as possible for them to discuss it.

Their conversation eased a lot of tension. He was no longer somber, at least not in his heart. Ira was nearing the end of his journey. He had run his race well and deserved whatever reward was in store for him. His faith had cost him much. It had cost him both the love and respect of his family, whom he had never turned his back on.

Indeed, his wife died loving him, but not fully knowing him. Even Leila knew almost nothing about her grandfather, who lived only a couple of hours away. Michael was convinced that Ira deserved better than what they gave him. All he did was follow his heart, which led him to Yeshua. They made the decision that his Christian-like faith disqualified him from having them too. That was their great loss.

Ira wasn't bitter. He had come to accept the way things were. His incredible leap of faith had also brought him immense joy too, along with the assurance of knowing that his soul was secure. His secret tears and anguish were not in vain. His constant prayer before the Lord was for his family and for the marginalized peoples among us. Ira had taught Michael so many things in the short time they had together, things he would carry with him for the rest of his life.

Michael spent the following Saturday night with Leila at her apartment. She was more than a good distraction; she was his sweet inspiration. He had been at Ira's house all day and he was emotionally spent. Being with her grounded him and allowed him to reboot.

* * *

His aunt called on Sunday morning while he was driving home. She wanted him and Christopher to come for Thanksgiving dinner and she wasn't taking no for an answer. He wasn't in the mood for a family gathering and he would have preferred to hide away at home alone on his day off. But with his dad not being there to prepare dinner for them, he knew he was trapped. He had to go.

At Aunt Wanda's there were nine people there altogether. Both of his cousins were there. They were in their late twenties and very capable young women. One brought a boyfriend with her. There was plenty of food, which meant that Christopher was in hog heaven. Everyone was very complimentary about the changes that they could see in his appearance. Of course, he hated the attention.

"So, Michael, do you have a girlfriend?" one of his cousins asked.

"I'm trying to focus on graduating," he replied.

"Well, maybe you should be looking for a nice girl too," Aunt Wanda urged. "You're at that age, you know. They must all be lined up around the block to get to you, especially now."

"Michael has a lot of girlfriends," Christopher interjected.

Michael shot a deadly glare at his brother, who immediately put his head down.

"I know he does," their aunt commented. "So handsome! I know a nice girl from church. She sings in the choir and has a beautiful voice."

"I'm good. Thanks," Michael said quickly.

Everyone laughed.

"No, she's really sweet," Aunt Wanda insisted. "You would really like her."

"Christopher is the one who needs a nice church girl," Michael remarked. "Talk to him."

"Well, I haven't seen either one of you guys in church lately," she stated.

"I'm coaching on Sunday mornings," Christopher volunteered.

"Well, just don't forget that you need to make time for God too," she preached. "He wants to be first in our lives. You guys can run around doing all this other stuff. But you better believe that if you ever have to go through a real battle in your life, you will not want to have to fight it on your own. The enemy is real, and he will attack you at every turn. And he doesn't fight fair. Ain't that right, Christopher? Your mother would want both of you to be in church."

Christopher didn't say a word. He just sat there with a constipated look on his face. Any mention of their mother generally caused feelings of sadness and discomfort to arise.

"We know," Michael said. "You're right."

"Then act like you know it," she persisted. "Your mom and I used to pray so hard for you boys. TJ too. I know in my heart that God is not through with TJ or my brother yet either."

"How *is* Uncle Daniel?" Michael asked.

"Oh, he's good, I guess. I invited him and Fred to come for dinner, but he said Fred is getting ready for a show."

"How old is their daughter?"

"I think she's four…no five. She's the cutest little thing."

Overall, dinner was nice. It was good to see his cousins. Their aunt was not quite as good of a cook as their dad was, but homecooked meals were hard to come by these days. Christopher wanted to finish watching some football game, so Michael left him there. There were plenty of people there who could give him a ride home.

He wanted to stop by Ira's house just to make sure that everything was okay there. Although Ira was in the latter stages of heart failure, he didn't appear to be in any pain and the oxygen was helping a lot. There was a do-not-resuscitate order in place, and he was only getting comfort care at home now. It was the same treatment that he would receive if he was in hospice. But he was still taking fluids and eating a little, which were good signs.

However, Ira seemed to be hallucinating a bit. He kept pointing to the corner and asking who that person was. He wasn't upset, but he was constantly looking in that general direction. The aide said that happens sometimes when a person is getting a lot of oxygen.

Michael hadn't seen Becky in over a week. She had started coming in the mornings without Leila. She came about every other day, and she was always gone by the time that he got there after work. She was obviously avoiding him, and he was grateful for even that small blessing. Their silent war was an agitation he didn't need.

* * *

Exactly two weeks after Thanksgiving, Michael received an early morning call at the office from Sandra, who was with Ira. She said that Ira had taken a turn for the worse during the night and he needed to come right away. He told her to call Becky too.

When he arrived there, Ira was asleep. He looked the same. But he apparently had a rough night and struggled to catch his breath at times.

He called Rabbi Cohen just to give him an update. Becky got there around noon, approximately three hours after Michael did. She was on her phone too a lot, presumably touching base with different family members. She always left Ira's room and took her calls downstairs. Ira opened his eyes a couple of times, but he didn't say anything.

Michael was anxious, but he was holding it together pretty good. He and Becky rarely spoke directly to each other and mostly just sat there quietly watching Ira sleep. Sandra came in and out of the room regularly to check on him.

The overall mood in the house was dark. Michael felt bad because he knew that was not what Ira would want. But that was completely out of his control. His relationship with Becky prevented a different send off. Accordingly, he did not foresee an entirely peaceful exit for Ira.

Leila got there around five o'clock, just as the shift changed for the aides. They were both very happy to see her, but only her mother could show it. Michael could only nod modestly in her direction. By the looks of it, Leila was there to support her mom and to say goodbye to her grandfather. She played her role to perfection.

She had been there for almost an hour when Becky's phone rang, and she hurried out of the room and down the stairs. Alone at last, the two lovers dropped the facade and came together. He kissed her on the side of her face, and they embraced tenderly with her arms around his waist and his arms about her neck and shoulders.

"How are you?" she asked.

"Better now that you are here," he replied.

"I got here as fast as I could."

"This feels like slow torture," he related.

"I know. You look so sad."

"No, I'm okay," Michael assured. "I have been preparing myself for this. I am worried about you."

"I really do love you, you know," she whispered.

"I love you too," he said and kissed her lips, then gently pressed the side of her face into his chest. She sighed and rested her head there.

At that moment, Ira made a loud gasping sound from his bed. It startled them both to attention. As they turned, they saw him staring back at them wide-eyed. They both jumped back and let go of each other. But it was too late. Their thin veil of secrecy had been lifted enough for a dying man to clearly see. It was written all over his face, which was suddenly flush.

He was struggling to get up. They both moved closer to his bedside, and he reached out for Leila. She grabbed his hand, and he looked like he was fighting hard to talk.

"Okay, calm down," Leila begged. "You're okay. You're okay. We're right here."

"Leila," Ira pleaded.

"Yes, it's me," she said in a slight panic and leaned in closer. "What is it?"

"Leila," Ira repeated.

"Yes, it's me, Leila."

"Leila…Yeshua is Lord!" he said clearly.

Her eyes shot open wide.

"What's happening?" Becky suddenly asked from the doorway.

"Um…he's awake," Leila whispered.

"Dad? Hi, Dad," Becky said as she approached. "It's me, Becky."

Ira didn't say anything. His gaze remained fixed upon his granddaughter as he held onto her hand.

"Dad, it's me," she repeated and stepped next to Leila.

Ira just put his head back down on the pillow and closed his eyes. He was sleeping again. But he appeared to be more relaxed, and his countenance changed. Even his breathing seemed to even out a little.

"Leila, honey," Becky questioned. "What did he say to you?"

"Nothing," she lied. "He just said my name."

"I thought I heard him say something," Becky persisted.

"No, we thought he was still sleeping, then he opened his eyes, and he called my name."

"You okay, honey?" Becky asked. "He didn't scare you, did he?"

"No, he didn't scare me. I'm fine." Leila looked disgusted.

"I'm sorry, honey. I just want to make sure that you're okay."

"I said I'm fine," Leila snapped.

Ira never said another word. He opened his eyes a couple of times, but he never fixed them on anyone or anything. They could tell that he was getting more restless. His breathing changed again just after midnight. Suddenly, it had a rattle to it and Becky looked terrified. Then the sound stopped as quickly as it started. They each just looked at each other. Michael took a deep breath and stood to his feet. He walked over and grabbed Ira by the hand.

"Leila, can you go get Roberta?" he asked.

She jumped to her feet and rushed out of the room. Becky rose slowly and moved to the foot of the bed, but she didn't come closer. A moment later, Roberta came in and began to examine Ira.

There was a stillness in the room that somehow eased Michael. He was very calm.

"I'm sorry," Roberta said and looked at Michael. "Can I turn off the oxygen?"

Michael turned to Becky who was looking straight ahead. Her face was strained.

"Yes," he said. "It's okay."

Chapter 23

It was 7:00 am. and Michael was just getting out of the shower when the doorbell rang. He was supposed to meet Becky at the funeral home at 9:30 a.m. He slipped on a T-shirt and a pair of sweatpants and hurried to the door. Standing there was a short middle-aged white guy in a big winter jacket and hood.

"Are you Michael Johnson?" the man asked.

"Yes, I am."

"This is for you. Have a nice day."

He handed Michael a white envelope and turned and walked away. Michael closed the door and opened the envelope quickly. He easily recognized that it was some kind of legal document. Inside was a stapled packet of papers that looked like a lawsuit with the words "Order to Show Cause" captioned in the upper right-hand corner. The parties listed were "Ari Goldberg and Rebecca Bernstein, Petitioners, versus Michael Johnson, Respondent." It was signed by a judge, and it read:

ORDERED that Respondent show cause on November 30, 2018, at 4:00 p.m., or any agreed upon adjourned date or time, at 612 State Street, Schenectady, New York 12305, why an order should not be granted giving the petitioners the sole right and discretion concerning the handling of the remains of Ira J. Goldberg.

He put the envelope down on the coffee table closest to the door. He didn't want to forget to bring it with him. Otherwise, he was pretty much unfazed. It's not like he didn't know that Becky was up to something. Ira never knew when Michael's birthday was, so whoever gave her that information wasn't her father. She was getting her information from someone else.

Michael needed to stop at the funeral home prior to going into the office. It was closed when he arrived there at 7:55 a.m., so he just placed his envelope in the mail slot. After Ira died, he had sent text messages to both Rabbi Cohen and Rob, neither of whom had responded back yet. He knew that he was in for a long day.

Rob arrived at the office just before 9:00 a.m. Michael was in the backroom putting away supplies and was very surprised to see Rob there so early.

"Hey, I got your text. Sorry to hear about Ira," Rob said.

"Thanks. I got some kind of lawsuit this morning from Becky and Ari. I put it on your desk. I hope you wouldn't mind looking at it for me," Michael replied.

"Okay, come on in and let me take a look at it."

Michael followed Rob into his office. He hung his coat on the back of the door and opened the envelope.

"Okay, let's see… have a seat.

Michael sat in the chair across from Rob's desk.

"It's a show cause order," Rob explained. "Somehow, they got a judge to sign this yesterday before Ira died. They were probably working on it all day. I didn't think it was possible to get one returnable the same day. You have to go to court this afternoon to answer this."

"Today? Really"

"Yes, this afternoon at four o'clock."

"How am I supposed to do that?" Michael asked partly panicked.

"I am going to call Sean McCarthy over at Simon Dickson. They are Ira's lawyers and they're the ones who drafted the power of attorney and Ira's will. I think that they might represent you on this. As you know, I'm not a litigator."

"So, I need a lawyer," Michael asked.

"Yes, you definitely need a lawyer. You were right to be concerned before."

"Where is the body now?" Rob asked.

"It's at the funeral home that Becky said their family always uses. I didn't care. I talked to the guy at Ira's house and told him that I had some papers for him. I dropped them by this morning, but no one was there yet."

"Okay, I think you should fax those papers to the funeral home too. After that, they shouldn't do anything with the body until they hear from you or receive a court order."

Michael jumped to his feet and said, "Okay, I'll do that right now."

"And I will try to reach Sean," Rob offered.

"Thank you very much, Rob," Michael said.

"You're welcome. And I just want to say again how sorry I am about Ira. I know how close you were to him. I imagine that this must be very hard on you."

"Thank you."

Michael braced himself to not show any emotion.

"You know, he changed a lot after you started working here," Rob volunteered. "He was happier somehow and you did that. You should be proud. I think that you were in some ways like the son that he always wanted. After talking to Ari, I can see that this was at the heart of all of this for him."

"Thank you," Michael remarked. "I really appreciate it."

His heart twisted in his throat. He turned and hurried out of the office as quickly as he could so that he didn't have to reflect upon Rob's insight.

A little later, Michael was sitting at his desk when Rob came out and told him that he needed to be at the Simon Dickson Law Firm at 11:00 a.m.

"Let me know if there is anything else that I can do," Rob remarked.

Rabbi Cohen called, and Michael gave him an update on what was happening. Rabbi said that he wasn't surprised. His opinion was that it was going to get a lot worse before it got better.

He was also surprised that Ira didn't want a service and wanted his remains cremated. He said that traditionally Jews didn't prefer cremation. But he stressed again that if Michael was going that route that it needed to be done as soon as possible.

Michael arrived on time for his appointment. He was nervous. He didn't know anything about Simon Dickson, other than that it was one of the biggest law firms in the capital region. As he sat alone in the waiting room, he kept telling himself to stay strong. It didn't matter what it cost him personally, he was going to honor his promise to Ira.

A young man came out and directed Michael to follow him. He was led into an empty conference room and was told that someone would be with him in a minute. Almost immediately, another man walked in and introduced himself as Sean McCarthy. He was a middle-aged white man with a medium build, salt and pepper hair and round wire-framed glasses.

"So, you were served today with the show cause order at home?" he asked.

"Yes," Michael answered.

"Was there any argument yesterday concerning the arrangements for Ira?"

"No."

"I think that it's interesting that they were planning to go to court without even talking to you about it first. This is a pretty drastic move."

"I'm not surprised," Michael acknowledged. "It's not like we haven't had problems all along."

"What kind of problems?"

"Um, it started when Becky, Ira's daughter, found out that Ira made me his health care proxy."

"I see. Do you have specific final plans for Ira?"

"Yes. Ira didn't want any services and he wanted to be cremated."

"Did you talk to Ira's family about that?"

"No, I didn't."

"Why not."

"He died early this morning," Michael explained. "We didn't talk about anything other than what funeral home to use. They just don't want me involved at all."

"Well, I'm not sure that they can completely leave you out. But let me ask you this: Is there any wiggle room here? How set are you on following Ira wishes?"

"Shouldn't that be the most important thing?" Michael challenged. "They are only concerned with what they want. They don't care anything about what their father wanted."

"Well, let's hope that the judge sees it our way," Mr. McCarthy said. "I will represent the estate at the proceeding this afternoon since the estate's interests are aligned closely with yours.

Technically, we do not represent you personally though and you have a right to retain your own attorney."

"You mean that I need to hire my own lawyer by four o'clock this afternoon?" Michael questioned. He was agitated.

"No, that is not what I am saying at all," Mr. McCarthy clarified. "We will try to get the judge to honor Ira's wishes. We know how fond he was of you, and we trust that everything you are saying is the truth. I think we should just see what happens this afternoon. Then we can talk again afterward and evaluate our options. Okay?"

"Yes, that's fine," Michael uttered and sighed heavily.

"I just want you to know how sorry we are to hear about Ira's passing. I have known him for probably twenty years or so. He was quite the character, I must say. I considered him to be a personal friend."

"Thank you," Michael replied.

"Do you have any questions?" Mr. McCarthy asked.

"So, is this like a hearing?" he wondered. "Will I have to testify?"

"No, generally the judge will listen to the attorneys and try to resolve the matter without a hearing."

"The reason why I ask is because Ira's rabbi said that it is important that Ira's remains be returned to the earth as soon as possible."

"Yes, I know about that," Mr. McCarthy acknowledged. "My wife is Jewish. It's hard to say what will happen this afternoon."

"Do you know this judge?"

"Not really," the lawyer said. "He's only been on the bench for about three or four years. He's a republican. I think that his background is in criminal law. Maybe he was in the district attorney's office at one time. I don't really remember."

"I was just wondering," Michael remarked.

"No, it's a legitimate question," Mr. McCarthy said. "If there is nothing else, how about I just meet you at the courthouse at 3:45 p.m.?"

"Okay, I'll be there."

Michael left feeling more tense than he did when he first arrived there. It was nothing against Mr. McCarthy, who seemed nice enough. But it was hard to be confident about something that you don't really understand.

Specifically, it seemed unfair that Ari and Becky could drag him into court when they never even spoke to Ira about his final wishes. He was more than a little concerned that he was going to get screwed because he wasn't white or rich.

He was just getting in his car when his phone rang. It was Leila.

"How are you?" he answered.

"I'm good," she replied. "How are you?"

"Hanging in there," he offered. "Do you know about this court thing this afternoon?"

"Yes, my mom just told me."

"I'm just leaving Ira's lawyer's office now."

"I can't believe any of this!" she said.

"I know," he replied. "This is not what Ira would have wanted."

"Is there any way that you can just let my mom have whatever kind of service that she wants?" she inquired. "I mean, does it really matter? Not that many people are probably going to come anyway."

"It matters to me," Michael stated. "I promised him."

"I know," she acknowledged. "And I respect that, I really do. I'm not asking you to do anything that you really don't want to do. But I'm afraid that this is going to make things even worse for us with my family."

"I'm sorry, but I can't help that," he spoke. "I'm not sure that I could live with myself knowing that I went back on my word."

"That's one of the things that I love most about you," she whispered. "This whole thing just gets worse by the minute."

"Leila, I still think that you should just stay out of it as much as you can," he suggested. "This is not your fight."

"I don't know if that's possible," she expressed. "I get that my mom is high strung and all, but she leans on me a lot. She and my dad have a weird relationship and my sister isn't here."

"Are you coming to court?" he asked.

"No, I can't," she replied. "I have parent meetings."

"Good," he stated emphatically. "I don't think you should come. There is nothing that you can really do anyway. The judge will decide whatever he decides and that will be the end it."

"Yeah, you're probably right," she conceded. "But what about you?"

"What about me?" he asked.

"I'm worried about you too."

"You don't have to worry about me."

"But I love you," she argued.

"Then listen to me," he implored. "Stay as far away from this as you can. If you're okay, then I'm okay."

"I don't think it's that easy," she voiced meekly.

"It is for me," he asserted.

"Michael, you're almost too good to be true."

"No, I'm not," he dismissed summarily.

* * *

Michael had never been in a courtroom before. Obviously, he had been in the courthouse many times, mostly filing papers for Jeff in the clerk's office on the first floor. But he had never been in one of the courtrooms, although he was always curious about what went on in them. The security officer directed him to court-room number three.

He arrived early at 3:15 p.m. There wasn't anyone else there yet. In fact, the door to the courtroom was locked and he could tell from the window glass that the lights inside were off. He took a seat on one of the benches there and waited."

"God please help me!" he prayed quietly.

At 3:30 p.m., Mr. McCarthy came around the corner. There was another man with him, who was introduced as Trevor Sanders, an associate at their firm. He was well-dressed and appeared to be about the same age as Michael. They were there about ten minutes making small talk when a uniformed man walked up, unlocked the door, walked inside, and turned on the lights.

Mr. McCarthy led them inside into a rather ornate courtroom. With its high ceiling, it had the feel of one of those old catholic churches. There was a judge's bench upfront with several flags behind it. To the right was a seat for the witnesses and a jury's box was in the corner facing the bench. There were also two wooden tables upfront, each with two chairs. Several pews for audience seating lined the rear of the courtroom. They followed Mr. McCarthy to the front row and sat there quietly.

At exactly 4:00 p.m., five people entered the courtroom from the back, including Becky and Ari. The other three looked like lawyers. Two of them walked over and introduced themselves as Jameson Adams and Beckett Jones from McQuillan, Parry & Carter. They then sat down on the first row too, but several feet away from their adversaries. Mr. McCarthy whispered that he never heard of them, but he was familiar with their firm, which was in Albany. Ari, Becky, and the other guy sat together in the back of the courtroom.

Moments later, two women entered from behind the bench. One was apparently the stenographer because she sat down behind the machine that was in front of the bench next to the witness stand. The other woman just stood to the right of the bench leaning against the top of it. They were talking and laughing together quietly, and never acknowledged the others who were in the courtroom watching them.

Chapter 24

Schenectady County Supreme Court
Special Term: November 30, 2018: 4:00 p.m.
Honorable Aaron Chapman, Presiding

All rise! The Honorable Aaron Chapman, presiding."
They all stood.

A man in a black robe came in and took his seat on the bench. He was a white man of average height and weight. He appeared to be in his fifties. He had sandy-brown hair that he neatly parted on the side. He wore black-framed glasses and had a slightly crooked nose that looked like it had once been broken.

"Be seated!" the officer directed.

"Goldberg versus Johnson," announced the woman standing next to the bench. "Counsel state your appearance for the record."

"Jameson Adams of McQuillan, Parry & Carter, for the Petitioners."

"Sean McCarthy of Simon & Dickson, for the Respondent."

Both attorneys took seats at the tables upfront.

"Mr. Adams, you may proceed," Judge Chapman said.

"Thank you, your honor," Mr. Adams began, "The Petitioners have commenced this special proceeding requesting an order directing and declaring that they alone have rights to the final remains of Ira Goldberg. The Petitioners are the only surviving son and daughter of the decedent who died early this morning. The Respondent is in possession of a document purporting to give him the power of attorney for the decedent prior to his death. However, as the court is no doubt aware, that document no longer has any effect now that Ira Goldberg has died. Accordingly, the Petitioners wish to exercise their rights as the surviving next of kin and request that the Respondent, who is not a family member and who is essentially a perfect stranger, be precluded from having any role in the decision-making process related to the final arrangements for Ira Goldberg."

"Mr. McCarthy," the Judge said.

"Thank you, your honor," Mr. McCarthy replied. "First your honor, I would like to make the Court aware that one of the partners at my firm, Stanley Levy, is the executor of the estate of Ira Goldberg, the decedent herein, and that the executor opposes the request of the Petitioners in this proceeding."

"Duly noted," Judge Chapman said.

"Further, your honor," Mr. McCarthy continued, "With all due respect to Mr. Adams, we maintain that he has incorrectly represented to the court the rights of the Respondent to the remains of the decedent. Specifically, prior to his death, Ira

Goldberg executed an instrument pursuant to Section 4201 of the New York Public Health Law designating Michael Johnson as the person who has the legal right to control the disposition of his remains. This instrument, signed by both Ira Goldberg and Michael Johnson, duly executed, and witnessed, is legally binding. Accordingly, it is the Petitioners who have no right to make the final arrangements for the decedent."

"Mr. McCarthy, do you have a copy of that document for the court?" the Judge asked.

"Yes, your honor. And for the record, I am also providing a copy to counsel."

Mr. McCarthy walked up to the bench and handed a copy of the document to the judge. He then turned and walked over to the other table and gave one to Mr. Adams.

"Mr. Adams," the Judge said. "Have you seen this document?"

"No, your honor," he responded. "This is the first time that we have seen this. May we have a moment to examine it?"

"Sure, go ahead," the Judge said.

Everyone stayed in place while Becky and Ari's lawyers read the form and whispered back and forth. After a minute or so, Mr. Adams, looked up."

"Thank you, your honor," he said.

"So, based upon this instrument, are you now withdrawing your petition?" the Judge asked.

"No, your honor," Mr. Adams replied.

"Why not?"

"We would like an opportunity to delve further into the circumstances surrounding the execution of this document. Frankly, the Respondent Michael Johnson is a person of questionable character. He is a close associate of one Christopher Johnson, who is a twice convicted felon, who was just recently released from prison, and who has also been charged in the past with grand larceny and robbery. For over a year now, the Respondent has had complete control of the finances of the decedent, a man of some means. There is reason to believe that he has been exercising undue influence over the decedent for some time now all for his own personal gain. Accordingly, we suspect that considerable mismanagement has likely taken place and the Petitioners are intending to conduct an independent audit of the finances of their father and refer the matter to the district attorney's office for prosecution at the appropriate time."

"Your honor," Mr. McCarthy interjected. "These allegations are entirely baseless. This smear campaign is nothing more than a smoke screen. The fact is neither Petitioner had a very good relationship with the decedent prior to his death. Their father did not trust them to follow his wishes and was forced to rely on his friend to do just that. Any allegation to the contrary is entirely specious and self-serving."

"Let me ask you this, Mr. McCarthy," the Judge said. "What does your client plan to do with the remains?"

"Ira Goldberg requested that he be cremated."

"And where are the remains now?" the Judge inquired further.

"At the funeral home."

"Mr. Adams, what are the intentions of your clients?"

"Burial in the Jewish cemetery next to his wife. They really wanted the burial to take place today, which was the reason that this application to this court was expedited."

"What is your position on cremation?"

"No objection, your honor."

"Counsel approach," the Judge demanded.

While Mr. McCarthy and Mr. Adams were standing at the bench engaging in a prolonged conversation with the Judge, Michael fumed in his seat. He felt like he was just kicked in his chest. He couldn't believe what just happened. For the first time since all of this started with Becky and Ari, he really wanted to do something to hurt them. Previously, he mostly just felt sorry for them because they were both clearly lost and broken souls. But they were also horrible people and now he wanted to make them to pay.

He just looked straight ahead at nothing. He refused to turn around at all or to acknowledge their presence. He was very disappointed in himself for letting them get to him. All this time, he was thinking that he was one step ahead of them. For some reason, he didn't think that they would stoop so low as to try to publicly assassinate him with outright lies. He should have known better.

Eventually, Mr. McCarthy returned to where Michael and Trevor Sanders were sitting and leaned down next to them.

"Michael," he whispered. "The judge is going to allow Ira's body to be cremated. He is also going to order that the remains not be buried anywhere at this time. He wants you to get together with Ira's family and see if you can agree upon a burial place. If you guys cannot agree, then he is going to hold a hearing where both sides get to put on witnesses, and he will then make a final determination."

"Why should I listen to them?" Michael erupted while struggling to keep his voice down. "They just accused me of stealing in open court that they know is a lie. I have never taken one penny from Ira!"

"I know how you feel," Mr. McCarthy sympathized. "But the judge wanted me to tell you that he is concerned that all of this was not clearly settled before Ira's death. He feels that neither one of you have done enough to avoid this."

"Are you kidding me?" Michael cringed. "None of this is my fault. Becky could have just asked her father about his final wishes, but she never did. And that's because she doesn't care what Ira wanted. She wants what she wants!"

"I know that you're right, but it can't hurt you to hear them out," Mr. McCarthy proposed. "You don't want the judge to think that we are being unreasonable here."

"Um, alright," Michael forced himself to say. "But I already know that it is not going to work."

"Okay, all we can do is give it our best shot," the lawyer said.

When they looked up, the judge was gone. So was Becky and her pack of wolves. Mr. McCarthy went back up to his seat at the table and sat down.

The judge ended up having to send somebody out in the hall to get Mr. Adams, who looked like he had been roughed up a bit when he came back in. The two lawyers returned to the bench and another lengthy conversation ensued. Finally, the judge advised the stenographer that he wanted to go back on the record.

"Aright," Judge Chapman began. "After hearing the arguments of both counsels, we went off the record for a bit so that both lawyers could have an opportunity to confer with their clients. At this time, since there is an agreement among the parties that the remains of Ira Goldberg can be cremated, it is the ruling of this court that said cremation takes place as soon as possible.

"Further, the court is ordering that the ashes remain in the custody of the Faber Funeral Home until such time as this court shall make a ruling regarding the proper handling of the same. In this regard, the court will conduct a full hearing one week from today on Friday, December 7, 2018, at 1:00 p.m. The scope of the hearing shall be limited to the circumstances surrounding the execution of the Public Health document, including the mental capacity of the decedent to execute said document. The court will also hear proof specifically related to the expressed or inferred wishes of the decedent about burial. The court is also strongly encouraging all the parties to come together prior to the scheduled hearing to try to settle this matter amicably. Counsel is there anything further?"

"No, your honor," Mr. Adams said.

"No, your honor," Mr. McCarthy repeated.

"This court is adjourned."

Chapter 25

Michael was in a bad mood when he left the courthouse. He was completely drained and had no interest in talking about anything more with Mr. McCarthy at that point. They agreed to get together on Monday. He could only manage a glancing look at Ira's grieving children.

Leila called him that night. He now realized that he needed to be very careful about what he said to her. Not that he didn't trust her fully, because he did. He knew that she would never intentionally hurt him. But she could inadvertently let something slip that her mother could twist and turn in a way that hurt his case.

"How did it go?" she asked.

"Okay, I guess. We agreed that Ira could be cremated and that is supposed to happen in the morning."

"That's good, right?" she begged.

"I guess," he said. "There is another hearing next week for the judge to decide who gets to make the decision about burial."

"Oh, I didn't know that."

"Didn't you talk to your mother?" he wondered.

"No, she just texted me and said that it was over and that she would tell me about it later."

"You know that she hates me, right?" he griped.

"Yes, I tried to tell you. She is obsessed with all of this."

"But I don't understand why," he asserted. "She never really had anything to do with Ira before he got sick."

"He is still her father," she maintained.

"Then maybe she should have spent this past year trying to get to know him better," he argued. "All of this could have been avoided."

"That would have been very hard for her to do because she knows that he was disappointed in her," she explained. "Think about how that must feel. He could have rejected her even more and that would have crushed her. You represent that rejection to her."

"I tried to get Ira to talk to her," he defended.

"I know, but it doesn't matter. She blames you."

"Well, that's her problem," he said as he exhaled deeply and blew out his nervous energy. "I don't want to talk about this stupid stuff anymore. Tell me, how was your day?"

"Oh, it was okay. I probably shouldn't have gone to work today. I should have just called in and told them that my grandfather had died. But I had some parent meetings that it would have been a real pain to cancel. I was dead on my feet all day. I have no idea how you did it."

"I kept thinking about you," he flirted. "It got me through."

"Are you coming over tomorrow?" she wondered.

"Uh, I don't know. I have two papers due next week and I promised my aunt that I would go to church with her on Sunday. I think there is a woman there who she wants to hook me up with."

"Aw hell no!" Leila exclaimed. "Don't make me get up in that church and set it off!"

"Is that right?" he played along.

"Nobody touches my man!"

"You are so crazy," he joked.

Talking with her cheered him up a little. But in the back of his mind, he kept wondering who Ari and Becky had hired to dig up dirt on him and his family. Clearly, they hadn't uncovered anything about him and Leila yet or else World War III would be in full swing right about now. He just didn't know how much to tell Leila. He figured that the smartest thing for him to do was to stay home this weekend and work on his research papers.

There had been so many events packed into this one day whose impact on him had yet to be fully realized. Foremost among them, it hadn't truly hit him yet that Ira was gone. When his mom passed, initially he was just relieved that she was out of pain. There was also an immediate void in his soul that throbbed like a toothache and never completely went away. Over time, it made him bitter.

But this was different. It felt like Ira was still there with him somehow, which numbed the pain quite a bit, like painkillers after a root canal. He fell asleep that night as soon as his head hit the pillow and he slept soundly.

* * *

Sean McCarthy called Michael early Monday morning. He wanted a meeting. Michael reluctantly agreed to go even though he would have preferred to do it later in the week. He really wasn't sure that he fully trusted Mr. McCarthy since the lawyer had made it clear that "technically" he was only representing his firm, whatever that meant.

The meeting was at noon. Michael was taken to the same conference room as before. But this time he wasn't nervous.

"Hi Michael," Mr. McCarthy said as he walked in alone. "Thank you for coming over so quickly."

"No problem."

"I don't know where Trevor is, but let's just get started. I know that you are on your lunch break, and I don't want to keep you. Do you have any questions about anything that happened on Friday?"

"Yeah, I was hoping that you could clear up for me whether you are representing me or the estate. I heard what you said in court, but the problem with that is, the estate is not the one being sued. I am."

"Good question," Mr. McCarthy said with a smirk. "You are a pretty bright guy. But to answer your question, yes, we are representing you. Judge Chapman asked me the same question at the bench, and we committed to representing you up to a final judgment, free of charge, of course."

"But why?" Michael wondered. "I don't understand why you would do that?"

"I personally spoke to Ira last year when he asked us to prepare the power of attorney and health care proxy naming you as his agent," the lawyer explained. "We know that he was very fond of you and placed a lot of trust in you. He would want us to defend you."

The door creaked open. "Sorry," Trevor Sanders said as he rushed in. "I couldn't get off a phone call."

"It's okay," Mr. McCarthy said. "We were just getting started."

"Michael you never said what cemetery you wanted for the burial," Mr. McCarthy inquired.

"I don't exactly know," Michael admitted. "Ira told me to talk to his rabbi about it and I haven't had much of a chance to do that yet."

"So, you don't want to bury Ira's ashes next to his wife?" Mr. McCarthy questioned with a puzzled look on his face.

"No," Michael responded bluntly.

"Why not?" Trevor asked.

"Because Ira wanted to be buried with other Messianic Jews," Michael explained. "His wife is buried in the Jewish cemetery."

"Did he put that in writing anywhere?" Trevor questioned.

"Not that I am aware."

"So, you have no proof," Trevor asserted.

"I only know what he told me, and I am the person he named to follow through," Michael conveyed. "They have no proof that I am lying."

"You should know that I spoke to Jameson Adams this morning and his clients are adamant that their father's remains be buried next to their mother," Mr. McCarthy divulged.

"Why?" Michael asked.

"I don't know."

"Don't you think that the judge will ask them that?"

"You're right," Mr. McCarthy said with a bit of a grin on his face. "I apologize. I probably should have asked that question. But I just assumed that it is entirely for sentimental reasons."

"Well, good for them," Michael replied coldly.

"So, you don't want to give in on this one point. They agreed to the cremation. My understanding is that Ira purchased the two plots when his wife died."

"Well, he changed his mind." Michael shot back.

"I know that Ira's family have made several outrageous allegations against you," Mr. McCarthy indicated. "I'm very sorry about that. Is that why this is so personal to you?"

"It's not personal at all," Michael disputed. "At least not the way that you mean. Ira made me promise him, and I intend to keep that promise."

"Well, they have agreed to drop their investigation of you if you agree to the burial."

"That's no deal! They can investigate me every day for the rest of my life. I don't care. I have nothing to hide."

"But we want you to understand that you could lose and get dragged through the mud in the process," Mr. McCarthy expounded. "They are his children. It is going to be hard for the judge to ignore that."

"I don't care," Michael countered. "Are you telling me that I am going to lose? Is that what the judge told you?"

"No, I'm not saying that at all," Mr. McCarthy corrected. "But it is my job to make sure that you fully understand the situation so that you can make the best decision for you. The judge was pushing us hard to get this settled. He may take it out on you if he thinks that you are not being reasonable."

"Okay," Michael said without expression. "You can tell them that if they want to help me pick out a nice Messianic cemetery, then I'm open to their input. Otherwise, they can go pound salt."

Mr. McCarthy and Trevor stared at each other for a couple of seconds.

"Alright, then we should probably think about witnesses for the hearing," Trevor said. "Do you have the name of the aide who was present at the time that Ira signed the document?"

Michael reached in his pocket and handed Trevor a piece of paper.

"Here are the names of everyone who worked with Ira during the last month," he offered. "You will probably have to go through their agency to get their contact information. I also included the name and phone number of Ira's rabbi who came to see him a couple of days before he signed the public health thing. I don't know everything that they talked about, but he can talk about Ira's mental state and religious affiliation."

"This is great, thanks." Trevor said. "Michael, how would you feel if I handled the hearing instead of Sean? I appear in supreme court all the time. I have done several hearings before, and I will do my best for you."

"That's fine," Michael said. "I don't care."

"One more thing," Trevor stated. "And I'm very sorry to have to ask you this, but is there anything in your past that we need to know about? Anything that they could maybe use against you to make you look dishonest or undermine your credibility?"

"No, there isn't," Michael emphasized. "The Christopher Johnson who they mentioned in court is my brother. He is on parole, but that has nothing to do with me. He had a drug problem. He was never convicted of any kind of fraud as far as I know. My dad was a mechanic at the police garage for over thirty years. I have never been arrested for anything. I haven't even had a speeding ticket."

"Okay, good to know," Trevor said. "I hope that you understand that I needed to ask."

Michael nodded his head.

"You will have to testify at the hearing," Trevor advised. "I will need to meet with you one more time this week to go over your testimony."

"Okay, just tell me when," Michael replied.

* * *

Ira's obituary was in the Schenectady newspaper on Tuesday. It was several paragraphs long and it went into depth about his long and distinguished law career. They used an old photograph. He looked good. It occurred to Michael that Ira would have really liked it. He assumed that Becky had given all the information to the funeral home. It mentioned only that no services were planned, and that burial was private.

The rest of the week leading up to Friday was slow and agonizing. Michael went to Ira's house just to check on it. He was the last one to leave after Ira's body was removed and he was wondering if he had shut everything down properly. There was mail in the mailbox, and he brought it in and dropped it in the cardboard box in the kitchen corner without looking at it. Mr. McCarthy told him that the firm would take immediate control of all of Ira's assets.

The house seemed exceptionally quiet, like it was sad. He only walked through the ground floor, not really wanting to go upstairs near Ira's bedroom. The small photograph on the mantelpiece above the fireplace caught his eye. It was a closeup of Ira sitting on a golf cart with a big smile on his face. It was taken long before Michael ever met him, but he had always been drawn to it. Perhaps it was because it portrayed a young, vibrant, stronger version of his friend. It was the way that he would always choose to see Ira. Thus, without any forethought, he took the photograph off the mantel, put it in his pocket and walked out of Ira's house, presumably for the last time.

* * *

He spoke to Leila every night that week. Their conversations were his saving grace. They purposely didn't talk about the upcoming court hearing at all. He just enjoyed being silly with her and hearing her laugh and giggle.

In his whole life, he had never aspired to be special or elevated. He had only ever wanted to be a "normal guy", even though he wasn't exactly sure what that entailed. But she made him feel special, probably because suddenly he wasn't lonely anymore. Indeed, it felt good to smile now.

Chapter 26

Schenectady County Supreme Court
Special Term: December 7, 2018, 1:00 p.m.
Honorable Aaron Chapman, Presiding

Matter of Goldberg versus Johnson. Counsel state your appearance for the record."

"Jameson Adams present for the Petitioners."

"Trevor Sanders present for the Respondent."

Judge Chapman began by addressing the court, "First, the court would like to remind counsel that the purpose of this hearing is two-fold. One, I want to hear testimony about the circumstances surrounding the execution of the document that has already been marked and introduced into evidence as Respondent's Exhibit A. Secondly, I'm also interested in testimony about the expressed or implied wishes of the decedent, Ira Goldberg, concerning possession and the handling of his remains. In other words, this court will not allow any other areas to be addressed in this special proceeding. Mr. Adams, you may call your first witness."

Mr. Adams replied, "Thank you, your honor. At this time, we call Ari Goldberg."

After swearing under oath, the witness was seated, and the direct examination began by Mr. Adams.

Q. Would you state your full name for the record?

A. Ari Benjamin Goldberg.

Q. Are you currently employed?

A. I am a board-certified plastic surgeon in New York City. I am in private practice and my office is located on Park Avenue.

Q. How long have you been practicing medicine in the State of New York?

A. Since 1985.

Q. What is your relationship to Ira Goldberg?

A. He is my father.

Q. What about your mother?

A. My mother died in 2006.

Q. How long were your parents married?

A. 52 years.

Q. Where is your mother's body buried?

A. Beth Israel Cemetery in Rotterdam, New York.

Q. Who purchased the plot?

A. My father did. He purchased two plots. One for her and one for him.

Q. He told you that one of the plots was for him?

A. Yes. He told that to both me and my sister.

Q. Let me show you what has been marked as Petitioner's Exhibit A and previously admitted into evidence by consent. Do you know what this is?

A. Yes, it's the title to the two plots at Beth Israel Cemetery.

Q. When did your father purchase those plots?

A. In 2006. He bought them a couple of days before my mother died.

Q. Do you know Michael Johnson?

A. I know who he is. I met him once about six months ago.

Q. And where did that meeting take place?

A. At my father's law firm. Mr. Johnson is the receptionist there.

Q. What was the purpose of the meeting?

> A. My sister had expressed some concerns to me about the amount of influence that Mr. Johnson was exercising over my father. My dad had just been diagnosed with a terminal condition and he had supposedly given Mr. Johnson both his health care proxy and his power of attorney.

Judge Chapman interrupted, "You say 'supposedly'. Do you have any information that your father did not intend for the Respondent to have his power of attorney?"

Ari responded, "Just what my sister told me."

Judge Chapman continued, "Well, I am not interested in what your sister told you, doctor.

Did you ever ask your father about whether he gave his power of attorney to Mr. Johnson?"

Yes.

Judge Chapman pressed, "What did he say?"

Ari explained, "He said that he did it because Mr. Johnson was his only friend. He seemed delusional."

Judge Chapman redirected the attention of the court, "Continue Mr. Adams."

Mr. Adams continued his direct examination.

Q. What happened when you spoke to the Respondent at your father's office?

> A. I asked to speak to him privately. We were in Rob Epstein's office. He is the managing partner there

since my father retired. And he called Michael in. I told him that I was very concerned with his increased role in my father's affairs. I asked him to leave our private matters to me and my sister because we know what is best for our father.

Q. And how did Mr. Johnson respond?

A. He came charging at me and he threatened to punch me in the face.

Q. Then what happened?

A. I tried to explain to him that I was only trying to protect my father. But he was irate. He started calling me names and he stormed out of the office.

Q. Anything else happen after that?

A. No, just that I asked Rob to escort me out because I was worried that Mr. Johnson might try to attack me.

Mr. Adams concluded, "Thank you, I have no more questions."

Judge Chapman summoned Mr. Sanders for the cross-examination. Mr. Sanders began.

Q. Dr. Goldberg, how many times have you seen your father since he was diagnosed with a terminal illness?

A. Just once. I have a very busy practice.

Q. And how many times would you say that you have spoken to your father on the telephone in the past year?

A. I don't know.

Q. On average, how many times would you say? Once a week?

A. No, not that much.

Q. If I told you that a log was kept of all the visitors who came to see your father at his house and who called him and your name only appears there once, would you agree with that?

A. I told you that I am very busy. My patients are very important to me. I spoke to my sister on a regular basis, and she kept me fully apprised of everything that was going on with him.

Q. Well, it's a good thing that you have your sister. Suffice it to say, you never spoke to your father about his final wishes, isn't that correct?

A. Yes.

Q. Dr. Goldberg, did you threaten Michael Johnson the day that you spoke to him in Rob Epstein's office?

A. No, he is the one who threatened to assault me.

Q. So, you never threatened to do anything to him?

A. No, I didn't.

Q. Did you try to get Michael fired that day?

A. No, I may have complained to Rob that his reception-ist had threatened to beat me up, but I never asked Rob to fire him.

Q. Okay. You said that the one time that you saw your father at his house that he seemed delusional. Do you remember saying that?

A. Yes.

Q. What exactly do you mean when you say that your father was delusional? Was he hallucinating?

A. No, I never said that he was hallucinating.

Q. Did he know who you were?

A. Yes.

Q. And he was able to carry on a conversation with you and answer your questions?

A. Yes.

Q. How would you describe his emotional state?

A. Well, he didn't like it when I asked him about signing over his power of attorney.

Q. But he knew that he had done that, right? I mean he knew that he had given Michael his power of attorney.

A. Yes.

Q. So, can you tell me exactly what you mean when you said that your father was delusional that day?

    A. My father has a lot of people in his life who love him very much. He has a brother in New York. He has four adult grandchildren and four great grand-children. He has me and my sister. The idea that Michael Johnson was his only friend was absurd. He sounded brainwashed.

Q. Doctor, when your father died last week, early Friday morning just after midnight, where were you?

    A. I don't understand the question?

Q. I'm sorry, let me rephrase it. Were you with your father when he died?

    A. No, I wasn't.

Q. Were you with a patient?

    A. No, I don't think so.

Mr. Sanders turned to the judge and declared, "I have no other questions."

Judge Chapman turned his attention to Mr. Adams, "Call your next witness."

Mr. Adams proceeded, "We call Rebecca Bernstein." The witness was sworn and seated. Mr. Adams began the direct examination.

Q. Could you state your full name please?

    A. Rebecca Ruth Bernstein

Q. Where do you reside?

    A. 3586 Silver Coach Road, Manlius, New York.

Q. Are you married?

    A. Yes. My husband Ben and I have been married for 35 years. We have two beautiful daughters and two grandchildren.

Q. Are you employed?

    A. I work part-time doing interior design in Syracuse.

Q. Are you related to Ira Goldberg?

    A. Yes, I am. He is…was… my father. [Crying]

Q. I am so sorry for your loss. Do you need a moment?

    A. No, I'm fine. Thank you.

Q. Were you with your father when he died?

    A. Yes, me and my daughter Leila were with him.

Q. Was Michael Johnson there too?

    A. Yes, Michael was there too. He was always there keeping an eye on everyone who came to see my father.

Q. How often did you go and see your father over the last year?

    A. I went as often as I could. I would say on average two or three times a week. My daughter Leila came with me a lot of the times.

Q. Now, did you ever ask your father about his final wishes?

    A. No.

Q. Why not?

    A. Because I just assumed that he wanted the same arrangements that he wanted for my mother. I was with him when we bought the two plots at Beth Israel. He never said anything that would have led me to believe otherwise.

Q. When did you first meet Michael Johnson?

    A. I don't remember. Maybe a year before my dad got sick. He called me one day and told me that my father was in the hospital.

Q. Did you ask your father about Michael?

    A. Yes, of course I did. My understanding was that they were friends. I knew that Michael was much younger than my dad and that he worked at my father's law firm. I thought it was harmless at first.

Q. Then what happened?

A. It seemed like he was too involved in my father's affairs. I was concerned that he was taking advantage of my father who was in his eighties and not as sharp as he used to be.

Q. Did you do anything about your concerns?

A. There wasn't much that I could do. My dad was always a bit eccentric, you know, so I decided that I would just keep an eye on the situation as best as I could.

Q. When did you find out that your father had given Michael Johnson his power of attorney?

A. When he was first diagnosed with this terrible heart condition. It was terminal in a man my father's age. His doctor said that he only had about a year. Obviously, I was distraught, and I wanted to get him into assisted living so that he could have full-time care. I couldn't bear the thought of him being neglected in any way. Michael refused to let me do that. He told me that if I didn't back down, he would make sure that I didn't see my dad at all...I'm sorry for getting so emotional...I'm trying my best. [Crying]

Q. No need to apologize. I'm almost done. After your mother died, did your father ever frequent her grave site?

   A. Yes, the first year after she died, he used to go there every weekend. I was very worried because he was grieving so hard. He loved her so much. He stopped going so much after a while, but I know that he still went there on her birthday and on their wedding anniversary.

Q. Becky is there any doubt in your mind that your father wanted to be buried next to his wife?

   A. No. No doubt at all.

Mr. Adams addressed the judge, "I have no more questions."

The cross-examination was continued by Mr. Sanders.

Q. Mrs. Bernstein, your father didn't want to go to assisted living, isn't that true?

   A. He said that he didn't want to go, but that was because Michael didn't want him to go.

Q. Are you aware that there is a note in your father's hospital record discharge summary that reads, "Patient is very concerned that his family will try to put him in a nursing home. Says that he wants to go home"?

   A. I never said that we were going to put him in a nursing home.

Q. Didn't you try to persuade your father to go into assisted living shortly after your mother died, and he refused you?

A. I don't recall that specifically, but all I ever wanted was the best for my father. He is the only dad that I will ever have.

Q. Isn't it true that neither you nor your brother had a very good relationship with your father?

A. No, that is not true! He was difficult a lot. But I was always there when he needed me.

Q. You said that you came to see him about twice a week after he got sick, but you rarely saw your elderly father in the years prior, isn't that correct?

A. I called him regularly.

Q. But Manlius, New York is less than two hours from Schenectady and sometimes you went several months without seeing him. Isn't that true?

A. I saw him as much as he wanted me to.

Q. Which wasn't that often. Wasn't that the case?

Mr. Adams interjected, "Objection your honor, argumentative."

Judge Chapman agreed, "Sustained."

Q. You were angry with your father that he gave Michael Johnson his health care proxy and power of attorney, correct?

A. Yes, I felt that he was manipulating my dad.

Q. Isn't it true that Michael accompanied your father to every one of his doctor's appointments over the past year?

A. It was easier for him because he lives in Schenectady, and I don't.

Q. Now Mrs. Bernstein, your father was never in a coma before he died?

A. Coma? No.

Q. And even up to his last day, there were periods when he was fully conscious and communicative, isn't that right?

A. He slept a lot near the end.

Q. And by fully communicative, from the logs at his house, it would appear that he recognized visitors and was able to talk to people, including the aides.

A. Yes.

Q. Now, your father had twenty-four-hour care at his house for the last year of his life after he was released from the hospital, isn't that true?

A. Yes.

Q. In fact, you are the one who found this Senior Home Care Agency that Michael retained to care of Mr. Goldberg.

A. Yes.

Q. Now, as you sit here today, you do not have any specific information about Michael Johnson ever taking any money or property from Ira Goldberg for his own personal use.

A. I can't answer that because there is no way of knowing what he did without an audit.

Q. That's fair enough. So, let me ask you this. Beth Israel is a Jewish cemetery, right?

A. Yes.

Q. And your mother was born Jewish?

A. Yes, she was.

Q. And she died in the Jewish faith, correct?

A. Yes.

Q. And your father was also born Jewish, am I right?

A. Yes.

Q. But he did not die in the Jewish faith, did he?

A. No.

Q. What was his faith when he died, if you know?

    A. I think he was Christian or something. I don't really know.

Then, Judge Chapman questioned the witness with his own examination.

Q. You don't know if your father was Christian?

    A. I said he was eccentric.

Q. Do you know for certain that Beth Israel Cemetery permits Christians to be buried there?

    A. I have contacted them, and they said that they could accommodate us.

Q. Even after you specifically told them about his change of faith?

    A. It never came up.

After a pause, Mr. Sanders stated, "No more questions."

Judge Chapman responded, "Call your next witness."

Mr. Adams announced, "Petitioners call Robert Epstein." The witness was sworn and seated. Mr. Adams continued with the direct examination as he questioned Mr. Epstein.

Q. Are you employed?

    A. Yes, I am a partner at Goldberg & Epstein, a law firm here in Schenectady.

Q. You were partners with Ira Goldberg?

A. Yes, we both inherited the business from our family. I have known Ira for most of my life.

Q. Do you know the Respondent Michael Johnson?

A. Yes, he is an employee at the firm.

Q. He is your receptionist?

A. He is really more than the receptionist. He's more like our office manager. He does some bookkeeping too.

Q. How long has he worked for you?

A. I'm gonna say around five years.

Q. Now, let me show you what has been marked as Respondent's Exhibit A. Have you ever seen this document before?

A. Yes, I prepared it and that is my signature there on the bottom.

Q. How did it come about that you became involved in preparing this document?

A. Michael asked me to.

Q. Did he tell you why he wanted you to prepare the document?

A. He said that he thought that Ari and Becky were planning something to prevent him from arranging for Ira's final arrangements. It was my idea to have Ira sign this.

Q. Your idea?

A. Yes, Michael was pretty upset. He just wanted to know if there was something that he could do to stop them from not following Ira's final wishes. I drafted the document, and I had Michael sign it in the office. That same afternoon, I drove to Ira's house and I had him sign it.

Q. Did you call either one of Ira Goldberg's children or tell them that you had prepared a document giving Mr. Johnson the right to make the final arrangements for their father.

A. No, I didn't.

Q. Weren't you concerned at all that Michael was trying to pull a fast one on the family?

A. No, not really. I knew that he and Ira were close.

Q. Do you remember telling Ira's son, Dr. Goldberg, that you didn't fully trust Michael?

A. Yes...yes, I do.

Q. Do you remember saying that you found their relationship to be very strange?

A. Yes.

Q. And wasn't it you who suggested to Dr. Goldberg that they consider auditing their father's business and personal records in order to see whether Michael was stealing from Ira?

A. Yes.

Q. So at least at that point, you thought that stealing from your business partner was something that Michael was capable of doing?

A. I guess that's true... yes.

Q. And didn't you tell Dr. Goldberg that you were planning to fire Michael because you didn't trust him.

A. Ari wanted me to fire him.

Q. You also said that Michael had a knack for getting Ira to do things that he didn't want to do. Isn't that right?

A. Yes

Q. Did you ever speak to Ira about your concerns about Michael?

A. Yes, I spoke to him about it right after he got out of the hospital. I was very concerned about the firm… about the power of attorney.

Q. What was Ira's response?

A. He just laughed and said that he trusted Michael. He told me that I needed to calm down and talk to Michael.

Q. Is one of the reasons that you agreed to help Michael with this document because you were afraid that he would retaliate against you by harming the firm in some way?

A. No, not really.

Q. But you never followed through on what you said you were planning to do about this situation. Something must have happened with Mr. Johnson that made you change your mind. Did he threaten you in any way?

A. No. In the end, it really wasn't my fight. I realized that I still had to work with him regardless, so it was better to try to resolve our differences like Ira said.

Mr. Adams concluded his examination, "I have no more questions for this witness."

Judge Chapman began his examination of Mr. Epstein.

Q. Did you speak to Mr. Goldberg about this document before he signed it on December 1, 2018?

A. Yes, I sat down with him, and I explained to him what it was.

Q. What was his state of mind?

A. Honestly, he looked and sounded pretty good to me. At least better than I thought that he would. I had been to the house before to see him, so I pretty much knew what to expect. They had him in the living room, and he was on oxygen. He was just sitting on the sofa there. He knew who I was, and he asked me how things were in the office. I told him that Michael wanted me to talk to him about signing this document about his final arrangements. I asked him if he wanted to sign it and he said yes. That is his signature there.

Q. Did you read it to him?

A. Yes, I did.

Q. Did he have any questions about it?

A. No, not that I recall.

Q. Just so that I am clear, is it your testimony today that Michael Johnson was forcing or manipulating Mr. Goldberg to do things that he didn't necessarily want to do?

A. No, that's not what I meant. They were friends outside of the office. I don't know all they did together, but they were always talking when Ira came into the office, which wasn't that much really. I always thought that they were good for each other, if I can say that. But I was just worried about how their relationship was going to affect the business that I have spent most of my life building. I didn't want to get caught in the middle of all of Ira's family drama.

Q. But then you drafted this document and took it to Mr. Goldberg's house to get him to sign it. Isn't that putting yourself in the middle?

A. Yes, I know how it looks. As I said, Ira was my partner for years. We weren't always on the best of terms, but he was a good guy. I did it for him.

Judge Chapman completed his questioning. He called for Mr. Sanders to cross examine Mr. Epstein, "Mr. Sanders, your witness."

Mr. Sanders began.

Q. Mr. Epstein, you were asked on direct examination about a conversation that you had with Ari Goldberg about Michael?

A. Yes.

Q. When did that conversation take place?

A. I don't remember the exact date. Several months ago.

Q. How did that conversation come about?

A. Ari called me several times at the office before I called him back. I knew what he wanted, and I didn't want to get involved.

Q. But you finally did call him back?

A. Yes, he said that he was coming to town and wanted to meet with me. We met for breakfast. He was really angry that Michael was calling the shots about Ira's care. He asked me what I was going to do about Michael thinking that he could tell everyone what to do. I told him that I was just trying to stay out of it. I had previously told Becky the same thing when she called me earlier.

Q. You were present when Ari Goldberg met with Michael in your office?

A. Yes, I brought Ari to my office. We came in through the back door so that nobody would see us. And then I called Michael in, and I left them alone.

Q. But you didn't really leave them alone, did you? You stood in the hall outside the door, isn't that correct?

A. Yes.

Q. And you heard the conversation?

A. Yes, I heard most of it. I wasn't eavesdropping. The door was open. I knew that this was going to be a problem and I just felt like I needed to stay close.

Q. And could you tell the court what you heard?

A. They mostly just got into an argument. Ari demanded that Michael get out of his family's business and Michael basically refused.

Q. Did you hear any threats being made?

A. I would say that they both threatened each other. Michael did not back down from Ari at all.

Q. So Ari was the aggressor?

A. He wanted the meeting. But it was unpleasant all around.

Q. How did it end?

A. Michael just walked out.

Q. One last thing, what religion was Ira Goldberg when he died, if you know?

A. I believe that he was Christian.

Q. Did his family know that he was Christian?

Mr. Adams interrupted, "Objection, your honor. It's speculative."

Judge Chapman denied his request, "No, I'll allow it. You can answer."

A. Yes, they knew. They hated that he converted.

Q. When did he convert from Judaism? If you know?

A. I don't know. Many years ago, for sure.

Q. Before he met Michael?

A. Yes. Michael had nothing to do with that.

Mr. Sanders completed his inquiry of the witness, "No more questions."

Judge Chapman asked Mr. Adams, "Do you have any more witnesses?"

Mr. Adams replied, "We want to call Michael Johnson."

Judge Chapman inquired further, "Do you have any other witnesses beside the Respondent?"

"No, your honor," Mr. Adams responded.

Judge Chapman pursued further, "What about you, Mr. Sanders? Do you have any additional witnesses?"

Mr. Sanders offered, "Yes, we were planning to call one of the people from the agency who was working in the house with Ira Goldberg. She can testify to his state of mind when he signed the public health document."

Judge Chapman contemplated his request, "I'm not sure that will be necessary. However, I do want to hear from Mr. Johnson. Then I will decide whether either one of you can call any more witnesses. Mr. Johnson, please come forward and be sworn in. I will begin the questioning myself." After Michael was sworn in, he proceeded with the examination.

Q. Mr. Johnson, tell me how it is that your friendship with Mr. Goldberg began?

A. We had our faith in common. We used to talk about it all the time. I'm a Christian. Ira was Messianic. We both believe that Jesus is the Messiah and the Savior of the world. But he did not consider himself to be Christian.

Q. Why not?

> A. He said that believing in Jesus made him more Jewish, not less and that Jewish believers are proof that God's covenants are eternal.

Q. Was he open with his family about it?

> A. Most definitely. He thought that it was important that Jewish believers be visible so that everyone can see the oneness of Jews and Gentiles. He also believed strongly that Yeshua is not going to make his triumphant return to the earth until Israel fulfills her calling to represent to the world that God's word is true.

Q. Did he tell you specifically that he did not want to be buried in the Jewish cemetery next to his wife?

> A. Yes, he said that he wanted to be buried with other Messianics.

Q. Did he tell his family about his wishes?

> A. I doubt it. He knew that they would be opposed.

Q. So, he was estranged from his family?

> A. That's not the way he saw it. He loved his children very much and he died believing that God will show his faithfulness by saving a remnant of his family.

Judge Chapman concluded his remarks, "Mr. Adams, do you have any questions for this witness?"

Mr. Adams proceeded with his examination and began with his first question.

Q. Mr. Johnson, it is your testimony that the place of burial was very important to Mr. Goldberg?

A. Yes it was.

Q. Something that he had given considerable thought?

A. Yes.

Q. And yet something that he told only you?

A. Yes.

Q. In all the years since he converted from Judaism, he only confided in you?

A. I can't answer that.

Q. And even though you knew how important it was to him, you didn't tell anyone else of his expressed wishes to only you?

A. No.

Q. Not his daughter.

A. No.

Q. Not even Mr. Epstein, who you got to draft papers giving you the right to decide the place of burial?

A. No. I didn't tell anybody.

Q. Is it your testimony that Mr. Goldberg swore you to secrecy about it?

A. No.

Q. And isn't it true that Mr. Goldberg never asked you to get someone to draft this document?

A. No, he didn't.

Q. So, despite his nearly 55 years of practicing law, he needed you to tell him what document he needed to sign in order to allow you to do something that was very important to him?

A. I never spoke to Ira about the document. Only Rob, um…Mr. Epstein did.

Q. But my point is that Mr. Goldberg, despite being an esteemed member of the bar for almost six decades, and even though he had his own private lawyer available to him as well, he never asked you, or anyone else for that matter, to prepare a document giving you the exclusive right to make all the decisions about his burial?

A. No, he didn't.

Q. Well, I must say that it is a good thing that he had you to do his thinking for him.

Mr. Sanders intruded, "Objection, your honor. It's argumentative."

Judge Chapman agreed, "Sustained."

Q. Now, on the day that Mr. Goldberg signed this document, you were literally controlling everyone who could come to his house to see him?

A. No, that's not true.

Q. But didn't you order the caretakers to keep track of everyone who came to the house and report back to you what happened during the visit?

A. I only wanted to make sure that no one was getting Ira upset. I never told anyone that they couldn't come see him.

Q. So, your intention was to keep everyone away from him who might get him upset?

A. I don't know. Maybe.

Q. And if anyone would have raised any subject or asked him a question that Mr. Goldberg might have found unpleasant, then they faced being permanently barred by you from ever seeing him?

A. Yes, I guess that's true. I would have done anything to protect him. He was dying. I just wanted to make sure that he died with dignity and in peace. That's really all I cared about. His daughter, in particular, liked to try to push him in order to get her way. I stopped her and I'm glad I did.

Q. That is all well and fine, but in so doing you prevented his family from talking to him about things that were important to them, like what happens when he dies, for fear that you would retaliate against them. Isn't that right?

    A. I don't know anything about that. Becky and her daughter are the only ones in Ira's family who ever came to visit him regularly or whoever called him, and I can tell you that the issues with her father went much deeper than trying to get him to talk to her about his final wishes.

"Nothing further," Mr. Adams concluded.

Judge Chapman turned to Mr. Sanders, "Mr. Sanders, do you have any questions for this witness?"

The cross examination commenced by Mr. Sanders.

    Q. So Michael, is it fair to say that you and Mrs. Bernstein are not on the best of terms?

    A. Yes, it's fair to say.

    Q. Why is that?

    A. Because Becky was only interested in getting even with Ira and shaming him, rather than coming to terms with him.

    Q. Shaming him?

    A. Yes, like she would refuse to leave the room when the aides were dressing him even though she knew that he didn't want her there. She wanted to expose his nakedness.

Q. I see. Michael, you heard the allegation of financial mismanagement against you by the Petitioners.

    A. Yes, I heard it.

Q. And how do you respond?

Mr. Adams interjected, "Objection. This goes beyond the scope of this proceeding."

Judge Chapman denied his request, "Overruled. You may answer."

    A. I never took one penny from Ira, and I am offended that they would say that.

Q. You have been controlling his finances now for over a year?

    A. Yes and no. Let's not forget that Ira was pretty much aware of everything until about the last week of his life. All I did was pay his bills. I took the power of attorney that he gave me to the bank, and they told me what account to use to pay everything. I paid the utilities, the housekeeper, the maintenance guy, and the home care company. I never made any purchases other than the stuff that he needed for his care, like his oxygen and medicine.

"Thank you, no more questions." Mr. Sanders had completed his examination.

Judge Chapman pensively questioned, "Anything else from either counsel?"

Both attorneys shook their heads.

Judge Chapman directed his attention the witness then to the attorneys, "Mr. Johnson, you may step down. I don't want to hear from any more witnesses. I understand that it is important that the remains of Ira Goldberg be buried as soon as possible. It is my intention to take a brief recess and then I will render my decision."

* * *

The Judge stood up abruptly and walked off the bench. Michael looked to his lawyer for some insight.

"Let's go out into the hall and talk," Trevor said.

Michael followed Trevor. Ari and Becky were already huddled together with their team in the far right-side corner of the courtroom. He was able to avoid making eye contact with any of them.

"That was great," Trevor said.

"Really, because they didn't ask me anything," Michael complained. "I was expecting it to be much worse."

"I don't think that the judge believes them," Trevor said. "But that doesn't necessarily mean that we win. I have been through this enough to know that you can never really tell."

"If we lose, is it over?" Michael questioned. "I mean, can we appeal?"

"Yeah, but Ira will be buried already so it will probably be a moot point by then, don't you think?" Trevor reasoned.

"But the same thing goes if we win, right?" Michael suggested.

Trevor sighed deeply and said, "How about we not get too far ahead of ourselves? Let's just see what the decision is before we start talking about that stuff."

Trevor wanted Michael to sit with him at counsel's table while the judge read his decision. Michael wasn't nervous at all when he was on the witness stand. But sitting there now, watching the judge purposely avoiding eye contact and shuffling steadily through his papers, he felt sick to his stomach and his heart raced as the decision was read into the record:

Judge Chapman gave his final, conclusive remarks about the case, "This court finds that in unfortunate disputes such as this one, that the wishes of the decedent, as they can be established, are paramount. That is, they must be given great weight and prevail over those of all interested parties, including the next of kin. Generally, the family has a right to possession of a decedent's remains and to make all the decisions related to burial. But such is not the case if the decedent has executed a binding written instrument pursuant to NY Public Health Law, Section 4201 (2), designating an individual of suitable age and discretion to make those decisions. Based upon the testimony of all three of the named parties, and attorney Robert Epstein, it is the determination of the court that the decedent was of sound mind when he freely and voluntarily signed the instrument that provided the Respondent Michael Johnson the exclusive right to control the disposition of his remains. Furthermore, based upon the forgoing, it is the decision of this court that the Respondent can take immediate possession of said remains and make the appropriate arrangements for burial at any Messianic cemetery, at any location, in or outside the State of New York, that he alone concludes best satisfies the final wishes and desires of Ira Goldberg, with all costs to be incurred by the decedent's estate. This is the decision of the court and judgement can be entered accordingly."

The judge jumped to his feet and, without so much as a glance outward, he exited the courtroom through the door behind him.

Michael was relieved, but he didn't react openly. He was in no mood to gloat. This was never about winning a lawsuit or putting Ira's children in their place. He always knew that it was much bigger than that.

He thanked Trevor and the two walked quietly out of the courtroom together. Simultaneously, the petitioners retreated to their corner once again to no doubt conspire further about how they might disrespect their father's memory in the days to come.

Chapter 27

Outside the courtroom, Trevor Sander's parting advice to Michael was to get the burial completed as soon as possible. But there was a small glitch that only Michael knew about. It was time to come clean. He walked to his jeep, sat down and took out his phone. He only hesitated slightly before dialing the number.

"Rabbi, this is Michael Johnson. The judge just decided that I can bury Ira's ashes any place that I choose."

"Congratulations! That's outstanding! How can I help you?"

"Well, Ira wanted to be buried in a Messianic cemetery."

"Upstate or downstate?"

"He didn't say," Michael answered.

"Well, that shouldn't be a problem. I know of several around the state."

"There is one problem," Michael stated.

"There is?" Rabbi inquired.

"Um, I'm wondering if …you know if… it would be possible to bury Ira in Israel?"

"Where?"

"Israel," he repeated. "Near Jerusalem."

"Are you serious?"

"Yes, I'm serious," Michael replied nervously. "I promised Ira that I would bring him home."

"But that's easier said than done."

"So, it's impossible?" Michael asked.

"No, I didn't say that. I have heard of people doing that."

"Then I'd like to try, please," Michael solicited.

"Hmm…okay, let me make a few phone calls," Rabbi said. "How soon do you want to do it?"

"As soon as possible," Michael divulged. "But I have to go there too. I have to witness the whole thing. It's an important part of it."

"I would think that's going to delay things a bit, don't you?"

"I know," Michael acknowledged. "I'm sorry."

"And you're sure about this?"

"Yeah, I'm sure."

"Then how about this?" Rabbi began. "I will work on finding the cemetery and you talk to the estate lawyers about the arrangements."

"Okay," Michael agreed. "Thank you for everything. I know that this is asking a lot."

"No, it's okay, Michael. Now I see what's going on. I must say that you and Ira are in a league of your own when it comes to gamesmanship. But I think that it is wonderful what you are doing. I really do."

Unfortunately, when Trevor got wind he didn't agree. To the contrary, he thought it was a very bad idea because he suspected that the judge would have a problem with the burial taking place outside of the USA. He sounded upset and said that he needed to talk to Sean McCarthy. He indicated that he would call back momentarily.

Five minutes later, the phone rang.

"Hi Michael, this is Sean."

"Hi," Michael answered.

"I have you on speaker with Trevor. He tells me that you want to do the burial outside of the country."

"Yes, that's right. In Israel."

"Michael, we don't think that that is such a great idea. Can't you find a cemetery in New York State?"

"Probably, but I don't want to, and the judge said that it was my choice."

"Yes, but I think that he was assuming that you meant to do it within the U.S."

"But that's not what he said," Michael contested.

"Also, how do you know that the country of Israel will even allow that sort of thing?"

"I just spoke to Ira's rabbi, and he is working on it," Michael disclosed. "Ira told me to talk to his rabbi."

"How come you never said anything about this before now?" Mr. McCarthy demanded.

"Because I didn't think that it was necessary for my case," Michael shot back. "I didn't want to give Becky and Ari one more reason to oppose what their father wanted."

"Well, I really don't like it. I think that we need to run it past the judge."

"Okay, but this is the same judge who just listened to both Becky and Ari lie on the stand," Michael argued. "I don't think that he is going to suddenly be sympathetic to their crap."

"Okay, assuming we do this, how would it work?" Trevor asked.

"I want to take Ira's remains to Israel and bury them in a Messianic cemetery somewhere near Jerusalem," Michael calmly asserted.

"You want to go to Jerusalem?"

"Yes."

"Do you even have a passport?" Trevor asked cynically.

"No, I don't," Michael admitted.

He could hear them getting restless on the other end of the phone.

"Are you sure that you don't want to reconsider?" Mr. McCarthy pressed. "They have a good argument that you are making it very difficult for them to pay their respects at their father's grave site."

"Pay their respects? Gimme a break," Michael rebuffed. "They never even visited him when he was alive."

"You sound like you want to get even with them for taking you to court," Mr. McCarthy reflected.

"Well, I can't help how it sounds," Michael responded with an edge. "The way I see it, I am just exercising my legal right to bury Ira wherever I see fit."

"But if you drag out the burial, then they might be able to get a stay order while they file an appeal," Trevor interjected.

"I'll take my chances," Michael commented. "This is what Ira would have wanted. Sean, you said that you knew him. Then you know that he was a fighter. I owe it to him to at least try."

"Okay, but like I said, I feel like we have an obligation to advise the court. Then we will go from there."

* * *

Michael couldn't believe that it was just 4:00 p.m. It seemed much later than that. He debated with himself whether he should go back to the office or just call it a day and go home. Even though he was exhausted, he ultimately decided to go to the office. It was easier that way since he was already downtown.

"What are you doing here?" Rob said when he discovered Michael sitting at his desk. "We didn't expect you to come back today."

"I know, but there are a couple of things that I needed to do."

"Congratulations. I heard," Rob said.

"Thank you," Michael replied.

"You got a second?" Rob asked.

"Sure."

Michael followed Rob to his office. He closed the door behind them.

"I just want to explain my testimony to you," Rob began.

"That's really not necessary," Michael protested. "I probably would not have won if it was not for you."

"But I know how it must have sounded to you and I am embarrassed," Rob disclosed. "I never intended to be unfair to you. I wish that I hadn't listened to Ari that day. I feel bad and I want to apologize."

"I understand, and I want to thank you for everything you did to help me," Michael spoke. "I have no hard feelings."

"So, now what? If you don't mind me asking," Rob inquired. "You know that you can work here as long as you want."

"Thank you, I really appreciate that. I was planning to…"

Michael's cell phone rang again. It was Sean McCarthy.

"I'm sorry, I have to take this," Michael said.

"No, it's fine," Rob said.

Michael walked back to his desk and sat down.

"Yes, I'm here," he said.

"Michael, it's Sean again. I called chambers and luckily the judge was still there. He said that his decision does allow you to pick any Messianic cemetery that you want without limitations. But he cautioned that his decision also requires you to be fast about it."

"Okay, but we can do it right?

"Yes, I think so."

"Great!"

"He also said, off the record, that if he were you, he wouldn't tell Ira's family about your plans until after the burial is completed."

"He said that?" Michael asked.

"Yes, he did," the lawyer relayed. "He also told me to tell you that he was really impressed by the way that you handled yourself."

"Really?" Michael responded with some skepticism.

"Yes. It seems that we all agree with Ira that you are pretty remarkable," Sean complimented.

"Thank you."

"So, I am going to see what we can do to get you an expedited passport," Sean offered. "You need to follow up with the rabbi about how fast he can find us a cemetery. I don't think that you should tell anyone about this until you get back."

"Okay," Michael agreed.

"Alright, you have a good weekend, and we will circle back on Monday."

* * *

Michael didn't call Leila until late. He ended up taking a two-hour power nap when he got home. When he woke up, he had a tension headache. He took two aspirins and started preparing dinner. He hadn't eaten anything since breakfast. He was starving.

It was just after 9:00 p.m. when he called his girlfriend.

"Hello stranger," she answered.

"I know. I'm sorry. I fell asleep."

"That's because you are trying to be superman."

"I am superman."

"If you say so."

"How are you?" he wondered.

"I'm okay," she replied. "I heard that the judge decided in your favor."

"Yes. Um… how does that make you feel?"

"I was secretly hoping that you would win," she revealed. "Is that bad?"

"No, but maybe we should just add that to the things we have to keep secret."

"Good thinking," she said and chuckled. "My mom is pretty sour."

"Well, it just happened. Maybe she just needs time to cool off."

"You don't know her," Leila argued. "One time she gave my dad the silent treatment for a month. And she supposedly loves him."

They both laughed.

"Well, hopefully it will work itself out," he said. "This is a pretty big secret that we are keeping. But your grandfather figured it out. Your mom will too eventually."

"Only if she's in the same room with us. I can't help that I have a hard time keeping my hands off you."

"Now you tell me. Are we getting together tomorrow?"

"Yes, you better come!" she urged. "Is pizza okay for dinner?"

"Perfect," he replied.

The week ended much better than it began. But it was always easy when it was just the two of them. But eventually they had to face the world.

One of the things that Michael was fairly certain about now was that it was highly unlikely that Leila's family would ever fully accept him short of a supernatural act of God. As a result, his over–riding concern was whether he and Leila had any chance at a real future together.

* * *

He woke up and it took a second before he remembered where he was. Leila was sleeping soundly. The clock on the nightstand read 3:14 a.m. He rolled out of bed because he needed to use the bathroom. He was careful not to wake her.

The living room was completely dark, and he couldn't see anything. He fumbled his way along and he hit his knee on a small table that he didn't recall was there. It really hurt too! Some papers fell on the floor. Fortunately, there was a light switch above the table that he managed to find, and he flicked it on. As he was picking up the papers and putting them back on the table, he noticed that they had been covering a small black book. He couldn't help but notice that the gold letters on the front cover read, "The Holy Bible."

* * *

Rabbi Cohen called Michael first thing Monday morning. He said that he had been working all day yesterday trying to find an appropriate burial site. He mentioned, for the first time, that burial places in and around Jerusalem were hard to come by and, even with Ira having been cremated, finding something wasn't going to be easy. Apparently, because of the shortage there, burial plots were often stolen, and bodies dug up. But rabbi did happen to find one place that he liked. It was in the city of Beit Shemesh, which was situated approximately 19 miles west of Jerusalem.

"Well, I trust your judgement," Michael said. "I have no way of knowing."

"I think that this might be it then," Rabbi presented. "My contact says that even though Beit Shemesh is a fairly big city, and it is largely orthodox, that it is unlikely that anyone will desecrate a grave site."

"But is it a Messianic cemetery?" Michael questioned.

"Not officially, if that's what you mean," Rabbi responded. "But as you probably know, we are far from being accepted by mainstream Jews or the government in Israel. Most of our meeting places are not advertised as such. I'm told that this cemetery is where many Messianic Jews are buried and that it is kind of an open secret. I'm not sure that we can do much better."

"Okay, then it works for me," Michael professed. "I can call Ira's lawyer and make arrangements once you get me the information."

"I'll text that to you right now."

After that, the plan quickly came together. Michael went to Boston the next day to get his passport. Sean had to make special arrangements for that to happen. He also needed a hepatitis A shot and he was able to squeeze that in the following afternoon. They also purchased airline tickets and made hotel reservations for him.

Additionally, Ira's remains were mailed to an individual in Jerusalem who Rabbi Cohen had identified. If everything went as planned, the burial would take place next Wednesday, December 19, 2018.

Michael had never been anywhere, and he was very nervous about taking a flight halfway around the world. He kind of felt about flying the way that he used to feel about driving. But he couldn't let on to anyone that he was afraid or that he didn't have a clue what he was doing.

Sean's secretary put an itinerary together for him and joked about wishing that she too could go to the Holy Land at Christmastime. While he appreciated the sentiment, he just really wanted to get this last part over with. He knew that there still was a lot of things that could go wrong.

Altogether, he was going to be out of the country for eight days. There was so much that needed to be done before he left. He didn't even own any luggage suitable for international travel, which meant that he had to go shopping. He also needed to get Christmas gifts for his aunt and for Leila.

On top of everything else, he didn't know what to tell Leila about his absence. He felt strongly that he needed to protect her and that meant that she couldn't know anything beforehand. But he also couldn't lie to her. He decided to split the difference.

"What do you want for Christmas?" she asked over the phone.

"All I want for Christmas is you," he replied seductively.

"You already have me."

"Then I think I'm all good," he insisted.

"You're no help at all."

"Besides, how is it that you celebrate Christmas?" he wondered. "Ira didn't."

"Growing up, we never did either. At least, not at home. We celebrated Hanukkah. But we always celebrated Christmas with our friends too," she explained.

"Listen, since you brought it up, I need to talk to you about something," he began cautiously.

"What is it?"

"I have to go away this week. But I will be back before Christmas."

"Where are you going?" she asked.

"I can't tell you that," he asserted.

"What do you mean you can't tell me?"

"I can't tell you," he reiterated. "It's for your own good. It's called 'plausible deniability'."

"What? Are you planning to rob a bank or something?"

"My lips are sealed."

"Hmm, wait a minute," she paused. "Does this have anything to do with my grandfather?"

"I said I can't tell you that," he repeated.

"Will you tell me when you get back?"

"I promise to tell you everything when I get back," he replied.

"How long are you going to be gone?" she wondered.

"I leave Sunday. I'll be gone eight days."

"Eight days!" she repeated in overstated shock. "Are you kidding me? Well, you really owe me big time buddy!"

"You just tell me how I can make it up to you," he remarked.

"Well, maybe we can figure out something," she joked.

His phone rang the second he hung up with Leila. It was Christopher. He really didn't feel like talking to anyone else, but he hadn't heard from his brother since Thanksgiving.

"Hey," he answered.

"Bro, where have you been?"

"End of the semester stuff," Michael said. "What's up?"

"Nothing much," Christopher replied. "We haven't worked out in a few. You got any time?"

"How's tomorrow?"

"Ah no, we have the playoffs tomorrow," Christopher advised. "How about Saturday?"

"Saturday is going to be tough," Michael confessed. "But I do need to talk to you. How about we get something to eat tomorrow after your game?"

"Yeah, that's good," Christopher replied. "We should be done around nine o'clock. Is that okay?"

"Yeah, that's good. I'll pick you up at the club."

* * *

Michael was worried that he wasn't going to be able to get everything done by week's end. He hadn't even begun to pack yet. Fortunately, the short–term weather forecast did not include any snowstorms so leaving the house unattended for a week wouldn't be a problem. But he needed to call his credit card company and get a haircut. He was feeling overwhelmed.

He shouldn't have gone into the office on the Friday before he was scheduled to leave but he had been out a lot lately, with the hearing and all, and he felt guilty. Fortunately, things were expected to be slow in the office for the next two weeks because of the holidays. There was only one real estate closing scheduled and it was a small residential sale that was already set up. Because business would be undemanding, Jeff was taking the entire week off between Christmas and New Year's.

Since there was not much going on at the office, Michael decided to leave work early to get a jump on things. That turned out to have been a good decision. There was a line of guys waiting to get haircuts at the barber shop, as a result he was there for over two hours. He then went home and started packing his clothes in his new luggage. Rabbi warned him not to bring a lot of stuff with him because getting through security and immigration at Ben Gurion Airport was already going to be a nightmare.

He managed to get most of the things on his list done before he met up with his brother. He arrived at the gym promptly at 8:30 p.m. It was a nice facility, much bigger than it looked from the outside. There were two basketball courts, and two games were being played simultaneously. There were bleachers set up all around for spectators with quite a few people in attendance. He spied Christopher almost immediately and walked over to that side of the gym and sat down.

Michael knew even less about basketball than he did about football. He still hadn't acquired an affinity for sports and seriously doubted that he ever would. It was one of the things growing up that had separated him from his father and his brothers. He always ended up in his room or in the kitchen with his mom while the guys were in the other room screaming and hollering over some game.

He didn't think Christopher knew he was there yet because his brother was completely immersed in the game from the sidelines. All the kids appeared to be nine or ten years old and there was about ten of them on Christopher's team. The score was nineteen to twenty-seven and Christopher's team was losing.

Michael wasn't really watching the game as he had a lot of things on his mind. He just happened to look up as one of Christopher's players stole the ball and dribbled down the court toward the basket when a boy on the other team undercut her legs from behind and knocked her hard to the floor. She immediately curled up into a fetal position.

A hush came over the gym. He watched intently as his brother sprinted onto the court, dropped to his knees, and was hovering over the young girl like a lioness with an injured cub. He was there next to her before anyone else had a chance to fully react. No one was moving on either court.

Michael could clearly see the sheer anguish on his brother's face as he was trying to tend to his player. She was whimpering softly. People began to circle around them, and it became difficult to see exactly what was happening. After several minutes, Christopher stood up with the girl in his arms and tenderly carried her off the court. He was whispering in her ear while she had her head buried in his massive chest. He looked like a guardian angel.

Michael was moved with compassion for the girl, and he instinctively began to pray for her. He was completely transfixed watching the events unfold. He could not take his eyes off his brother, who displayed equal amounts of strength and compassion. It was clear that Christopher genuinely cared for his player and in that moment, he was fully capable of reckless love. It was at that exact moment that Michael realized just how special his brother really was. Apparently, his heart was every bit as big as his biceps.

But it was also true that his soul was severely damaged and overshadowed by his deeply rooted insecurities. Michael was suddenly very proud of him and, perhaps for the very first time, he started to believe in Christopher's saving graces.

Fortunately, the injured player recovered enough that she was able to come back to the game and play a little. But their team lost, and Christopher did his best to console his players afterward. Michael sat patiently as his brother did his thing. He was in his element, and it was inspirational for Michael to watch.

"Hey, you got a second?" Christopher asked as he approached. "There is somebody that I want you to meet."

"Yeah, sure," Michael answered.

He followed his brother off the court and down an open corridor to a small office. In it was one cluttered desk with opened boxes of uniforms piled up all around on the floor. Sitting there was a young woman. She was light skinned with shoulder–length hair pulled back tightly into a ponytail. She was somewhat full-figured and appeared to be in her late twenties.

"Hey Rita, I would like for you to meet my brother Michael."

She stood up and extended her hand.

"Nice to meet you," she said. "I have heard so much about you."

"Nice to meet you too," Michael responded.

"Rita runs this whole place," Christopher remarked with a big smile on his face. "She is amazing."

"Oh, don't listen to him," she said. "I'm just one of the staff supervisors."

"No, she's really great," Christopher insisted. "She taught me everything I know."

He was clearly infatuated.

"We just love your brother," she said. "I wish that we had more like him."

"Well, that's good to hear," Michael admitted. "But I don't think the world could handle any more Christophers."

She laughed.

"I tell him all the time that he needs to learn to be patient," she volunteered. "He's so good with the kids."

"I am patient," Christopher lied.

"No, you're not," Rita argued. "You need to listen to me. I know what I am talking about."

"Michael is buying me dinner," Christopher announced.

"Well, it was very nice to meet you," Michael said again.

"Nice to meet you too," she responded.

"See you tomorrow," Christopher commented and leaned in and whispered something in her ear.

She giggled and blushed.

Michael wondered if this kind of fraternizing was permitted. As soon as they were out of ear shot, he turned to his brother.

"Is she Spanish?" he asked.

"Puerto Rican," Christopher responded with a big smile.

After they left the Boy's and Girl's Club, they went to one of the diners that Ira used to like, and Michael was saddened.

Christopher was in a good mood despite his team's defeat. He never mentioned the game. He talked mostly about Rita.

Over dinner, Michael finally told Christopher about his trip.

"You're going where?" Christopher asked with a puzzled look on his face.

"Israel," Michael repeated.

"Is that even safe," Christopher questioned. "Aren't they at war or something?"

"No, there is no war," Michael responded and rolled his eyes.

"But why you? Doesn't this guy have family who can do that?'"

"He specifically asked me to do it before he died. I have to go."

"Does Dad know?" Christopher wondered.

"No, he doesn't and I'm not going to tell him," Michael articulated. "I'm only telling you. And you better not tell anybody else."

"How long will you be gone?"

"Just a week," Michael advised. "I'll be back on Christmas eve. I will have my cell phone and it will work over there if you need me."

"Is there anything you need me to do here while you're gone?"

"No, I don't think so," Michael replied. "Just don't tell anybody. Especially don't tell Daddy or Auntie. If she calls you, just make up something."

"Okay," Christopher promised. "But just tell me this, should I be worried?"

Christopher stopped eating for a second and looked his brother squarely in the eyes. Michael was suddenly uncomfortable.

"No," he quickly answered. "Some people wait their whole lives for an opportunity like this. It's supposed to be a beautiful country. It's the place where most of the major things in the Bible happened."

Christopher shrugged as he took a bite of his sandwich.

"Sounds boring," he said.

"No, it doesn't. You just got love on your mind. You can't think straight."

"I know, right," Christopher admitted with wide grin. "Hey, do you think that we can maybe do what we talked about when you get back?"

"Oh, yeah, for sure," Michael replied.

Chapter 28

Sean's office arranged for a driver to pick Michael up at 5:00 a.m. and drive him to JFK Airport in New York City. The driver was very nice, but Michael was in no mood to talk. He sat in the back seat and tried to sleep. But he was too revved up to relax enough to sleep. Although his flight wasn't leaving until 11:45 a.m., they said he needed to be there several hours beforehand in order to fly El Al Israel Airline.

He didn't get to board the flight until 11:00 a.m. He had spent most of the time standing in one line or another. Security was intense. They went through his bags and interviewed him for about thirty minutes. Rabbi told him to tell anyone who asked that he was just a college student on break and not to mention the burial. At first, he wanted to bring Ira's ashes with him. But now he understood why that was a bad idea.

The plane was gigantic. He wasn't expecting that. It was a Boeing 787-9 Dreamliner. Most of the passengers appeared to be of middle eastern descent and the plane was completely full.

He was stuck in the middle of the row. He would have really preferred an aisle seat, but none were available.

The ensuing twelve hours were like a nightmare. People were constantly moving about and the guy next to him snored. He couldn't figure out why his nose kept running. The little sleep he managed to get was not very restful.

Further, he thought the takeoff was terrifying, but that was before he experienced the landing. There was a second there when his life flashed before his eyes. He just closed them and prayed quietly to God. He wondered if it was possible for him and Ira to be buried together.

Once off the plane, there was armed security everywhere. He figured that he wouldn't have to go through security again after he landed, but he was wrong. Although the security was worse, at least he was off the plane and could move around a bit. However, three hours later, he still had not been cleared. His body ached and he felt a little like one of the walking dead.

Finally, through security and out of the airport, he met his driver at the pickup area. The man was holding a small cardboard sign with "Johnson" written on it. He waved to the guy and followed him to a small car, whose make and model he did not recognize. The fresh air felt good. It was warm, compared to the cold winter air that he had left back home. His body had no idea what time it was, but it appeared to be late at night. It was dark and there was only light traffic leaving the airport.

The hotel in Jerusalem was nicer than he expected. The clock on the wall behind the front desk read 11:45 p.m. He couldn't wait to get to his room and take a shower. This was probably as tired as he had ever been in his whole life. He fell asleep as soon as he crawled into bed.

He woke up to his cell phone beeping. It was 10:50 a.m. He checked his phone after he first landed, and he had no messages. But now there were several. There were two messages from Sean wondering about him. He also had messages from Rabbi Cohen, Leila, and Christopher. He responded to them all with the same generic response and ordered room service. He was famished.

It was Tuesday. The burial was the next day, which meant that he had the day to kill. He wasn't really planning to leave his room. But after a couple of hours of napping, he was starting to go a little stir crazy. He had been cramped up on the plane for what seemed like an eternity, and he really needed to move his body. Besides, Rabbi told him that it was important that he get out and appear to be like every other tourist. So, he decided to go for a walk.

Jerusalem was a modern city. It had tall buildings and all the hustle and bustle that one would expect in a city with a population of almost a million people. There were people everywhere. It was sunny and clear. The temperature was 65∘F. He didn't want to go too far, but he walked around and took in the local color.

The thing that shocked him the most was the number of teens he saw walking around in military uniforms. These girls and boys couldn't have been any older than eighteen or nineteen years old. They were literally armed with guns.

All things considered, he felt safe. He went into a bookstore and looked around. He also ordered something to eat and drink in a small coffee shop. It turned out that he didn't like falafels.

Back at the hotel, he signed up for a tour of the city on Thursday and a trip to the Galilee region on Friday. Sean had given him one thousand dollars cash for expenses and encouraged him to take full advantage of his time in the Holy Land. Michael was hesitant initially, but Sean reminded him that Ira would have wanted him to enjoy himself.

"Think of this trip as a going away gift from your friend," Sean said.

Back at the hotel, he came to discover it had a weight room. Too bad that it never occurred to him to bring workout clothes. A good workout would have done his body good. Instead, he had an early dinner in the hotel restaurant. It was buffet style. Although he was hungry, he refused to try anything new or anything that looked too different. He discovered that the fruit and the ice cream were especially good. After dinner, he just went back to his room and turned in early.

At 8:00 a.m. the next morning he called Leila. It was 3:00 p.m. back home. She was just getting home from work.

"Hi there," she answered.

"Hey, you," he said.

"Where are you?"

"In my hotel room," he disclosed.

"But where?" she pressed. "Come on, you can tell me now. You're already there."

"I'm in Jerusalem."

"Where?"

"Jerusalem," he repeated.

"You're kidding, right?"

"Nope."

"You're in Israel?"

"Yes, and I'm seriously jet lagged."

"But what are you doing there?" she probed.

"Ira is going to be buried here tomorrow."

"What? Oh, wait. I get it now. Why didn't you want to tell me? How is it?"

"Nice," he offered. "I walked around a little yesterday. I guess it's like any other big city."

"But is it safe?" she asked. "I mean, aren't you nervous?"

"Not really," he replied. "There are a lot of people here and it's Christmas. I think that I like it. I want to see more places before I leave. Never know if I will ever be here again."

"My grandfather really wanted to be buried there?" she wondered.

"Let's just say that it was his first choice," Michael stated.

"Hmm," she remarked.

"What?"

"Nothing."

"No, what?' he pressed.

"I think that I just realized how much you loved him."

He was quiet. He wasn't sure how to respond.

"Promise me that you will be careful," she begged.

"I will. Please don't worry about me."

"I still can't believe you did this," she reflected.

"Just so you know, I love you," he spoke.

"You do?"

"Yeah, I think I might," he whispered. "Seems like I miss you."

"Good, I miss you too."

* * *

After their phone call, he headed down to the lobby. He was supposed to be picked up at 10:00 a.m., but he was anxious, so he arrived there at 9:30 a.m. At 10:15 a.m., a man with a scruffy beard wearing jeans and a brown corduroy jacket walked in the door and began looking around the lobby in a harried fashion. Michael stood up and he approached.

"Michael Johnson?" he asked.

"Yes."

"Hello," he said. "I am Jacob Mizrachi. Please come with me."

Michael followed the man to a car parked out front. There were two-armed "baby soldiers" casually watching them from across the street as they got in the car. It was an old Toyota which clearly had seen its fair share of accidents and fender benders.

He suddenly became nervous about the car's ability to safely navigate the streets.

Michael did his best to ignore his feelings and sat in the front seat. There wasn't a lot of leg room. As soon as Jacob started the car, the radio began to play some weird music. He lowered the volume. They had been driving in traffic for about fifteen minutes or so before Jacob spoke.

"Have you been to Israel before?"

"No, this is my first time," Michael answered.

"You like it here?"

"I really haven't seen that much. But it is beautiful."

"You are Christian?" Jacob asked.

"Yes."

"Me too," Jacob disclosed. "It is not easy to be a Christian if you are Israeli."

"I heard that. How long have you been Christian?" Michael asked.

"Many years now. My wife is Estonian. She was already a believer of Yeshua when she arrived in Israel. She is the one who led me to the Lord."

"Do you have to hide your faith?"

"Not hide. But we are quiet about it," Jacob explained and lowered his voice. "We meet with other believers in our homes or temporary places. It is not too bad if you do not draw attention."

"Your English is very good," Michael complimented.

"Thank you. I studied at the university," Jacob explained. "I own a coffee shop in Beit Shemesh with my brother Asher."

"Do you have children?"

"Yes, I have two boys and a girl," Jacob said. "We teach our children the truth about Yeshua so that they will know. But they do not talk to the other children about this because if their parents find out then there will be trouble."

"Do you ever worry about them?"

"A little maybe," Jacob acknowledged. "But this is my home. I was born right here in this city. I love to worship Yeshua and to help where I can. But it is not for us like it is for you in America where you can worship freely out in the open."

"I saw a lot of Christian churches on the map in my hotel room," Michael reflected. "Looks like most of them are Catholic churches."

"Yes, but no one cares as long as no Israelis attend those. It draws in good business when Christians come to visit here and spend money."

"How long is it going to take to get there?" Michael asked after a few moments of silence.

"Not long," Jacob answered. "Thirty more minutes maybe. So, this man you bury, he is your friend?"

"Yes, he is my friend."

"He is Christian?"

"Messianic. Is this a good place to bury him?"

"Yes, it is very good," Jacob advised. "The people who live in Beit Shemesh are mostly honorable and hard-working people. This is a middle–class community. Of course, some are bad. But there are bad people everywhere, yes?"

Suddenly, Jacob took a turn off the main highway and proceeded down what appeared to be a more rural roadway. There were some rather steep inclines and the small car seemed to struggle a little trying to make it over them. After a few turns, they pulled into a parking lot that was only partially paved. Jacob parked the car and directed Michael to come with him.

Jacob raised the car's trunk and reached inside an opened cardboard box and took out a small wooden box. He handed it to Michael.

"This is for you," he said.

Michael stared at the box, which resembled a jewelry box. He swallowed hard. It never occurred to him that they were carrying Ira's remains with them. Jacob clarified that he picked up the ashes on way to the hotel.

It didn't appear that there was anyone else there. The parking lot was empty. The sun was shining bright in the sky and the temperature was comfortable. Michael followed Jacob across the parking lot and down a narrow path. About fifty yards in, marked gravestones began to appear in random fashion. The grounds were hilly and rocky and there weren't any written signs indicating that they were in a cemetery.

They came across a man with a wheelbarrow working underneath a tree.

"David, can you tell Rabbi that we are here?" Jacob called out.

The man nodded but did not speak. They proceeded another hundred yards to a row of graves. Only a few had headstones. The writing on them was in Hebrew. At the end of the row was a hole with a small mound of dirt next to it and a shovel sticking out of the ground.

"Here we are," Jacob said. "What do you think?"

"It's nice," Michael replied. He didn't know what else to say. It was different than he expected.

"I knew that you would like it," Jacob stated. "My father and my sister are buried down the way, not far. It is a very peaceful location, yes?"

"Yes, I can see that," Michael said.

"You already paid for the headstone, but that won't come for a while."

"Okay."

"Ah, here comes Rabbi."

Michael turned to see a man walking toward them. He was tall and thin. He was wearing a black coat and a yarmulke.

"Hello," he said. "I am Rabbi Samuel Goshen. You know my friend Ben Cohen."

"Yes, I do."

"Good man, Ben," the rabbi said. "We met when I was in New York City when I was a student. Please give him my best."

"I will," Michael said.

"Shall we begin?"

Michael nodded his head.

"You can put that in the hole there."

Michael walked over and gently placed the wooden box in the hole, which was harder to do than it looked because the floor of the hole wasn't level, which caused him to be a bit unsteady. He took a couple of steps backwards. Now the only part of the box that was visible was the very top.

The rabbi began reading in Hebrew from a small prayer book. He then transitioned to English. Michael recognized some of it as being from the New Testament. The rabbi had a stronger accent than Jacob and it was difficult to make out some of the words. His entire remarks lasted no more than ten minutes. He ended with readings from the book of Psalms and then from the prophet Isaiah:

> The Lord is my light and my salvation-
> So why should I be afraid?
> The Lord is my fortress, protecting me from danger,
> So why should I tremble?
> When evil people come to devour me,
> When my enemies and foes attack me,
> They will stumble and fall.
> Though a mighty army surrounds me,
> My heart will not be afraid.
> Even if I am attacked,
> I will remain confident.
> The one thing I ask of the Lord-
> The thing I seek most-
> Is to live in the house of the Lord all the days of my
> life,
> Delighting in the Lord's perfections

And meditating in his temple.
(Psalm 27:1-4 NLT)

And he continued on:

No longer will you need the sun to shine by day,
Nor the moon to give its light by night,
For the Lord your God will be your everlasting light,
And your God will be your glory.
Your sun will never set, your moon will not go down.
For the Lord will be your everlasting light.
Your days of mourning will come to an end.
All your people will be righteous. They will possess
Their land forever, for I will plant them there with my
Own hands to bring myself glory.
The smallest family will become a thousand people,
And the tiniest group will become a mighty nation.
At the right time, I, the Lord will make it happen.
(Isaiah: 60:19-22 NLT)

There was a light breeze that was very soothing. The rabbi stood motionless for a moment before he smiled warmly, shook Michael's hand, and slowly walked away. Jacob then approached him and gently touched his shoulder.

"That is for you too," he said and pointed to the shovel. "Stay as long as you like. I will be waiting in the car."

Michael stood there alone for several minutes. He wasn't really thinking about anything. Nor was he especially grieved or saddened. He was mostly just relieved. Without a doubt, God has never forsaken the Jews as his chosen people. The fight for their restoration has never been physical. Ultimately, it is a spiritual war and Ira had believed God to the end. And according to Scripture, history will end in Israel and Ira will be there when it happens.

The truth is that he was truly honored to do this for Ira. And this was probably the proudest moment in his life thus far: he had to fight his own demons every step of the way to get there. Only by the grace of God was he still standing. He was comforted because he knew in his heart that he had been chosen for this and divinely protected. He knew that the Psalm the rabbi just read was for him, and hence forth it would always be his song of praise. In this moment, he finally realized that fear was mostly an illusion and God could give him the edge to overcome anything.

He almost forgot that Sean wanted him to take photos of Ira's final resting place. He pulled his phone from his pocket and took several shots of the grave from different angles. There was complete silence all around except for the wind hovering and stirring about like an expectant father. Thus, he felt safeguarded.

He grabbed the shovel, picked up some dirt from the mound, and began dropping it into the hole. It only took a minute to move it all. He stepped back to examine his handiwork. "For it is written," he recited. "Wherever you die, I will die and there I will be buried." He took a few more photos, and then he turned and slowly walked back down the path.

Jacob was sitting in the car. Michael opened the door and got in. "How was it for you?" Jacob asked.

"Good," Michael replied soberly.

"Rabbi always says that there are no endings, only new beginnings," Jacob encouraged.

"I know. Thank you, for everything."

"It is a very important thing that you do today," Jacob exhorted. "The more Jewish believers who come back to their first love and find their peace, the sooner the Lord will return to deliver all of the nations of the earth… Amen?"

"Amen," Michael echoed and smiled to himself.

Chapter 29

ichael really did enjoy his time in the Holy Land. But it was good to be home.

Traffic out of New York City was a nightmare due to an accident near Grand Central Parkway, and he didn't get home until almost 6:00 a.m. Christmas morning. Leila had to spend the day with her family, which meant that he wasn't going to see her until the 26th. So, he was planning to rest and relax all day.

He slept until noon when he was awakened by his phone ringing. It was Christopher calling to see if he had arrived home safely. They only spoke briefly as it sounded as though his brother had company.

Shortly after he got off the phone with his brother, he called his dad who was very happy to hear from him. Witnessing firsthand Ira's struggles with Becky had made Michael appreciate his own father more. He saw clearly now that his own anger and rejection of his father were the primary reasons that they weren't closer. His father was a man after God's own heart. Without a doubt, he should have done more to help his dad after his mother died, like he told her he would do. He knew he was wrong. He was intent on finding a way to properly honor this man: a father who had loved him and covered him spiritually while he hid from the world.

Most people probably would have hated spending Christmas day all alone. But he only felt blessed. He knew that he was at a crossroad in his life and that he was probably in for many more challenges up ahead. He readily accepted that there was no looking back. At this juncture, he was already much stronger than he ever knew he could be.

* * *

"What! New Year's in Boston! What an amazing idea!" Leila exclaimed as she finished reading over the itinerary in her Christmas card that Michael gave her. He got the idea when he had gone to Boston to get his passport. Sean told him about a place his wife really liked. Leila then opened the small velvet box he gave her. "Wow!" She gasped as she opened it. "Oh, Michael they're beautiful! I'm going to try them on right now!" She loved the diamond earrings that he got her in Jerusalem. Turns out that Jacob knew a guy.

Several days later they were walking around downtown Boston holding hands and being together in a way that they never had before. They didn't have to hide, and they had more time together than just one night. In fact, they had three nights. They slept in each morning and stayed out late into the night. She had been to Boston several times before and thoroughly enjoyed leading him around the city and showing him her favorite places. Everything was perfect.

Unfortunately, her mood changed dramatically toward the end of their getaway. She was quiet for much of the drive home.

"Is something wrong?" he finally asked.

"No, I'm okay," she said and gently touched his arm.

"You sure?"

"I probably should tell you something," she began.

"What?'

"I had a big fight with my dad when you were away. The holidays were really awful."

"About what?"

"About us. I told him about you." she confessed.

"What on earth possessed you do that?"

"I thought that maybe he could help us. See, I always got along with my dad. I was always daddy's little girl. Heather is better with my mom."

"So, what happened when you told him?" he asked and braced himself.

"He lost his mind," she disclosed. "I could hardly believe what I was hearing. He said that I was being foolish and that you were just using me. He was saying all this crazy stuff too. He threatened to hurt you if he ever laid eyes on you!"

"Is he going to tell your mother?" He was trying hard to hide his growing panic.

"No, he would never tell her."

"How can you be so sure?"

"Because he knows that she would go completely off the deep end and make everyone's lives miserable, including his. No, he is a part of the secret now, whether he likes it or not. He just ordered me to end it with you. It was kind of like an ultimatum that I still don't really understand."

"I'm sorry, but I don't get why you told him in the first place," Michael complained. "It seems like you took a big chance and lost."

"Because I just can't do this anymore! I hate all this sneaking around and I was just trying to figure out a way for us to be together. Me and Heather both thought that my dad was my best chance. If we got him on our side, then he could maybe help to get my mom to come around."

"Okay, but I would rather have you like this then not have you at all," he articulated. "It's better this way. Believe me, even if your dad wanted to help, it is still way too soon to tell your mother. She made that very clear in court."

"I know," she agreed. "I made a mistake."

"So, what do you want to do now?" he asked.

She shook her head and pouted.

"I don't know. He said some awful things. Even about you being black. I never really heard him say anything like that before. I don't even know if I like him anymore. He made it seem like I was like this big tramp."

"I'm sorry," he whispered. "He probably didn't mean everything he said."

"No, he meant it," she lamented.

She was quiet the rest of the way home. He knew that she needed space and he felt bad for her. Obviously, Leila was going to have to make some difficult choices at some point. But he just didn't see why she had to press the issue now.

Although he would never admit it, especially to Leila, he had been preparing himself all along for the day that she will break it off with him. This was not his insecurities haunting him—not even close. He was just being realistic because he couldn't see her ever choosing him over her family. They meant everything to her. While she still had a youthful persona and rebellious spirit, it had really never been tested before. For the most part, she had pretty much always gotten everything that she ever wanted. Unfortunately, that probably wouldn't be the case this time around.

He couldn't deny that he loved Leila with his whole heart, but the greatest love has always been sacrificial love. In a perfect world, he would choose her every time and they would be together forever. However, this world is anything but perfect.

Unlike the fictional Romeo, he was not a naive teenager and he simply refused to live his life that way. If his heart inevitably got ripped out of his chest and torn into a thousand pieces, he would fight with all that was within him to live and not die. Out of love, he would have to pick up the pieces and move on. That's the secret promise he was forced to make to himself.

Chapter 30

Michael pulled his jeep into the one small parking space left on the street. He was not familiar with Albany, and he had never been in this part of the city before. But once they got the address from their father, Christopher knew exactly how to get there. Michael was a bit apprehensive, and he never would have come here alone, especially at night. He just followed Christopher across the street into the apartment building.

The main door was broken and unlocked. The elevator didn't work. The foyer was dirty and there was debris and garbage thrown about. They took the stairs to the 4th floor. The narrow hall was poorly lit and the smell of something foul permeated the air. The number on the door read, "408." Christopher looked at Michael and then knocked twice with two of his knuckles on his right hand.

"Who is it?"

"Christopher and Michael," Christopher said.

They could hear the lock on the inside being manipulated. The door opened slowly. They barely recognized their brother. He was maybe twenty pounds heavier than he was the last time that they saw him. He looked like he hadn't cut his hair in years and his face was broken out with acne or something. The dingy t-shirt that he wore was stained and ripped on the sides and his pants were filthy.

"Hi," TJ said cautiously. "What are you guys doing here? Is something wrong?"

"No, nothing is wrong," Christopher said. "We haven't seen you in many moons. We wanted to come check on you."

"Oh," TJ said.

"Can we come in?" Christopher asked.

"Yeah, come in."

They both shook hands with TJ. There were no warm embraces. All three were uncomfortable.

Michael could not believe his eyes. The small studio apartment was completely trashed. There was a broken recliner facing a small television that was placed on top of two cardboard boxes in the middle of the room. An unmade bed was in one corner and there was a sink and small refrigerator in the other corner. The tile floor was broken in several spots, and it looked like there was rotting wood underneath. Christopher later said that he saw roaches crawling on the walls, but thankfully Michael never saw them.

"How are you?" Christopher asked.

"I'm doing good," TJ replied.

"Man, how long have you lived here?" Christopher inquired.

"Not long."

"How come you didn't call somebody if you needed help?"
"I said that I'm okay," TJ insisted.

"C'mon man, you can't live like this," Christopher argued.

"Look, I don't need any help," TJ said defensively. "I can take care of myself."

"How can you say that?" Christopher pressed. "If mom could see you now, she would be hurt bad. I don't understand what you are doing here. It looks to me like you are trying to kill yourself. Is that it? You want to die?"

"No, that's not it at all!" TJ shouted. "I never asked you …"

"Then what is it?" Christopher yelled back. "Because this is just dumb stuff! I would rather go back to prison than live in a place like this!"

TJ was clearly hurt and embarrassed. He looked uncomfortable standing there and put his head down, refusing to make eye contact with them.

"Can you believe this?" Christopher asked turning to Michael.

"Wait a minute," Michael finally said. "Let's just calm down. TJ tell me this. Are you stable with your medications?"

"Yes," TJ insisted. "I haven't been in the hospital in like two years. I'm telling you guys that I am okay."

"That's excellent," Michael remarked. "I'm so proud of you for staying on top of your health. That's the most important thing."

"Thank you," TJ mumbled.

"But we are your brothers, and we are here to bring you home. You have been gone away too long. There are people there who love and care about you. Auntie asks about you all the time. You deserve to have a good life with people you love. Don't you think?"

"Well, I don't know." TJ hesitated. "I can…"

"Yes, you do," Michael pressed. "You know that we were not raised to live below a certain standard. Daddy worked hard his whole life to make sure that we had everything we needed. We had the best mother ever. She loved you with all her heart. We were taught to love each other and to love God. What about God? I bet you can't remember the last time that you went to church."

"You don't know," TJ resisted. "I still know God. I pray all the time."

"Well, he sent us here to get you," Michael begged. "It is time for you to come home. What do you say? Please, TJ? Aren't you tired of all of this?"

"I can't go right now," TJ maintained. "Can you guys maybe come back and get me on Saturday? It's just two days from now."

"No!" Christopher unleashed. "Just leave this stuff. You need…"

"What time on Saturday?" Michael jumped in.

"Eleven o'clock?"

"Okay, we will be here then," Michael said. "Thank you so much for doing this for us. This is so awesome!"

There was an awkward goodbye too. Michael and Christopher did not speak until they got to the jeep.

"Oh my God!" Christopher exclaimed. "I'm in shock. I mean, are you kidding me?"

"I had no idea what to expect, but I have never seen anything like that," Michael expressed.

"What do you think happened to him?" Christopher asked.

"I don't know."

"Do you believe that he hasn't had an episode in two years?" Christopher posed.

"I don't know what to believe," Michael admitted. "It looks to me like he just had one this morning."

"Word," Christopher echoed.

"But first things first," Michael emphasized. "I say first we get him home and then we figure out what he needs."

"Okay, but we probably need to call Daddy."

"Yeah, I'll call him as soon as I get home," Michael agreed. "I don't think that he will have a problem with us getting TJ out of that hell hole."

"By the way, I saw the way you handled him," Christopher remarked. "You got skills. I gotta give it to you. I could learn from you to help me with the kids at the club."

"If it wasn't for you, I would never have come here," Michael confessed. "You were right in wanting to come and check up on him. So, you deserve all the credit."

"I just hope that he is there on Saturday," Christopher stated.

“I guess we’ll see.”

Michael was more than a little concerned about TJ coming home. He could recall vividly how much of a handful TJ was before he left home when he was eighteen years old. His mood swings were epic, and he was literally out of control. Hopefully, the treatment for bipolar disorder has improved over the last few decades. Regardless, having his brother living with them was going to be complicated.

His dad didn’t answer his phone, so Michael ended up just sending a text. He called his aunt too who spent ten minutes scolding him for not coming over to her house on Christmas. Apparently, Christopher had gone there for Christmas dinner, something he neglected to mention.

“Auntie, the reason that I’m calling is because I want to tell you about TJ.”

“What about him?” she recoiled.

“Me and Christopher found him,” he said. “He was living in this roach-infested apartment in Albany. It was disgusting!”

“Lord Jesus!” she prayed.

“Well, we talked him into coming home,” Michael said.

“Supposedly, we are picking him up on Saturday. But he’s in pretty bad shape physically. I don’t know how he is emotionally.”

“Okay,” she acknowledged. “I’ve been thinking about that boy. I just woke up the other night and I started praying for him. This is an answer to prayers.”

“You are gonna have to help me with him,” he solicited. “I don’t think that I can do it by myself without Daddy.”

"You know I'll help," she promised. "I would love to get my hands on him."

"Thank you."

"You don't have to thank me," she reflected. "I love you guys like my own children. I would do anything for any one of you. Don't you ever forget that."

"I won't."

He felt a little better after he hung up with her. The return text from his father just said, "ok." He didn't ask any questions probably because he was distracted. Michael erupted in laughter. Apparently, he and Christopher weren't the only ones with a love jones.

* * *

TJ kept his word. He was waiting for them when they arrived. Surprisingly, he had enough stuff to fill up the back of the jeep. Most of it was junk crammed into several cardboard boxes. It became abundantly clear once they were closely quartered in the car together that TJ needed a shower in the worst kind of way. In addition, Michael was really concerned that his brother was transporting vermin with him.

"Welcome home TJ!" Michael said as he pulled into the driveway. "We can put your stuff in the garage for now."

"Alright," Christopher said. "I got it."

Michael led TJ into the house.

"I cleaned out your room," he said. "It's all set for you. Why don't you go up and check it out?"

"Okay," said an expressionless TJ.

He slowly walked upstairs. Then, Christopher came inside.

"Hey," Michael said. "I'm going to run to Walmart and get him some stuff. You go up and put him in the shower. There are toiletries underneath the sink."

"What are you gonna get for him?"

"Looks like he pretty much needs everything, don't you think? But for now, I figure that I'll just get some t-shirts, underwear, socks, and pants. What size do you think? 2X?"

"Yeah," Christopher advised. "Get sweatpants with elastic."

"Okay, I won't be long. Auntie is coming over around two o'clock."

Michael hurried out. He didn't want his aunt to see TJ in his present condition. It was important that nothing was forced upon TJ too soon. At this point, there was no way of knowing how he would react to anything.

When Michael returned an hour later, his brothers were still in the bathroom. The door was closed. He shouted to them through the door that he was putting TJ's stuff on the bed. Just then, he heard the front door downstairs open, and Aunt Wanda call out.

"We'll be right down," he shouted back.

She was in the kitchen, and she brought food.

As Michael walked down the stairs she asked, "You guys didn't eat, did you?"

"No, we didn't."

"I didn't think so," she commented. "I made you something. Honey, there's one more bag in the back seat of my car. Can you go get it for me, please?"

"Yeah, sure."

He ran out and came back in and placed the brown paper bag on the counter.

"How's TJ doing?" she asked.

"I really don't know," Michael replied. "He was very quiet in the car. I feel a little bit like we kidnapped him and forced him to come home. But we had no choice. He's a hot mess."

"What's he doing now?"

"Christopher is helping him get cleaned up a bit."

"Well, get them down here," she said. "Poor thing probably hasn't had a real homecooked meal in years. I fried up some chicken. I remember how much he used to like it."

"Alright, let me go see what they are doing."

Michael was starting to walk up when Christopher came down the stairs. He had a large garbage bag in his hand that he was holding away from his body with his arm extended out and his head turned to the side.

"This is all of the clothes that he was wearing," Christopher whispered. "I'm just throwing them out. He is finishing getting dressed. You did a good job. Everything fits. He should be down in a minute."

"Did he say much to you?" Michael wondered.

"No, he's being really quiet. But he did everything that I asked him to do… Oh, and somebody needs to clean the bathroom," Christopher smirked then smiled wide.

They went into the kitchen and sat down. A few moments later, TJ walked in.

"TJ! Oh, my goodness!" Aunt Wanda squealed in delight. "You better get over here boy and hug me around my neck."

TJ let her hug him instead.

"You look good," she lied. "You hungry? I made you a special lunch. Have a seat right there."

TJ sat down. He looked lost.

"You cut his hair?" Michael whispered.

"Yup," Christopher mouthed back. "Looks good too. Doesn't it?"

He had a proud look on his face.

"Michael, say grace," Wanda directed.

Michael lowered his head and prayed, "Father God, we are so grateful to you for your loving kindness and your faithfulness to us. Thank you for this food that we are about to receive and for the hands that prepared it. Thank you also for bringing our brother TJ home to us. In Jesus name. Amen."

"Okay, you guys eat up!" she ordered. "I already ate. This is way too late for me to be eating lunch. I'm really trying not to eat between meals."

"This is great!" Christopher said as he put three pieces of chicken on his plate.

"So, Michael, what's this I hear about you having a Spanish girlfriend?" she asked.

Michael's eyes got big, and he began to choke on his drink. He was coughing and trying not to gag.

Christopher let out a roar of laughter.

"What did you tell people?" Michael demanded.

He was suddenly fired up.

"I just said that you were spending Christmas with your girlfriend," Christopher teased. "What? Did I say the wrong thing?"

"Don't listen to him," Michael urged. "He never knows what he's talking about. But that doesn't stop him from running his mouth!"

"Not true," Christopher refuted. "You just have too many secrets. Don't blame me because you want to act like a secret agent all the time."

"You're the one with the Puerto Rican girlfriend," Michael shot back. "Bet he didn't tell you about her, did he?"

"I don't care what nationality she is as long as she is a Christian," Wanda stated emphatically. "Neither one of you guys better bring home no worldly woman. That's just asking for trouble."

"I can't believe you," Michael fumed. "I swear Christopher, you're such an idiot!"

He was glaring at his brother. He had made the mistake of letting Christopher get under his skin and now he was seeing red.

"Auntie, did you hear what Michael just called me?" Christopher protested. "Is that allowed at the table?"

"It most certainly is not!" Wanda asserted and gave Michael a hard look.

"I didn't think so," Christopher taunted. "I think you should make him apologize to me for his sudden outburst of anger. So uncalled for."

"Apologize?" Michael shouted. "Something is seriously wrong with you!"

"No there isn't," Christopher rebutted. "You're the one being disrespectful to me. TJ, you better watch out, Michael still acts like he's the little prince."

"You're the one who…"

"Enough, the both of you! I mean it!" Auntie hollered. "Don't make me get up! This don't make no sense!"

TJ laughed.

Chapter 31

Michael had no idea why Sean McCarthy wanted to talk to him. A few days after he brought TJ home, McCarthy's secretary had called and wanted to know if he had some time to come in. She didn't offer any specifics regarding the purpose of the meeting. The thought occurred to him that Becky and Ari had sued him again for something. Frankly, he was hoping he would never have to step foot in Sean's office again.

This time he was taken directly to Sean's office and not to the conference room. Sean was sitting at his desk and stood to his feet just as Michael walked in. The two men shook hands.

"How are you adjusting to being back on Eastern Standard Time?"

"Pretty good. I was a little out of it those first couple of days back."

"Did you go to Boston?" Sean asked.

"Yes, we did and thank you again. It was a really nice place."

"My wife loves it there," Sean indicated. "I always take her there when I need to get out of the doghouse."

"I'll have to remember that trick," Michael joked.

"Anyway, I don't want to take up too much of your time, but I really needed to talk to you about Ira's will."

He gestured for Michael to sit.

"His will?" Michael questioned with a puzzled look on his face.

"Yes, as you know, we are the attorneys for his estate. We will be proceeding shortly to surrogate's court to get his will probated."

"Okay," Michael responded in a dismissive fashion.

"Aren't you at all curious?" Sean asked.

"No, not really."

"We have received several calls from Ira's family about the status of his will, but nothing from you."

"Because I don't care," Michael stated bluntly. "This part of it has nothing to do with me."

"Oh, but it does," Sean contended. "Ira didn't tell you then?"

"Tell me what?"

"He left you his share of the law firm."

"He did what?" Michael reacted.

His stomach did a backflip. He could hardly believe his ears.

"Yes, you own…er, you will own 52% of Goldberg & Epstein," Sean reported.

"You're kidding!" Michael responded in disbelief. "But that doesn't make any sense. He always said that he wanted to keep the firm in the family."

"Obviously, he considered you to be his family."

"But you don't seem to understand," Michael said. "Becky and Ari are going to go crazy all over again."

"Yes, I'm sure that they will," Sean acknowledged. "But that's not really your problem, is it? Ira left everything else mostly to his grandchildren. He gave the house to his daughter and nothing to his son."

"I'm sorry, but my head is spinning," Michael expressed.

"I know that it's a lot to take in," Sean sympathized.

"Does Rob know?"

"No, we haven't told anyone. Rob did call me right after Christmas, but I haven't called him back yet. I'm pretty sure that is why he is calling, and I wanted to talk to you first."

"Do I have to take it?"

"Frankly, I don't see why you wouldn't," Sean opined. "We don't know the exact value of the firm right now, but it is worth a pretty good sum. Besides, Ira really wanted you to have it. I spoke to him at some length about it, and he really wanted this for you. He said that you are planning to attend law school?"

"Yes," Michael answered quietly. "He wasn't supposed to tell anyone."

"None of his family are lawyers," Sean continued. "There are some strict rules in New York prohibiting nonlawyers from being a partner in a law firm. And there are some stipulations in the will about what you can do with Ira's share. For instance, you can't change the name of the firm and you can only sell it under certain conditions. Obviously, all the income generated is yours to do with as you please. But other than that, you can run the business however you want… along with Rob Epstein, of course."

"I think that Rob is hoping to buy out Ira's share," Michael offered.

"You get along with him, right?" Sean inquired. "I mean, Trevor said that he testified mostly for you as I recall. Is this really going to make that much of a difference for him?"

"I honestly don't know the answer to that," Michael stated.

"You two guys are going to have to just figure it out," Sean concluded.

"So that's what Ira meant," Michael said out loud to himself.

"What?"

"Nothing…but this ties me to Ira's family for the rest of my life."

"Not really," Sean answered. "They have no involvement in the firm."

"Can anybody contest the will?"

"Yes, but they won't win," Sean asserted. "Ira knew exactly what he was doing. He trusted you with his professional legacy. That must mean something to you."

"It does," Michael admitted. "But he never…"

"Honestly, I wasn't sure myself that Ira was doing the right thing at first. I tried to persuade him to go a different route. But now I think this could work out perfectly for everybody. I'd say that your friend Ira was a wise man."

Michael was in quasi-shock when he left Sean's office. He wasn't quite sure if this was a good or a bad thing. Even if he got into law school, that doesn't mean he would want to work in a small private firm, or even stay in Schenectady his whole life. More importantly, this could negatively impact his relationship with Leila by making him the permanent family nemesis. This could literally be the last nail in his coffin.

But when he told Leila the news that night, she just laughed.

"How come I suddenly feel like I'm sleeping with my uncle?" she asked in jest. "Are you sure that you aren't actually my grandfather's illegitimate black son?"

Because she wasn't worried, he was forced to at least consider that he might be overreacting. Most people in his position would be overjoyed. But everything since Ira's death has caused his thinking and his emotions to be all over the place. He needed to take a step back and just wait and see what would happen. Sean said that it was going to take several months to get Ira's will through probate. In the meantime, he wasn't going to sweat it.

* * *

Surprisingly, TJ was a good housemate. He kept his room clean, and he helped with the chores. Michael had forgotten that his middle brother was always better at that kind of stuff.

Because TJ was used to being alone, he was okay during the day and on those nights when Michael stayed at Leila's apartment. For the most part, Michael hardly heard a peep from him.

However, the goal was much more than just getting TJ back home. They needed to help him find his way to the place where he was living a productive life. The first part of that was to help him become physically healthy and stable. It was obvious that he hadn't been under a doctor's care for anything other than his mental health issues for some time. He needed a physical. His acne was bad. He also needed to go to the dentist.

Michael checked things off his to-do list for his brother one by one. He got TJ all new clothes, including a winter coat and boots. Several prescriptions had to be refilled, and TJ needed new eyeglasses. He also had four cavities. Christopher still didn't have his driver's license since being out of prison, which meant that Michael had to do all the transporting. Aunt Wanda mostly just brought them meals and groceries and preached to them every chance she got.

One morning when they were returning from running an errand, Michael noticed TJ staring at the silk flower arrangement that was on one of the coffee tables in the living room.

"What's up?" Michael asked.

"I made that," TJ informed. "I gave it to mom just before she died."

"I don't remember that."

"They're lilies in honor of her passing and rebirth. I had Daddy give it to her for me."

"Do you ever think about her?" Michael asked.

"Are you kidding me?" he answered. "I think about her all of the time."

"Me too. Christopher still can't talk about her without crying."

"How bad was it? Was she really scared?" TJ asked timidly.

He looked like he was afraid of what the answers to his questions might be.

"Um, I don't think so," Michael said. "She was worried about us. She was in a lot of pain. She got to the point where she was ready to go."

"I wanted to come see her, but I couldn't," TJ articulated.

"Why not?"

"Because I was too embarrassed," TJ confessed.

"About what?"

"About how I turned out," he explained. "I didn't want her to remember me that way."

"But she was your mother!" Michael challenged. "She was literally on her death bed. You really think that she cared what you looked like? The way I see it, you shouldn't have let anything in this world keep you from getting to her."

TJ looked stunned.

"Since we are talking about it, you need to know that I was very angry with you about this for a long time," Michael poured out from his heart. "When you left home, you never once looked back."

"That's not true."

"You have been thirty miles from here all this time and you never came home, not even once. You never even tried to call anyone—like we just disappeared or ceased to exist. Like we did something to you and deserved to be punished for it!"

TJ was now staring at his brother defiantly.

"So, you want me to leave?" he asked. "Is that what you're saying?"

"No, I don't want you to leave!" Michael yelled. "We came and got you, remember?"

"Then what?" TJ erupted. "Okay, maybe I made a mistake. But I wanted to prove I could make it on my own and I was only doing the best that I could! I was tired of people worrying about me and I didn't want to be a burden to anyone anymore."

"On second thought, you're right," Michael responded. "You should be embarrassed. But not because of how you look or because you are bipolar. Now I see that you and me and Christopher got broken somewhere along the way. We only ever thought about ourselves…ever! We never stopped and thought about how our choices were impacting those around us. Daddy saw that *that* something was missing in all of us, and we almost killed him too. I'm embarrassed for my part. You should be too."

"I don't know what you want from me!" TJ protested.

"Mom said that all she wanted was for us to find a way to be happy," Michael continued. "Don't you see that having bipolar disorder doesn't have to define who you are. Why can't you live a normal life and just be bipolar?"

"But I don't know how to do that," TJ argued. "I never had a chance to find that balance."

"Mom's whole life was about giving you a chance and she would have helped you find that balance too, if you let her," Michael countered. "We weren't babies when she passed. We were grown men!"

"I know and I can see that you are different," TJ acknowledged. "How did you do it?"

"I just decided that I couldn't take being me anymore," Michael recalled. "I wanted more for my life. And when I see mom again one day, I want her to be proud of me."

"Don't you think that I want that too!" TJ voiced.

He was clearly shaken, but he was also still obstinate and defensive.

But there was a fire in Michael's belly. He took one step closer. They were toe to toe.

"Then I am going to tell you the same thing that I told Christopher," Michael declared. "If you are tired of being a loser, then fight your way through!"

TJ eyes got big and began to tear up.

"I don't think that you understand what it's like to be bipolar. It's different for me."

"Yeah, I'm sure it is," Michael responded coldly. "But I don't think you understand how much you were loved by this incredible woman and by an awesome God. You have to reimagine a world with you happy in it."

"You make it sound so easy when it can never be that way for me," TJ argued.

"It's not easy for anybody. That's the big lie that we tell ourselves to keep from trying."

TJ nodded his head in agreement.

"Look," Michael continued. "Mom died still believing that her kids were special. All three of us! You tell me, was she wrong about you?"

Michael sensed the impact of his words. It was like a bomb went off in the room. He could see that TJ was struggling. He began to second guess whether he was doing the right thing in confronting his brother head on. TJ obviously felt cornered and under attack. They always knew that he often played up his condition when it suited his purposes.

Suddenly, TJ reached out and grabbed Michael and pulled him close. Michael was caught off guard. He couldn't believe how strong TJ was. As TJ pressed his face into his brother's neck and shoulder, he sobbed uncontrollably.

"I'm sorry!" he cried. "I'm so sorry!"

Michael returned his embrace. But he never shed a tear himself. Weeping is only acceptable for a night. For the Johnson brothers, it was now morning.

* * *

Sean called. He wanted Michael to know that he had sent a letter to Becky and Ari's lawyers setting forth the provisions of

Ira's will. He was calling Rob next. He didn't want Michael to get caught off guard.

Other than Leila, Michael hadn't told a soul about his inheritance. He wished that Ira would have discussed it with him before he changed his will. At least then, he would have known what the expectations were. It would have also put him in a better position to deal with the expected fallout.

Rob arrived at the office at 9:15 a.m. He called out to Michael at 9:25 a.m. As soon as Michael entered the office, he could see that Rob was not happy.

"I just spoke to Sean McCarthy," he said. "Looks like you and I might be in business together."

Seated at his desk, Rob's whole body was shaking-almost like he had a nervous twitch. He had already unbuttoned the top button on his shirt and his tie was askew. He looked fit to be tied.

"Yeah, I heard," Michael replied cautiously. He didn't know what else to say.

"How long have you've known about this?" Rob demanded.

"Not long," Michael disclosed.

"Really?" he questioned. "Because it occurred to me that you might have known about this all along."

"That's crazy!" Michael said. "Ira never said anything to me. I'm just as surprised as you are."

"Well, this is gonna be a pretty tough pill for me to swallow," Rob said. "Talk about being stabbed in the back!"

"I understand how you feel."

"Do you?" Rob mocked. "I have carried this firm for years by myself. I thought that Ira respected me for that. Now I feel like I have been blind-sided. Even beyond the grave, he has found a way to really stick it to me."

"Wait a minute. I don't think that Ira was trying to hurt you," Michael defended. "I don't think that it has anything to do with you. Would you feel better if he left his half to Becky?"

"Frankly, I would," Rob contended. "Because at least then she could sell it to me. You can't even do that."

"I'm sorry," Michael expressed. "What do you want me to say?"

"When did you decide to go to law school anyway?" Rob diverted. "This is the first that I'm hearing about that."

"I haven't told anyone other than my girlfriend," Michael answered. "…and Ira."

"Do you even want to work here as a lawyer?" Rob asked.

"Honestly, I don't know the answer to that," Michael admitted. "I'm just as surprised as you are. Look, I get why you are upset. I really do. But Ira never told you he would allow you to buy him out. Can't we just let the dust settle before we start trying to figure everything out? Who knows, maybe Ira's children will contest the will and I'll get nothing."

"Not likely," Rob said with a disheartened look on his face.

Michael felt bad for Rob. But Ira's father is the one who started the firm, and he had every right to do with his half whatever he wanted. Rob inherited his share of the firm too, so he benefited from the same process. Regardless, Michael was more concerned about the reaction of Leila's family. Even if she herself didn't care, he seriously doubted that the others would be as accepting.

Moreover, there was no guarantee that he was going to get into law school, at least not this time around. He only applied to one school, and he still hadn't heard anything. He feared that he would have to tell everyone that he didn't get in. It was bad enough when Ira kept asking him about it. At least, it made sense now why Ira never let the topic go.

* * *

Once again Michael and Rob were at odds with each other. But this time, it was Rob's anger that was the driving force behind it. It's easy to say he was being childish, as he certainly was not hiding his feelings. He refused to look in Michael's direction when he walked by, and he kept his office door closed all day. It was just uncomfortable all around and Michael was getting tired of being treated that way.

Rob erupted at Jeff one afternoon for no reason at all. Suddenly their work environment was becoming increasingly hostile. Obviously, Michael couldn't just quit his job now because his boss was acting like a jerk; thus, it was hard to see how he and Rob could ever be business partners.

As luck would have it, Rob caught a cold or something, and he didn't come into the office for the next three days. They were all grateful because it gave them a reprieve from his miserable disposition. Michael felt especially sorry for Jeff, who bore the brunt of it. Rob knew better than to blatantly disrespect his employees. But he apparently had concluded that Jeff was fair game. Michael had decided that he was going to say something to Rob if he didn't let up soon.

Chapter 32

There was a noticeable change in TJ following their heart-to-heart conversation. His energy level increased immediately, and his overall mood improved. He was no longer self-absorbed and zombie–like. He was suddenly present and making great strides.

As evidence, he completely took over management of the household. He cooked and cleaned. He reorganized the kitchen and regularly hounded Michael to get someone to come in and fix some of the things that needed to be repaired. And he started talking to their dad on the phone.

It turns out that TJ's acne was a reaction to one of the medications that he was taking. His skin quickly cleared up after they changed his prescription, and he looked a lot better. He was receiving social security disability payments due to his disorder and therefore had income of his own. Because he wasn't paying rent anymore and his expenses were few, he started accumulating funds and he opened his first savings account.

He also bought a laptop and Michael taught him how to use it. He was a pro within an hour's time. He loved the internet and sat in front of his screen for hours daily. He really liked science and was obsessed with the environment so he started watching and studying everything he could get his eyes on. Suddenly, all he wanted to talk about was climate control and natural disasters. It got to the point that Michael almost liked it better when TJ wasn't talking.

Michael had a standing date with Leila on Saturday nights, which he was determined to make every effort to keep. He usually came home early Sunday afternoon. Sometimes TJ wasn't there since he had started going to church with Aunt Wanda, who was thrilled beyond words to have a new church buddy.

"Are you ever going to bring your girlfriend home to meet us?" TJ asked one Sunday afternoon.

"Maybe. I told you that she lives in Syracuse."

"What's her name?"

"Leila."

"What does she do?"

"She teaches first grade."

"And she's Spanish?"

"No, she's not Spanish!" Michael reacted. "Will you please stop listening to Christopher. You know he's stupid."

TJ was amused.

"How long have you been seeing her?"

"Like four months."

"Are you planning to get married?" he asked.

"No, we haven't talked about it."

"Why not?"

"Because it's complicated."

"Complicated how?"

"It just is," Michael responded and turned away.

"Does she have kids?" TJ persisted.

"No, she doesn't have any kids."

"Is she white?"

"Why are you asking me all these questions?" Michael posed and squirmed noticeably.

"Yup, I knew she was white," TJ commented.

"Actually, she's Jewish."

"Oh, this gets better," TJ said facetiously. "She's white and not a Christian? Can I please be there when you tell auntie?"

"You're dead if you tell," Michael threatened.

* * *

Leila revealed that her mother told her she and Heather were beneficiaries in their grandfather's will. She was obviously happy about her inheritance, but like Michael, she wasn't overly focused on her windfall. She was still very upset about her father. Apparently, Becky never mentioned the other aspects of the will to her. He was relieved to hear that.

However, they had one close call. Becky texted Leila early one Sunday morning and said that she was going to drop off a package that was delivered to her house for Leila. Typically, they slept in and just enjoyed their free time together without checking their phones. That morning, Leila accidentally knocked her phone off the nightstand and was examining it when she discovered the text. They both jumped up and he quickly got dressed and headed out the door. He was careful not to exit the building until he was sure that there was no one in the parking lot.

He felt foolish. Leila told him later that her mother never actually showed up until the afternoon. It would have been an absolute nightmare if Becky would have found him in her daughter's apartment. He hated the sneaking around just as much as she did. At their age, it was demoralizing. But their hands were firmly tied as there didn't appear to be anything they could do to end this cold war.

* * *

It was a slow day at the office and Jeff said that he was going to leave at 4:00 p.m. He looked beat. That left Michael by himself. The phone didn't ring all afternoon and he started shutting everything down a little early because he needed to leave right at 5:00 p.m. He had a class and he needed to go home before heading out.

On the walk to his jeep, there was a brisk wind and the cold air sliced right through him. He walked quickly. His nose was starting to run, and he wondered if he was getting sick. He always parked in the same place, on one of the side streets several blocks away where parking was free. He made the extra effort because the firm didn't pay for his parking. Just as he was approaching his jeep, he thought he heard someone coming up behind him. He turned his head slightly to the right to see who it was, and everything faded to black.

Chapter 33

Michael opened his eyes slowly. There were two people kneeling over him. One of them was talking to him, but he couldn't really understand what the man was saying. He could feel the hard cold ground against his backside. Instinctively, he tried to get up. They pushed him back down. His head was throbbing. When he closed his eyes, he lost consciousness again.

He vaguely remembered being put in the ambulance and hearing people talk. However, his first clear memory was waking up in the hospital. He tried to look around, but he had a screaming headache. He suddenly felt nauseous and vomited.

They kept shining a light and looking into his eyes and poking and prodding him. He had no idea how long he had been in the emergency room before a nurse said that they were taking him for a CT scan. He was lying there alone for what seemed like an eternity. Once he tried to lift his hand to feel the back of his head, but even that slight movement made him feel dizzy.

Then, they finally found a room for him. There was no one in the other bed. He was just getting settled in when two men walked in and said that they needed to talk to him. They were policemen. They looked the part. One was tall, mid-thirties and muscular with a receding hairline. The other was a slightly younger black guy.

"Mr. Johnson, I'm Detective Lawrence and this is Detective Cranston," the tall detective said. "We need to ask you a couple of questions. Will that be alright?"

"Okay," Michael said.

"Did you see who hit you?"

"No."

"Did you see or hear anything at all?"

"No, I don't remember any of it," Michael explained. "The last thing that I remember is closing the law office where I work. I don't even remember leaving the building."

"Can you think of anyone who might want to hurt you?" Detective Cranston asked.

"No," he uttered with hesitation.

"Your girlfriend's ex-boyfriend? A guy you got in a fight with at a party, maybe? Anybody at all?"

"No, no one," Michael asserted.

He was becoming more anxious.

"Whoever it was didn't take anything. We found your wallet and your phone. Are you sure that you can't think of anyone, anyone at all, who had reason to want to hurt you?"

"You think that someone was trying to hurt me?" Michael asked slightly panicked.

"No, we are not suggesting that at all," Detective Lawrence replied. "We don't want to scare you. Most likely, it was just an attempted mugging, and the guy got spooked for some reason and didn't have time to go through your pockets. Usually, that's what it is. We are just looking at all the possible angles here."

"Did anybody else see?" Michael inquired.

Detective Lawrence shook his head.

"No," he replied. "The woman who found you saw someone running away, but she only saw the back of him. Her husband called 9-1-1."

"Am I in danger?" he asked.

Michael was suddenly afraid. He felt like a sitting duck and that he needed to go somewhere but his headache was still intense.

"Let's not jump to conclusions," Detective Lawrence spoke. "You're safe now. We will let you know if we come up with anything else and get back to you."

"Okay."

"In the meantime, here's my card," Detective Cranston said. "Please call me if you remember anything. Sometimes that happens. Otherwise, try not to worry about it. The good thing is that your injuries do not appear to be life–threatening. It could have been a lot worse. So, I'd say that you are pretty lucky."

"Right," Michael agreed.

"Okay, so here is your wallet and your phone. You will probably be needing these."

"Thank you," Michael said.

He was worried. He lied about having enemies because he didn't know what else to do. But he was having second thoughts already. He just needed a moment to clear his head and to think things through. He can always come clean later.

He was just nodding off when Christopher, TJ, his aunt, and his uncle came rushing in. They crowded the bed in one swift motion.

"Michael, how are you feeling?" Aunt Wanda emoted. She looked scared.

"I'm okay," he said. "My head hurts a lot, but I think that I am going to live."

"What happened?" TJ probed.

"I don't know. I guess I was leaving work, and someone tried to mug me."

"Did you see who it was," TJ questioned further.

"No, I don't even remember getting hit," Michael said. "I just remember being in the office."

"Do you have a concussion?" his uncle asked.

"I don't know. I haven't seen the doctor yet."

"Baby, do you want me to call your father?" Aunt Wanda asked.

"No, let's just wait and see what the doctor says," he stated. "I'm sure that I am fine, and I don't want to worry him. How did you guys know that I was here?"

"The police called the house," TJ advised. "They scared me half to death."

"Do you need anything?" Aunt Wanda asked.

"I don't think so."

Christopher was noticeably silent. He looked angry and Michael wasn't sure what that was all about. It put him further on edge.

A young Asian doctor in a white coat eventually walked into the room. "Hello, I'm Dr. Wu." He was tall, thin, and handsome.

"Hi," Michael said.

"So, how do you feel?" the doctor asked.

"My head hurts and I'm a little nauseous."

"I can give you something for your stomach. On a scale of zero to ten, how bad is the pain?"

"About an eight," Michael answered.

"Alright, we'll see if we can do something about the pain too. The good news is that the CT scan was negative. There is no skull fracture or intracranial hematoma. I think you just have a closed head injury. You will probably have some pain and dizziness, and maybe some fatigue for a couple of days, but you should make a full recovery."

"Praise the Lord!" Aunt Wanda said and sighed heavily.

She hugged her husband.

"When can I go home?" Michael inquired.

"I want to watch you overnight and do an MRI tomorrow just to be safe. If everything is okay after that, then you can go home."

"Okay," Michael said.

"Any more questions?"

"No, I can't think of anything."

"How many stiches did he get," TJ asked.

"I don't really know," Dr. Wu replied. "I didn't do it. There was not much bleeding. Anything else?"

They all shook their heads.

"Alright, I will get you something for your stomach and for the pain. It was nice meeting you all." He turned and walked away.

"Okay, I think that we should let you get some rest," Uncle Simon said.

"Yes, let's just pray before we go and we will let you sleep," Aunt Wanda suggested.

They held hands while she said a quick prayer. Then she walked up and kissed him on the forehead.

"I love you, baby," she said. "We'll see you in the morning."

"Okay, thank you," Michael said. "Would it be okay if I talked to Christopher for a second?"

"Yeah, we'll be out in the hall," she said.

TJ walked up to the head of the bed and leaned in.

"I'll bring you a change of clothes tomorrow."

"Okay."

"And call Leila," he whispered.

"Right," Michael responded. "Thanks."

Christopher stood there until everyone was gone. Then he walked up to the bedside. Michael could see clearly now. His brother was heated.

"What are you in to?" he ordered.

Christopher was breathing hard through his nose and his nostrils were flared. His eyes were wide open, his lips were trembling. Michael was taken aback.

"What?" he asked.

"Wrong answer!" Christopher said in a deep voice designed to keep him from yelling. "Did you forgot how long I was locked up? Do you really think that I don't know a hit when I see one? He didn't take anything. Did he?"

"No."

"Michael…I swear to God! You got five seconds!"

"Okay... okay! Remember I told you about my friend Ira who just died?"

"Yeah."

"He left me his half of the law firm in his will."

"What? You're kidding, right?"

"No, I'm not kidding. His family hates me. We've been going back and forth about stuff for a while. Both his son and son–in–law have threatened me. And his business partner is crazy mad too."

"Threatened you how?"

"Oh, I don't know," Michael fussed. "To beat me up or whatever. I didn't take any of it seriously."

"What else?" Christopher pressed.

"My girlfriend is Ira's granddaughter."

"And they don't like that either, I bet."

"Something like that," Michael admitted.

He was afraid to look directly at Christopher.

"How come you never told me about this before? I asked you what was going on."

"Like I said, I didn't take it seriously. I thought that I could take care of it myself. I'm not afraid of them."

"You don't have to be afraid to get shanked to death," Christopher argued. "You know what we used to call guys like you who think that they can do their time all by themselves without backup?"

"No."

"The walking dead."

Michael didn't say anything. He felt stupid.

"Did you tell the police any of this?" Christopher asked.

"No. They said that it was probably just an attempted mugging."

"Good, don't!" Christopher whispered and moved in closer. "Here's what we are going to do. Don't say anything to the police. You don't have any proof and they are not going to believe you anyway."

"That's kinda what I was thinking," Michael concurred.

"You just want to know what they know," Christopher instructed. "Right now, they want to help you. So, let them."

"Okay."

"What about your girl?" Christopher asked.

"What about her?"

"Can you trust her?"

"I love her."

"But can you trust her?"

"Yeah, I trust her."

"Okay, but don't tell her that you suspect that someone in her family tried to have you killed. That won't help anyone."

"Is that what...do you really think that they were trying to kill me?" Michael asked.

"Doesn't matter. You could have died," Christopher pointed out. "So, don't take any chances with anyone. As far as you are concerned, the police are right that someone just tried to mug you. That's all it was."

"That makes sense. Thanks, Christopher."

It felt good to be able to unburden himself and have his brother on his side.

"And Michael, just so you know, if you ever do anything like this again, I swear to God, I will kill you myself," Christopher threatened. "I don't think you understand that if something happens to you, this family won't survive. Me and TJ and Daddy, we won't make it. We're all dead."

"I'm sorry," Michael uttered. "I wasn't expecting all this."

He lowered his head and began to cry. It was just an emotional release. He needed to let it go. Christopher reached out and cupped his brother's right hand in his own. They were face-to-face.

"This never would have happened if you got a Spanish girlfriend like I told you," Christopher finally said with a sly grin.

Michael fell asleep as soon as Christopher left the room. But he kept waking up because the nurses were coming in every fifteen or twenty minutes. It was during one of those bed checks that he remembered Leila. He reached over to check his phone. She had called once and texted him once. It was just after midnight. Although he was hesitant, he called her. She answered on the third ring.

"Sorry to wake you."

"Is something wrong?" she asked. "I tried to call you earlier. I just thought that you got caught up with something."

"Well, I kinda did. I'm in the hospital."

"What happened?" she asked.

There was clear concern in her voice.

"I got mugged leaving work."

"Mugged?"

"Yeah, I was getting in my jeep, and someone came up behind me and hit me on the head. I guess I passed out and someone called the police."

"Oh my God!" she exclaimed. "Are you okay?"

"Yes, I'm fine," he reassured. "They are just keeping me overnight for observation."

"Did they catch the guy?

"No."

"Oh, poor baby! How do you feel now?"

"My head still hurts, but not as bad as before."

"Well, I'm glad you called me."

"I was going to call you earlier, but I fell asleep. I'm sorry. I have never been a hospital patient before."

"Is there anything that I can do? Are you sure you're okay?"

"Yes, I'm sure."

"I love you, you know," she said.

"I love you too."

He slept better after they hung up. Her love gently laid him down.

* * *

He texted Jeff at 8:00 a.m. The nurse had no idea when they would be taking him down for the MRI. He just wanted to go home. Rob called twice, but Michael couldn't make himself answer the phone. He spoke briefly to his dad, who was quite

364

composed. His aunt showed up with Christopher and TJ at 10:00 a.m. and they kept him company until they took him for the MRI at noon and then released him at 3:00 p.m.

Over everyone's objection, he went to get his jeep. Christopher, who had a driver's permit, insisted upon driving them home. They all made a big fuss over Michael when all he really wanted was to be left alone. He texted Leila letting her know that he was home, and he finally found the wherewithal to call Rob back at 4:45 p.m.

"How are you?" Rob asked.

"I have a big bump at the back of my head, but I'm fine other than that."

"I can't believe that this happened," Rob commiserated. "I'm just glad that you're okay."

"Me too."

"The police were here today," Rob advised. "They asked a bunch of questions."

"What kind of questions?" Michael wondered.

"Basic stuff," Rob said. "They wanted to know how long you have worked here and what kind of employee you are."

"I hope that you said good things," Michael joked.

"Funny," Rob replied. "But they did ask me if I knew of anybody who might want to hurt you. I thought that was an odd question."

"What did you say?" Michael asked and perked up a little.

"I just said that I didn't know anything about that."

"They asked me that too," Michael disclosed. "I think that they are just trying to cover all of their bases."

"You're probably right," Rob conceded.

"I won't be in tomorrow."

"Right," Rob said. "I didn't expect that you would be. We will be fine. Just take care of yourself."

Aunt Wanda came over to the house first thing Saturday morning and she stayed all day. That meant that there was no chance that he was going to Syracuse to see Leila. His heart was a little strained because more than anything he needed to see her face. In the end, he told his girlfriend that it probably wasn't safe for him to drive that far with a head injury. His pride just wouldn't let him tell her the truth—that he was afraid of his auntie.

* * *

Detectives Lawrence and Cranston came by the office on Tuesday morning. Michael met with them in the conference room. They showed him a photograph. It depicted a black male in his early 20s. He wore shoulder length braids or dreads. Although it was dark, the camera angle was looking down and he could see the man's face clearly.

"Do you recognize this guy?" Detective Cranston asked.

"No, I'm sorry," Michael replied. "Who is it?"

"We got this shot off the video footage a couple of blocks from where you were parked," Detective Cranston explained. "It was taken about fifteen minutes before you were attacked."

"Are you going to arrest him?"

"No, it is not a crime to walk down the street," the detective said. "We have nothing to tie him to your assault."

"What's his name?"

"We don't want to get into that," the detective said.

"Why not?" Michael challenged. "If you're not going to arrest him, then he is going to be out there running around Schenectady. I want to make sure that I recognize him if we end up at the same party or something."

"Cunningham," Detective Lawrence disclosed. "Charles Cunningham. Have you ever heard the name before?"

"No."

"Well, he's not a nice guy," the detective said. "You might want to go the other way if you run into him."

"I will."

"Hey, by the way, I know your father from the police garage," Detective Cranston said. "How's he doing?"

"Good. He spends the winter in Arizona. He should be home in a couple of weeks."

"Good for him. He's a good guy, your old man. Tell him that Danny Cranston said hello."

Rob approached Michael at his desk as soon as the detectives left.

"What did they want?" he inquired.

"They wanted to ask me some more questions and see if I remember anything more."

Michael was careful not to say too much. Although Rob's disposition had improved considerably since the attack, it would be foolish to trust him. But Rob did offer him Ira's old parking spot, which was only one block away and the firm was still paying for it.

Seemingly, both Sarah and Jeff knew about Ira's will. Rob must have told them. Michael would have preferred to have kept that between them for the time being, if for no other reason than because he wasn't ready for anything to change in the office. In many ways, this job was one of the best things that ever happened to him. It was how he met Ira, and Leila, of course.

Moreover, Jeff was the one who really got him interested in law as a possible career. Without him, it is doubtful that he would have ever considered it. Not only did he find the work interesting, but he could envision himself venturing beyond the central focus of the firm. For instance, he was very interested in litigation—something like what he saw Trevor Sanders doing.

He was thinking a lot lately about what Christopher said to him in the hospital about living in social isolation. The truth is that he had become so accustomed to doing life alone in his own head that he now needed to learn how to let other people in. For sure, he had made a lot of progress in that area, especially as far as Ira was concerned. But he was still far behind where he needed to be.

Indeed, God is relational. He made us to be in positive relationship with him and with each other. It is not good for us to live alone. Trusting God means trusting other people because God places people, flaws and all, in our lives for a reason.

In this regard, it was particularly important that he trust Leila. Like he told Christopher, he did trust that she had nothing to do with the attack that was made on him. That was easy. But he didn't trust that she could ever love him as much as he loved her. And if it came to it, he also wasn't sure if she would choose him over her family. Not that he ever wanted her to choose. There was still a lingering hesitancy in their relationship. Clearly, he continued to struggle with both giving and receiving fully.

A day or so later, there was an article in the newspaper about the mugging. He received several phone calls and text messages from people, most of whom he only casually knew. In fact, both Sean and Trevor called him separately. He had to admit that it was nice to know that people cared enough to reach out like that.

He dutifully reported to Christopher everything that the detectives told him about this guy Charles Cunningham. Christopher had no real response. He just reminded Michael to keep his guard up.

Things quickly returned to normal as his family eased up and stopped hovering around him. However, he was aware that TJ remained very worried about him.

"Can I ask you something," TJ asked one night.

"Yeah."

"Are you worried that maybe the doctors missed something?"

"What do you mean?" Michael pressed.

"I mean, I don't know if you know but blows to the head can cause traumatic brain injury, which can be difficult to diagnose and to treat."

"No, but I'm not worried," Michael spoke calmly. "I haven't had any problems since I left the hospital. I only took the pain meds they gave me one time. I feel good."

TJ continued to look troubled.

"Um…but I was reading about this one guy who got hit on the back of the head and was fine at first and then he slowly started losing feeling in his body until he was paralyzed and became a quadriplegic."

"I know that you are worried about me," Michael acknowledged. "But I feel like God was really protecting me that day," Michael replied. "My doctor said that I was pretty lucky."

"Yeah, but I just think that it wouldn't hurt to go get a second opinion from a neurologist," TJ pressed. "You never saw a neurologist, right?"

"If I have any symptoms at all, I promise that I will make an appointment. Okay?"

"Okay, I'm not trying to make a big deal out of it," TJ said in earnest.

"No, I know, and I appreciate it. But if anyone around here needs a doctor to examine his brain, my money is on Christopher."

"Mine too," TJ admitted.

* * *

Christopher was supposed to come to the house for dinner. TJ prepared most of their meals now. Michael didn't particularly like his cooking, but Christopher could eat anything—no doubt a byproduct of years of prison food. He was late as usual, and Michael was in his room doing homework when he finally arrived. When Michael eventually came down, Christopher was sitting at the kitchen table finishing his dinner. TJ was putting dishes into the dishwasher.

Michael took one look at Christopher and his blood started to boil. Christopher avoided his gaze.

"Michael, look at his eye," TJ said.

There was a large, bluish-colored raised bruise under Christopher's right eye and a small, reddened gash on the right side of his face. His bottom lip was busted in the middle.

"What happened?" Michael asked calmly.

"He ran into something at the gym," TJ answered. "I think it looks bad."

"I'll be okay," Christopher remarked. "It's nothing, it doesn't even hurt."

"Maybe, but I'm gonna get something to put on it right now so that it won't get infected," TJ volunteered.

"Look in Daddy's bathroom," Michael directed.

TJ turned and headed upstairs.

Michael sat down at the table. He just looked straight ahead without speaking.

"Okay, before you start, can I please just say something?" Christopher asked.

Michael didn't respond.

"I went looking for that Cunningham punk, right."

"You did *what*?"

"No, it's alright," Christopher quickly asserted. "Just listen. I know that family. You know them too. There was a bunch of them in school with us. Nothing but trouble, every last one of them. Well, I found Charlie, ole boy, and we had a little talk, me and him. And he admitted it."

"Yeah right, he just came out and told you that he attacked me," Michael dismissed.

"Not exactly, I may have taken out his boy first," Christopher said with a hint of a smile.

"*That's* what happened to your face?"

"The two of them together ain't worth one pack of cigarettes! But I got him to spill his guts, the little scumbag! He told me that someone hired him to teach you a lesson. He said that it wasn't personal."

"Who?" Michael demanded.

"He didn't know," Christopher reported. "He said a white dude he knows from some dive bar paid him, but someone else was behind it."

"Someone like who?"

"He swore he didn't know, but he thinks that it was a woman. I believe him. He was pretty scared."

Michael inhaled deeply and sat upright in his chair. He was turbo charged.

"Any idea?" Christopher wondered.

"Most definitely," Michael admitted to himself as he exhaled.

"Who?"

"Doesn't matter. I can take care of it from here."

"Not by yourself you won't!" Christopher barked. "I already told you…"

"I think that you have already done enough!" Michael roared back. "Or did you forget that you are on parole, and they could send you back to prison for the rest of your life?"

"Forget that!" Christopher protested. "I know how to handle these people!"

"Me too," Michael insisted. "I don't run from a fight anymore. You gotta trust me too!"

"Okay, but listen to me, Michael. I'm serious. This really is war now. Show no fear. Take care of business, or they will come back at you again. And next time, they just might kill you!"

Chapter 34

Michael drove slowly through downtown Syracuse to an area called "Armory Square." It reminded him a little of the neighborhood where they had stayed when they were in Boston. After parking, he sat in his jeep for a minute to get his head straight. Christopher was right, he needed to be on his game. He had been mulling it over for two days. Suddenly, he was ready and got out of the vehicle.

There was a chill in the air and there was almost no traffic. The place where Becky worked was on the second floor of a red–brick building. He took the stairs and followed the signs and arrows to the end of the hall to a set of big glass doors with the name "Studio Eleven Designs" with a logo that was prominently displayed in gold letters.

Initially, there didn't appear to be anyone there. It was a large brightly lit showroom with photographs and posters of fancy rooms in upscale homes and offices set up all around. Soft music was playing. When he called earlier in the week, the woman who answered the phone told him that Becky came in on Saturdays. As he stepped in further, she came around the corner.

"May I help you?" she asked before she recognized him. She was wearing a black V-neck sweater, slacks and fancy black leather boots that probably cost more than he made in a month.

"I'd like to talk to you please," he said.

She gasped audibly. She was suddenly red-faced.

"What are you doing here?" she demanded. "You need to leave now! This is my place of business!"

"I said that I want to talk to you," he repeated.

"Well, I have no interest in talking to you," she replied. "You need to leave before I call security."

"You can do that, but before you do, you should know that first thing Monday morning I'm planning to go the Schenectady County District Attorney's Office and I'm going to tell them *everything* I found out about you. And then I am going to file a complaint charging you with attempted murder."

"You're crazy!" she shouted.

"Am I really?" he taunted. "Maybe you haven't heard yet, but I'm a partner in a very prestigious law firm in Schenectady and I'm going to do everything I can to make sure that the only rooms that you are decorating from now on are in state prison. I'm pretty sure that the ladies there are going to just love you."

"You're bluffing," she exclaimed. "You got nothing."

"Try me," he dared.

Her eyes were darting back and forth in her head, and she was breathing hard. She looked like a trapped animal. Her carefully cultivated façade was crumbling before his eyes.

"If you try slandering me… or my family, I'll sue you so fast…"

"Your own father knew the truth about you being a lost cause," he interrupted. "And that's why you hated him. It had nothing to do with his religion or his personality. You're completely broken inside, and you know that he saw you for who you are."

"You don't know what the hell you're talking about!" she roared ferociously. "You don't know what it was like having a father who was impossible to please, who looked down on your every accomplishment and who cared more about helping other people's bastard kids than his own."

"That's not true."

"You don't think that it was strange that both of his children despised him. He was a real piece of work! A self-righteous, judgmental, hypocrite, just like all the rest of you religious fanatics! Let's be clear. He was far from this perfect, loving father you keep trying to make him out to be. Trust me, I would know."

"I never said that he was perfect," Michael deflected. "But you had no right to dishonor because he didn't live up to your warped idea of who you wanted him to be. None of us are perfect. Tell me this Becky, are you happy with your life?"

"Okay, that's enough," she shouted and pointed behind him. "Get out! Get out now!"

"See you in court," he teased. "I beat you once and I'm going to beat you again. Only this time you are going to prison."

He began to turn away.

"Alright…alright," she reluctantly conceded. "Say whatever you came here to say and then get the hell out!"

"I know what you did, and I can prove it," he said with an icy cold stare.

"I don't know what you are talking about," she lied.

"You hired someone to try to kill me."

"What? You're insane," she said and laughed to herself.

"You're a liar!" he yelled. "I found the guy."

"You're lying!" she pushed back.

"Here's the thing," he said. "I didn't come here to have a debate with you about this. I knew that you hated me, but I didn't know just how evil you really are. But now that I know, I'm coming for you."

For a second, she almost looked frightened… and sympathetic… almost.

"You're just a hood rat trying to pass yourself off as somebody," she attacked with a vengeance. "But you're a nobody! Isn't that the real truth, Michael? You can change the way you look and how you dress. You can even take over my father's business. But underneath it all, you're still just an insecure little boy without any class and with no chance of ever having any! Refurbished garbage is still just that, trash without the stink!"

She pointed her nose at him and sniffed the air.

"Matter of fact, you're smelling a little rank right now, I must say," she ridiculed. "I think you're slipping a bit Michael."

"I know that you know about me and Leila," he countered. "I'm going to tell her tonight what you did."

She paused momentarily. Her eyes were cold and dark.

"What do you want from me?" she asked defiantly.

"I want you to give me one good reason why I shouldn't tell Leila what a monster her mother is."

"Are you trying to set me up or something?" she asked with a smirk. "Because I have to say, this little interrogation act of yours, or whatever this is supposed to be, is boring me to tears."

"I'm trying to give you a way out!" he snapped.

"By making me beg?" she quipped. "No thanks!"

"I don't want you to beg," he refuted. "I want you to put your daughter's happiness above your own for once in your life! I want you to pretend like you support her and love her! We both know how good you are at pretending, don't we?"

"You're wrong!" she fired back. "I do love Leila!"

"No, you don't!" he challenged. "Not like I do!"

"I'm not giving you my daughter if that's what you are asking."

"Who Leila ends up with is her decision, not yours or mine!"

"So why don't you just come out with it, Michael?" she shouted. "What exactly do you want?"

He took one step closer, and he tore into her with his eyes. They revealed for the first time the depth of his contempt for her.

"If you, or your weak-assed husband, so much as whisper one single word against me to Leila or try to pressure her in any way or cause trouble between us, I'm going to tell her, Heather, the district attorney, and whoever else will listen to me exactly what you did to me," he unleashed. "I know Leila well enough to know that she will believe me. I also know that she will hate you when she finds out."

"You're wrong! My daughter could never hate me," she resisted.

"I guess that we will just have to see, won't we?"

"What if she comes to her senses and dumps you on her own?"

"Then I'll leave her alone with her demon–possessed mother. Either way, she deserves better than you and we both know it. But having you in her life is her decision too. Take it or leave it! That's the deal."

"Do I have a choice?"

"No, you don't!" he declared. "And you should also know that if anything happens to me, a friend of mine is going straight to the district attorney with this information."

They just stared at each other. She was still dug in. But she dared not utter another word. They both knew that he had won. He slowly turned and headed for the door.

As soon as he got to his jeep, he threw his body inside and exhaled deeply. Nothing about that was fun. He sent Christopher a text message:

Bomb dropped. Mission accomplished.
Thx bro!

Christopher responded immediately:

Who da man?

* * *

Leila jumped into his arms as soon as she opened the door. His heart was delighted. She held him so tight that they almost fell over. They just laughed and kept gushing over each other. He felt safe and at home with her.

She made a big deal about his stitched-up wound, and he loved the attention from her. Although he didn't want to talk about it, she wanted to hear everything about the investigation. He told her most of it. Of course, he never mentioned his attacker's name…or the fact that her mother was an unindicted co-conspirator.

It was another perfect evening. They were lying close together in bed. She had her head on his chest.

"Um… Michael, I have something to tell you, but I don't want you to be mad."

"What is it?"

"Promise?"

"I promise," he said.

"I'm pregnant."

"What? You're pregnant?"

"I'm afraid so."

"You sure?"

"Yes, I'm sure."

"How did this happen?"

She raised her head. "Boston happened," she answered.

"Oh… Well, what are we going to do?" he wondered aloud.

"I don't know," she whispered into the darkness.

"I guess that our little secret is out now," he acknowledged. "There's no hiding this."

"I know," she said. "I have to tell my parents. I don't care anymore. I am a grown woman and I intend to live my life however I like. They can choose for themselves whether they are in or out. I'm prepared for whichever way it goes."

He was stunned. He could hardly believe what he was hearing,

"Are you sure?" he asked.

"You and our baby are my life now," she declared. "I love you both so much. That's all that matters to me."

"I don't know what to say," Michael said in amazement.

He was trying to gather his thoughts. His super–charged emotions just wouldn't let him think clearly.

"Are you happy about the baby?" she asked. "You never said."

"Of course, I'm happy," he said. "I'm sorry, I'm just in a bit of shock here. But this is amazing! I'm trying to get my head around the idea that I am going to be a dad. I mean…wow!"

"I know, I feel the same way," she acknowledged and giggled. "I feel like I'm flying!"

"Uh oh, wait a minute!" he exclaimed.

"What is it?"

"My dad! Oh my God!" he cried out.

He sat straight up in bed and put both of his hands on the top of his head.

"What about your dad?" she asked.

"He's going to kill me!" Michael declared.

"Michael, you're overreacting," she rebuked. "You're almost 40 years old."

"Huh, doesn't matter!" he refuted. "This dude ain't no joke. He doesn't care how old I am. When my brother got his girlfriend pregnant in high school, my mom literally fasted and prayed all day before she told him. We were all convinced that he was going to shoot Christopher dead on the spot."

"We'll, if I can face my two parents, then you can face your one."

"I'll trade ya," he joked. "Maybe we should just leave the country now. I got friends in Israel. We could move there."

"Not funny. I think that you are taking this way too far," she reflected. "Together we can face anyone."

"Okay, maybe you're right," he considered. "From now on it's me and you together against the world forever. What do you say?"

"Agreed," she said.

"Let's shake on it."

They shook hands. And then they kissed on it.

The next morning, they lingered in the afterglow of their passions and lifetime commitment to each other. They just kept touching and teasing one another and laughing. Michael felt like he wanted to run through the streets of Syracuse shouting at the top of his lungs that he was in love. He was completely out of his mind.

He hated to leave her, but there were things that he needed to do at home. Their goodbye rivaled that of a soldier going off to war. They literally clung to one another until the very last second. He got home at 2:30 p.m. TJ was in his room, and he came down the stairs when he heard Michael walk in.

"Hi," TJ said.

"Hi."

"How was your day with Leila."

"Good. How are you?"

"Good. If you want lunch, there is stuff in the refrigerator. I could warm it up for you."

"No, I can get it later," Michael spoke. "How was church?"

"I didn't go. Auntie had a migraine."

"Oh… is she okay?"

"I think so," TJ replied. "Can I talk to you about something?"

"Can you please stop asking me that?" Michael requested. "You can ask me anything or tell me anything. Just say it, alright?"

"Well, it's not really a question. It's more like a statement."

Michael just looked at him.

"Okay," TJ continued nervously. "I feel like you and Christopher shut me out. You guys have secrets, and you keep things from me. I'm not fragile or something, you know. I know that I've been gone for a long time, but I am a part of this family too just like you guys are."

"We know that you're not fragile," Michael defended. "I don't think that we do that on purpose."

"Yes, you do," TJ maintained. "You guys do it all the time and it makes me feel bad. Auntie noticed it too."

"I'm sorry," Michael said. "I honestly didn't know. You should have said something before. You haven't really been home that long, and I guess that we just got used to doing our own thing. I'm sorry. We'll do better with that. I promise."

"Okay."

"We good?"

"Yeah, thanks."

"So, can I tell you a secret now?" Michael asked.

"What?"

"Leila is pregnant," he announced with a big grin on his face.

"Pregnant?" TJ responded. "You're kidding?"

"Nope, I just found out," he added. "Can you believe it?"

"No, I can't… Daddy's gonna shoot you."

Chapter 35

A part of him wished that he had proposed to Leila in Boston. However, although it seemed like the right place, it really was the wrong time. It would have been premature as it would have put undue pressure on her, especially considering what had happened with her father. He was ready. He just needed help planning the perfect moment to pop the question.

It was hard keeping everything secret this time around. But he had waited this long, he figured he could hold out just a bit longer. He was almost giddy, and he was distracted all week. He knew how it looked, but he didn't care. He never imagined it would all work out like this.

He was just getting ready to go to lunch on Thursday when Leila called him. She sounded panicked.

"Michael, there's a problem with the baby," she cried.

"What's wrong?" he asked.

"I don't know."

"Where are you?"

"I'm at urgent care," she said. "I am bleeding."

"Okay. I'm coming now."

"Okay," she said.

He jumped up and shouted to Jeff that he had to go. He didn't wait for a response, and he was out the door and halfway down the stairs when Jeff appeared. He just waved him off. His heart was racing as he ran to his jeep. He was out of breath, and he couldn't think straight. All he knew was that he needed to get to Leila. Nothing else mattered.

He made it as far as the Utica exit on the New York State Thruway before he was pulled over by a state trooper for speeding. He tried to explain that he was in a hurry to get to his sick girlfriend, but the female trooper clearly was not impressed in the least with his pleadings. It was as if she was moving in slow motion just to punish him even more for breaking the law. She had him parked there on the side of the roadway for nearly thirty minutes.

Leila called him just as he was pulling off. She said that she was going home and for him to meet her at her apartment. He had to resist the temptation to speed again. He told himself that everything must be okay with her if she was home already, but he wasn't fully convinced. He must have caught every traffic light on the Syracuse eastside.

He knocked on the door twice and stood there nervously. A middle-aged white man opened it. Face to face for the first time, Leila's dad raised both of his eyebrows, sighed heavily, and stepped to the side as he directed Michael to come inside with his right arm and hand extended. Michael hurried past him in one swift motion and found Leila lying on her back on the sofa. She had a pillow behind her head and a heating pad on her midsection.

As he rushed to her side, he saw Becky out of the corner of his eye standing in the kitchen.

"Leila, you okay?" he cried out.

"Yes, I'm okay."

"What happened?"

"Michael, I had a miscarriage," she said with tears in her eyes.

He felt like he was just kicked in the stomach. He dropped to his knees next to her. She reached out for him, and he kissed her on the side of her face.

"I'm sorry," she said. "I'm so sorry, Michael."

"You don't have to be sorry," he whispered as he wiped her tears away with his hand. "You didn't do anything wrong. These things just happen."

"This was going to be the beginning of a new life for us," she reflected. "We were going to be so happy." She began sobbing.

"Leila, baby please listen to me. We are happy. It's gonna be okay."

"But we were going to be a family and now it's gone!"

"We will be a family," he promised. "We will!"

"But we lost the baby!" she cried out.

"I know, but don't think about that now," he directed. "Just look at me. All I want to know is do you still love me?"

"Yes, I love you so much, but…"

"Do you believe me when I tell you that I still love you?"

"Yes, I believe you."

"Remember when we promised each other forever? We shook hands on it. Remember?"

"Yes, I remember."

"Did you mean it?"

"Yes, I meant it, but…"

"Then marry me, Leila."

"What?"

"With God as my witness, I swear that I will do everything that I can to make you happy. I am asking you to marry me."

"Really?" she whimpered.

"Will you?"

"Okay…I mean yes," she blubbered. "I will marry you!"

They kissed and held on tight to each other until their sadness had lifted and their love had new life.

Michael never heard the front door close.

It took a few minutes before he even remembered that her parents had been there. Even then, they were just a passing thought. She never said anything about them afterward and he certainly didn't want to revisit the drama.

That night they just talked about their hopes and dreams for their future. They made each other laugh like always. He promised to get her an engagement ring right away. She told him that she wanted four or five kids. His reaction was less than supportive, and she reminded him of his promise to do anything to make her happy.

"I think you were hearing things," he teased.

He had to go to work the next morning, which meant that he had to drive home first to change his clothes. He slid out of bed at 5:00 a.m. He tried not to wake her, but when he came out of the bathroom, she was sitting up in bed with the lights on.

"What are you doing?" he asked.

"I know that you have to go, but there is one more thing that I need to tell you."

"Okay."

He sat down on the bed.

"Do you remember what my grandfather said to me?"

"When?"

"What he said to me that night just before he died," she stated. "I know you heard it."

"Yes, I remember," he said.

"Well, I haven't been able to stop thinking about it," she disclosed. "I have been playing that scene over and over in my head ever since. It's like his words were carried on an arrow that was shot deep into my heart and was lodged there."

"Really?"

"At first, I was angry because I was really struggling with what he said, and I didn't know what to do about it. I started doing research online and I bought a Bible, of all things. I was still really confused, especially with the Jewish side of it. Honestly, I was having a problem with the case against Jesus. So, I called Rabbi Cohen."

"You did?" Michael remarked. "I didn't even know you knew him."

"He gave me his card one day when he came to see my grandfather and we were there," she conveyed. "We talked on the phone for a long time. He is wonderful, and very reassuring. And so now I feel better."

"When did all of this happen?" Michael questioned. "When did you call him?"

"When you were in Israel."

"How come you didn't tell me?"

"Because I felt like I needed to do this without you," she explained. "What did you call it? Plausible deniability?"

"What do you mean you feel better now?"

"I'm saying that I now believe in my heart that Jesus is the Jewish Messiah," she confessed. "I'm sorry, but it's really clear to me. I can't explain it and I won't deny it. I think that you should probably know before you marry me that I am Messianic."

Michael was dumbfounded. He didn't see this coming. Even when he saw the Bible on her table that morning, he wasn't quite sure what to make of it. He was truly amazed by the awesomeness of God. He just sat there staring at her, a gift that he didn't deserve.

"Leila, you do realize that this is going to put another wedge between you and your parents," he felt impressed to say. "Even Heather is probably going to have a hard time with this one."

She pulled her knees close to her body and grasped them with both of her arms. She suddenly looked like she was deep in thought.

"Yeah, I know," she said finally. "But Jesus asked what we really benefit if you gain the whole world but lose your own soul."

He was struggling to hide the impact of her words upon him.

"So, yeah, you might be my only friend... What do you think?" she asked. "You still want to marry me?"

He sat motionless.

"Can I think about it?" he asked with a straight face.

Then he touched her neck, and she squealed in delight.

* * *

Michael received a text message from Jacob. It was nice. He just said that he was in the cemetery the other day and noticed that there were some white lilies blooming near Ira's grave in a place where there had never been any flowers before. He sent a photo and wrote underneath:

Lilies in winter are a sign from heaven.

Chapter 36

TJ was driving them crazy. Their father was returning home on Sunday, and he somehow got it in his head that he wanted to have a special dinner in their dad's honor. He was running around like a chicken with its head cut off. Michael and Christopher were making fun of him behind his back.

Michael never made a big deal out of his dad's return before. And he certainly didn't clean the whole house or prepare a celebratory feast. It was overkill in his opinion. But he wasn't about to say that to his brother.

Early in the week, TJ texted them a list of things that he expected them to do. He also insisted that Leila come to dinner too. She was excited, but Michael was more than a little concerned that his brothers would readily avail themselves of this unprecedented opportunity to embarrass him.

Michael stayed at Leila's apartment Saturday night like usual and she followed him in her car to Schenectady so that he didn't have to drive her back to Syracuse. They arrived on time. Upon entering the house, Michael introduced his fiancé.

"Hey, TJ, this is Leila. Leila this is my brother, TJ."

"Hi," TJ said.

"Hi, how are you?" she asked.

"I'm good. It is nice to finally meet you."

"You too," she replied. "I have heard lots of good things about you."

"Where's Christopher?" Michael asked.

"I don't know," TJ answered. "But he has exactly ten minutes to get here before he is officially late. I'm sick of him already."

"Where's Daddy?" Michael inquired further.

"He's upstairs. He got in around midnight and went straight to bed. He came down this morning for coffee. I told him that dinner wasn't until four o'clock so he could go rest."

"Leila made this cake," Michael said. "Where do you want to put it?"

"Oh, I'll take it. Thanks Leila!"

"You're welcome."

"Why don't you guys just hang out here. Everything is ready. We just need Christopher and then I'll call Daddy."

"Okay," Michael replied. "Isn't auntie coming?"

"Later," TJ reported. "She dropped off her food earlier. You know how she is all over the place."

"Are you sure that you don't need help with anything?" Leila asked.

"No, we're good," TJ replied. "Have a seat please."

Michael and Leila sat down. She was asking him about the different photographs on the walls when Christopher stormed in.

"I know, I'm late," he whispered. "It's not my fault. Where's the drill sergeant?"

"I heard that!" TJ yelled from the kitchen.

"Leila this is my brother Christopher," Michael spoke.

"Hi," she said.

"Hi," Christopher echoed. "You're a lot prettier than I thought you'd be."

"Thank you," she replied and blushed.

"Michael usually likes ugly girls," he blurted out with a half-smile.

She erupted in laughter.

"Here we go," Michael said and shook his head. "You're lying already."

"I'm not lying," Christopher refuted. "Your last girlfriend looked like a man. She had back hair long enough to braid!"

"I already warned Leila about you," Michael advised. "None of your lies are gonna work. So, you can stop now."

Undeterred, Christopher rolled his eyes, turned sideways, and whispered, "Leila, we need to have a private conversation later without you know who. We find that it's hard to talk freely when Michael's around because he's mentally unstable."

"Okay," Leila played along. "I would love to hear anything you have to say."

TJ called for them to come into the dining room. He had set the table. It looked really nice. You could tell that he had worked hard on it.

"Now, take a seat wherever you want and when Daddy comes down, I want you to all stand up and give him a round of applause," TJ directed.

"Aw…I don't want to do that," Christopher protested. "Why can't we just act normal?"

TJ quickly spun his head around and gave Christopher the evil eye.

"Okay, we'll do it your way," Christopher immediately retreated and put his hands up. "I was just asking. Geez!"

"And could you guys not fight tonight at the table?" TJ insisted. "I want a nice family dinner."

"Good luck with that," Michael said under his breath.

"No, I mean it!" TJ loudly interjected. "This is important to me. All I'm asking is for you two clowns to pretend like you know how to act. Cheech and Chong, the both of you!"

Nobody said anything.

TJ stood there a moment expressionless for added emphasis before he abruptly turned in disgust and walked up the stairs.

"I say we make a run for it now," Michael whispered.

The three of them began chuckling.

TJ came back down and took his seat across from Michael and Leila. As instructed, they waited until their dad walked into the room and they stood up and applauded.

He looked surprised. He also looked great for a man in his sixties. He still had all his hair, although some grey was starting to show around his temple. It looked like he had thinned out a little even with his muscular frame. But he moved gingerly. No doubt, his chronic back problem was aggravated by the long drive home.

"What's all this?" he asked with a puzzled look on his face.

"We wanted to celebrate you coming home and say thank you," TJ spoke.

"Thank me?" their father questioned.

"Yes," TJ continued. "We know that this is long overdue, but we want to thank you for carrying us all these years. You are the greatest man that we know and the best father that anyone could ever have. You prayed for us when we didn't know enough to pray for ourselves. We are proud to be your sons."

Their dad was clearly caught off guard and he was visibly shaken. There was an atmosphere of quiet reverence.

"Thank you," he said and lowered his head momentarily while he fought to regain his composure.

Then he walked directly over to Leila and extended his hand.

"Hello, I'm Dale Johnson," he said with a warm smile.

"Hi, I'm Leila." She had tears in her eyes.

"It is an honor to meet you, Leila."

"It's an honor to meet you too," she whispered.

"I hear that you are going to marry my son?"

"Yes, sir," she nervously replied.

"Then I feel that I should probably tell you something," he spoke. "Michael's mother breast fed him until he was twelve years old which is when he got his braces. I only mention it because it's not too late for you to reconsider."

The Johnson men suddenly roared with laughter. Even Michael was laughing. Christopher and TJ were shaking their fists in the air and hooting and hollering like they were at a football game. Leila was laughing too.

Despite all of TJ's planning, dinner ended up being a loud raucous affair. All pretenses were off. The guys tore into each other every chance they got. They were suddenly teenagers again and even TJ got in his fair share of shots.

There was a rather extended conversation about TJ's cooking skills, or the lack thereof, that probably went a bit too far. But Michael was the one mostly in the hot seat. Their father had deftly and comedically turned the focus from himself and onto his youngest son.

Moreover, they were pretty much immune from any long-term offense of their harassment of one another. They each attacked at will and then simply moved on, without so much as a second thought. They were literally yelling one moment and laughing their heads off the next. Michael was very concerned about how his family's dysfunction was affecting Leila, and he kept touching her hand under the table.

However, things did get a little dicey there at one point after Aunt Wanda arrived.

"Leila is a very pretty name," she began. "What kind of name is that?"

"Um…it's Persian," she answered. "It just means 'night' or 'dark'."

"So, you like things dark, huh?" auntie interjected.

The guys laughed nervously.

"Yes, I guess I like some dark things," Leila responded with a half-smile.

"Auntie, please," Michael muttered in an attempt to rescue her.

"You just be quiet and mind your business," she rebuked. "I'm just trying to get to know your fiancé… Leila, so are you Persian?"

"No, my family is Jewish."

"So, you're not Christian?" she zeroed in.

"I'm Messianic."

"Really?" Aunt Wanda replied enthusiastically. "There is a program on Christian TV that has this rabbi teaching about Jesus. I think it's called 'Christ the Lord'. It's really good. Do you ever watch that show?"

"No, I've never seen it," Leila admitted.

"You really should check it out."

"I will."

"So… what kind of wedding do you want?"

"I don't really know," Leila responded and looked to Michael for help. "We haven't really talked about it much yet."

"Yeah, we still have a lot of things to figure out," he said. "Leila lives in Syracuse."

"Michael, how come Leila doesn't have an engagement ring on her finger?" his aunt shifted.

"Um… because I didn't know what kind to get her," he explained.

"Boy, what's wrong with you?" she reprimanded. "You're not supposed to propose marriage to a young girl without a ring in your pocket! Seems to me that you got this thing backwards."

"Don't blame Michael, auntie," Christopher chimed in. "He don't know no better."

"Shut up, Christopher!" Michael snapped.

"What did I say?" Christopher mouthed with a straight face. "I'm just trying to help you out."

"Shut up, Christopher!" his dad ordered.

TJ laughed heartily.

"Leila honey, let me give you a little advice," Aunt Wanda continued. "I think that you should march his little dark butt right down to the jewelry store tomorrow and get yourself the biggest diamond ring you see. Men come and go, but diamonds are forever girl!"

"Hey!" Michael protested. "Whose side are you on anyway?"

"Sorry, baby," Aunt Wanda spoke. "But we girls gotta stick together on some things. Ain't that right, Leila? You gotta work it girl!"

Leila was tickled.

"Okay, I hate to break up the fun, but I am still a little tired from the drive," the senior Johnson announced. "Thank you, guys, again for everything. I wasn't expecting this. Leila, very nice to meet you and welcome to the family. TJ, thank you. I have missed you all and I appreciate you very much."

"Uh, Daddy?" Michael said. "There is one more thing before you go."

He reached in his back pocket and handed his dad a folded piece of paper.

"What's this?" his father asked as he opened it.

He read it to himself and at one point he set his gaze on Michael. He began rubbing the top of his head with his free hand and was tearing up. Michael was crying now as he rushed around the table and the two men embraced.

Everyone just watched in silence.

"Okay, let me say this," their father insisted as he pulled away from Michael and gathered himself. "Your mother had faith and always said that you guys would one day 'Rise from the ashes and take your rightful places in the world'. Those were her words, not mine. I hate to say it, but I honestly thought she was dreaming. I wanted to believe her, but I just couldn't see it because of the way things were. When she died, I just felt like all hope was lost for us as a family. I have never been so low in all my life. Truth is, I almost didn't make it… But I am starting to see things differently. When I look at you now and see the changes in you, I know that she was right all along. I was wrong, and I repent before God… I guess what I am trying to say is that, even though I know God didn't *give* her cancer, I still hoped he could somehow use all of our suffering for his glory… and that you guys would be who he intended you to be. That would make all of the pain worth it. I can't believe that I am saying this myself, but it's true. I would definitely do it all over again… I swear I would do it for you!"

A fullness saturated the room as the air was unexpectedly charged like lightening.

"Amen!" Aunt Wanda exclaimed. "Praise the Lord! I tell you my God is so good!"

"What's in the letter?" TJ wondered.

"This letter says that my son has been accepted at Albany Law School," the Johnson patriarch declared. "*My* son! *My* son!"

After a slight pause, everyone erupted in jubilation. They were patting Michael on the back and grabbing for the letter to read for themselves. They were genuinely proud of Michael, and he was clearly proud of himself. They gave themselves completely over to the moment and were talking fast and furious over each other. Aunt Wanda began to praise dance like she often did during Sunday worship service. It was truly a glorious celebration.

But it didn't last long. It quickly faded like a summer rain shower in the Mojave Desert and the bickering promptly resumed when Christopher and TJ suddenly realized that they resented Michael for not telling them that he had applied to law school. They were relentless.

"You're a bum!" TJ insisted.

"What did I tell you about being *secret double agent no fun*?" Christopher scolded.

Once again, Michael just shook his head and laughed. And the evening ended the way that it had started. TJ began barking orders. That was Christopher's cue to get out of there and he left with Aunt Wanda, who said that she needed to get home because her husband was sick. Michael and Leila helped a little with the cleanup, but he insisted that she head back to Syracuse before it got too late. He walked her out to her car.

"Oh my God, that was an amazing evening!" she exclaimed. "I have never experienced anything like that before. I love your family already."

"I think that you were a big hit too."

"Now I get what you were saying about your dad. He has such a presence! I have so many questions, but I loved it."

"Really?" Michael questioned. "Because I know that we can get a little carried away."

"No, it warmed my heart to see how much you guys love your dad and love each other," she insisted. "It's a side of you that I never saw before. I liked it."

"Thanks," he whispered. "I'm glad."

"I wish that I could have met your mother. It sounds like she was an amazing woman."

"She was amazing," he reflected.

"I'm just so honored to be a part of your family. Thank you."

She pressed into him, and he kissed her gently goodbye. She started to get into her car and then she hesitated.

"Oh, by the way, tomorrow me and you are going ring shopping, buddy!" she spoke with glee. "I'm so excited! Yay me!"

* * *

Later that evening, Michael was in his room sitting at his desk going over his class notes when there was a knock on the door.

"Come in!"

It was his dad, who walked in and shut the door behind him.

"I'm sorry for bothering you," he said.

"No, it's okay, I wasn't doing anything."

"I just wanted to tell you that I like Leila. You chose well."

"Thanks. I really wanted you to like her."

"I think that your mother would have liked her too."

"That's good to hear," Michael softly acknowledged as he fought through the lump forming in his throat.

"I also wanted to thank you for helping out your brothers the way that you have been doing," his father continued. "Wanda told me that you have really been working with them and I can't thank you enough."

"Daddy, you don't have to thank me," Michael insisted. "They have been helping me too. I don't know if TJ told you, but he wants to start taking college courses online. That dude is really smart!"

"No, he didn't tell me."

"We really have just been helping each other," Michael explained. "We are family."

"Well, I couldn't be happier," his father said as he sat down on the edge of the bed. "I'm really proud of you guys."

"Thank you."

"And uh, there is something else that I need to tell you."

"Okay," Michael urged.

"About a couple of days before you were attacked, I was praying, and the Lord showed me something," he revealed. "I saw an image of you being chased by a dark cloud. Just as clear as day, I saw you get hit on the head from behind and I saw you spinning downward in slow motion. My heart was immediately gripped by fear, and I began to cry out."

"No kidding? You saw that?"

"Then the Spirit of the Lord arrested me and rebuked me for being afraid and I felt convicted. Then this blanket of peace fell on me."

"That's incredible." Michael reacted.

"I'm just so grateful these days for everything. I really didn't understand it, but I wasn't worried or surprised when Wanda called me. God was trying to tell me that something bad would happen, but it was going to be okay because he is in control."

"Oh, that makes sense," Michael said.

"Now, I don't need to know what that was all about," his father proclaimed. "My guess is that I'm better off not knowing. You are safe now and that's all that matters. But Michael, I just want to make sure that you understand something. Your whole life will be a series of battles, one after the other. And there is much more that will be required of you. Lord knows I've been fighting my whole life! But for some reason God has favored us. Our trials are how he teaches us. So, you must be fearless and courageous. And most of all, you must call upon the name of the Lord all the days of your life."

"I will, Daddy," Michael said solemnly. "I have been thinking a lot about mom lately. I didn't know much about God before she got sick. And I definitely didn't know him like you guys did. I still don't… But a lot has happened since she died. Not just getting hit over the head, but a lot of different things. And I have come to see that not only is God real and his love for me is real, but I want and need him in *my* life. So, yeah, I can honestly say that I will always trust him, no matter what."

"I know you will… That's really what I came in here to say."

He rose slowly from the bed and grimaced as he leaned back slightly to stretch his back.

"Have a goodnight, son."

"Thank you."

"Don't stay up too late," he said before turning away.

"Oh, Daddy?" Michael called out.

"Yes."

"No, never mind."

"What is it?"

"It's nothing really…"

"What?"

"Um… you think that maybe you could like…I don't know… warn a brother the next time you get a vision?" Michael contended.

They were both motionless.

Only their eyes revealed their shared amusement.

"Goodnight, Michael."

"Goodnight, Daddy."

Epilogue

Horatio looked at his reflection. He was just making sure that his uniform was even in the back. Sometimes it got bunched up, which would be unacceptable today. Angels and men are somewhat similar in appearance, but that wasn't always the case. It happened over time, after the creation of the earth and mankind. Prior to that, angels, as spiritual beings, were much more fluid in their appearance. The change was mostly a preference stemming from the practicality of regularly interfacing with men. However, the appearances of those hosts who are assigned to guard against sin or to serve in the inner courts are beyond human comprehension.

He hurried back to his office. It was located on the top floor. It was a large and spacious corner office with dark mahogany furniture that he had picked out himself. The view from his office window was spectacular. He loved to stand there and watch as the wind moved artfully and majestically over the mountains and across the valleys. It was really something to behold. It never lost its wonder!

Horatio sat down at his desk because he wanted to go over his notes one more time. His meeting with Michael, the general of heaven's army, was in an hour. He was always concerned that he would be asked a question about his sector that he couldn't answer. As a colonel in the lord's army, he was required to participate in the regularly scheduled general's briefings. Since the end of the church age on earth, these meetings had taken on added significance. The time of the Lord was at hand!

He breathed out and Mateo and Luca promptly appeared. They both held the rank of major. Their offices were next to his. It was their rank and file that engaged in the actual warfare and had prepared the report.

"Yes, Colonel," Mateo spoke.

"I just want to make sure that this is current," Horatio said.

"That's the updated version you have there," Luca replied. "We just doubled checked the numbers again. There has not been any recent active engagement on earth that I am aware of."

"And how do we compare with the other sectors?"

"Pretty good, I'd say," Luca expressed. "We were a little behind at first because of the power outages on the east coast of America and the Mexican Gulf. In the end, however, they worked out to our advantage because it forced people to shelter together to stay warm. It seems that the added distress made it easier to evangelize."

"What about all these places experiencing the extreme heat?" Horatio inquired.

"That has been a bigger problem," Luca divulged. "The enemy took away night too in most of those areas. That has meant that there is no reprieve from the stifling heat and oppressive conditions. People are irritable and much more focused on the cries of their flesh.

As a result, there are growing casualties, which frankly are to be expected.”

“Even if they are to be expected, they aren’t acceptable, Major!” Horatio expressed rather harshly.

“Yes, Colonel,” Luca responded.

“I want you mighty soldiers, who heard and witnessed the things that the seven thunders uttered, to find a way through. It’s not like we didn’t know that this was going to happen. All he is asking of us is to provide every man and woman with as many chances as time permits to acknowledge and seek him. That’s not likely to happen in extreme conditions.”

“Yes, Colonel.”

“Is there anything else that I should know before my meeting with the general?” Horatio asked.

“No, Colonel,” Luca said.

“No, Colonel,” Mateo, repeated.

“Stay tuned to my frequency until I close you out,” Horatio ordered.

“Yes, Colonel,” Mateo said.

“Yes, Colonel,” Luca repeated.

“Oh, wait.” Horatio said looking down at the report. “Tell me again what happened here, just outside the west gate? Why the sudden spike in new believers?”

“Oh, remember Colonel, I told you about the revival,” Mateo replied. “We used it for our ‘Operation Healer’.”

“Oh yeah, that’s right,” Horatio said.

"There were approximately 1,500 Jews saved in one day," Mateo reported.

"It says here 1,533 to be exact," Horatio corrected. "And it wasn't really scheduled, right? Wasn't it just impromptu?"

"Yes, Colonel, that is correct" Mateo replied. "Obviously, it was a huge victory for us in the heavenlies too. The Kingdom was advanced mightily."

"Who led it on earth?" Horatio asked.

"Uh, Jace Johnson, the evangelist. You may recall that he also held the crusades in Toronto and Kampala."

"Whose line?" Horatio questioned.

"Ira Goldberg's line."

"Whose?"

"You know," Mateo insisted. "Ira Goldberg from Ruth, 115th Generation."

"Ira Goldberg? Ah, yes, Ira. Quite the character," Horatio reflected. "That was one of the operations that the general himself initiated and commanded while on several bus rides. New York, right?"

"Yes, Colonel," Luca affirmed. "Upstate New York."

"Okay, the general is going to love hearing about this. Excellent! I think I'm just about ready now. Thank you both. You're dismissed."

About the Author

Ed Thompson is a lay minister in Syracuse, New York. He is also a trial attorney in New York, having practiced law in Syracuse for more than twenty-five years. He is a former federal prosecutor and a former assistant public defender. Additionally, Ed received a master's degree in biblical studies from Alliance Theological Seminary in 2020. Previously, Ed received a BA degree from Ohio Northern University in 1982 and a JD degree from Albany Law School in 1985. Presently, he resides in Baldwinsville, New York, with his wife and daughter.

Ed can be contacted at ethompson.esq@gmail.com.

Other Books by Ed Thompson

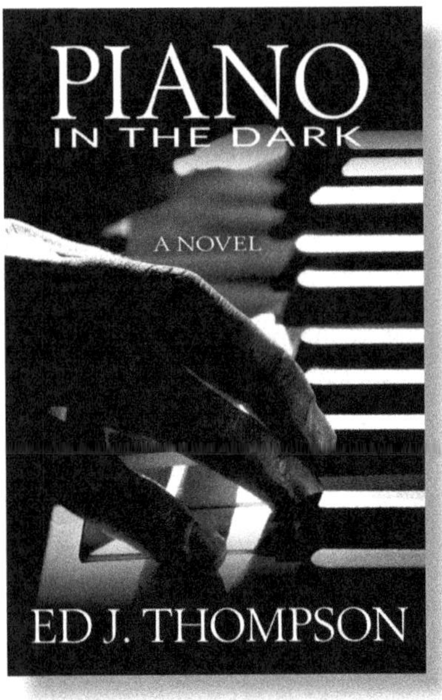

Sandy Coleman loved God his whole life. The only son of a Baptist minister, he grew up in the church playing the piano and leading worship every Sunday. His musical gifts are undeniable, and the people at Mount Moriah Baptist Church in Syracuse, New York, adore him. However, a chance meeting with Tony Moreno, a handsome, young legal aid lawyer would change his life forever. As their forbidden romance unfolds, Sandy's secret life is exposed and he is distraught when he is suddenly and mercilessly forced to leave the church. With virtually no friends and limited support from his family, his world slowly spirals out of control as he is painfully torn between his physical passions and his love for God. Nothing makes sense to Sandy. Doesn't he deserve to find love and be happy just like everyone else? Sexuality is not a choice, right? Could anything be worse than when the heart desires something that God might not want it to have? More than a love story, Piano in the Dark is a raw and honest look at the unresolved conflict between the church and homosexuality.

Other Books by Ed Thompson

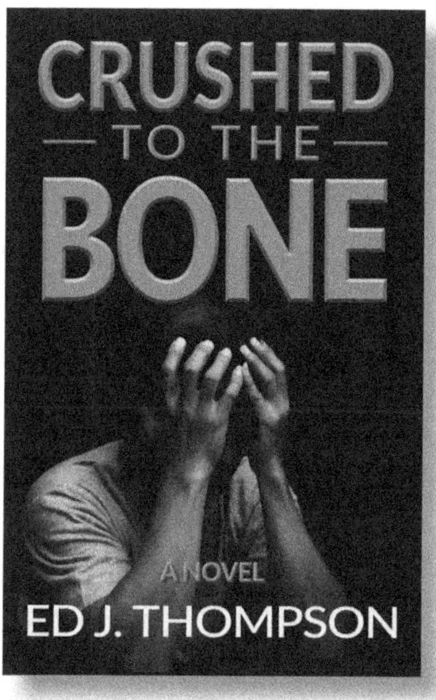

From an early age, Dale Johnson determined in his heart that he would make a real life for himself. Even more than the poverty and neglect, he hated the suffocating feelings of brokenness and inferiority.

Dale's life changed dramatically when he started dating Lizzy in middle school. She introduced him to a world that he had only dreamed about—one where people truly cared about each other and loved God. Lizzy was from a different background, and he adored her. Her love made him a true believer, and he was on top of the world the day she became his wife.

But life has a way of stripping one mercilessly of their hopes and dreams with its trials and storms. And when Lizzy was diagnosed with terminal cancer, Dale, already feeling depressed and dejected, began to doubt everything he thought he ever knew, including the meaning of life and the goodness of God. Why would anyone choose God if they end up a sad, broken mess?